space case

Also by Stuart Gibbs

STUART GIBBS

space case

A **moon base alpha** NOVEL

Simon & Schuster Books for Young Readers

New York London Toronto Sydney New Delhi

SIMON & SCHUSTER BOOKS FOR YOUNG READERS
An imprint of Simon & Schuster Children's Publishing Division
1230 Avenue of the Americas, New York, New York 10020
This book is a work of fiction. Any references to historical events, real people, or real places are used fictitiously. Other names, characters, places, and events are products of the author's imagination, and any resemblance to actual events or places or persons, living or dead, is entirely coincidental.
Text copyright © 2014 by Stuart Gibbs
Cover lunar surface photograph copyright © 2014 by Thinkstock.com
All rights reserved, including the right of reproduction in whole or in part in any form.
SIMON & SCHUSTER BOOKS FOR YOUNG READERS is a trademark of Simon & Schuster, Inc.
For information about special discounts for bulk purchases, please contact Simon & Schuster Special Sales at 1-866-506-1949 or business@simonandschuster.com.
The Simon & Schuster Speakers Bureau can bring authors to your live event. For more information or to book an event, contact the Simon & Schuster Speakers Bureau at 1-866-248-3049 or visit our website at www.simonspeakers.com.
Also available in a Simon & Schuster Books for Young Readers hardcover edition
Book design and illustration by Lucy Ruth Cummins
Map art by Ryan Thompson
The text for this book is set in Adobe Garamond.
Manufactured in the United States of America
0518 OFF
First Simon & Schuster Books for Young Readers paperback edition October 2015
10 9 8 7
The Library of Congress has cataloged the hardcover edition as follows:
Gibbs, Stuart, 1969–
Space case / Stuart Gibbs. — First edition.
pages cm
Summary: "Dashiell Gibson, who lives on Moon Base Alpha, has to solve a murder of one of the moon's most prominent doctors"—Provided by publisher.
ISBN 978-1-4424-9486-2 (hardcover) — ISBN 978-1-4424-9488-6 (eBook)
[1. Mystery and detective stories. 2. Moon—Fiction. 3. Space colonies—Fiction. 4. Human-alien encounters—Fiction. 5. Science fiction.] I. Title.
PZ7.G339236Sk 2014
[Fic]—dc23
2013033587
ISBN 978-1-4424-9487-9 (pbk)

For my grandparents,
Rose and Ralph and Annie and Herman

acknowledgments

This book wouldn't exist if it weren't for my good friend Garrett Reisman, who used to be an astronaut and is now the human spaceflight program manager at SpaceX. I've always been thrilled by space travel (back when I was thirteen, I wrote to NASA volunteering to be the first teenager in space) but having a friend who has actually done it is the next best thing to doing it yourself. Over the years, Garrett has given me an incredible window into the present and future of space travel, inviting me and my family to space shuttle launches, videoconferencing with me from the International Space Station (where he showed off his infamous "zero gravity juggling"), and, of course, letting me try the space toilet simulator at the Johnson Space Center. Those experiences inspired this book—as well as my son, Dashiell, who spent many days of his young life dressed as an astronaut. Even though Garrett is insanely busy these days, he was always available to answer any questions I had about what life would be like in space. (However, I should point out that my lead character's views on moon colonization are fictional; they are not the opinions of Garrett or anyone else at NASA or SpaceX.)

I am also indebted to Leah Ilan for teaching me about sign language, Tim Delaney and Danny Eisenberg for doing a tremendous amount of research, Kristin Ostby for her excellent editing, and Jennifer Joel, my extraordinary agent, for first suggesting that space might be a great location for a middle grade series. Finally, huge thanks to my dear friend and fellow science fiend Scott Lew, who went to superhuman lengths to give me some really excellent notes on this book.

contents

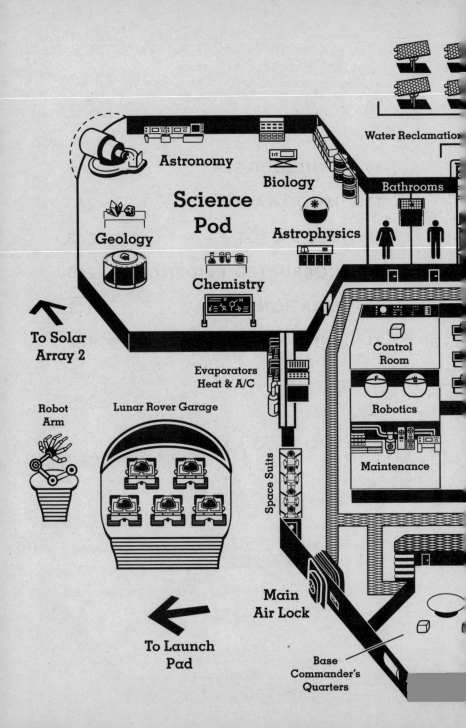

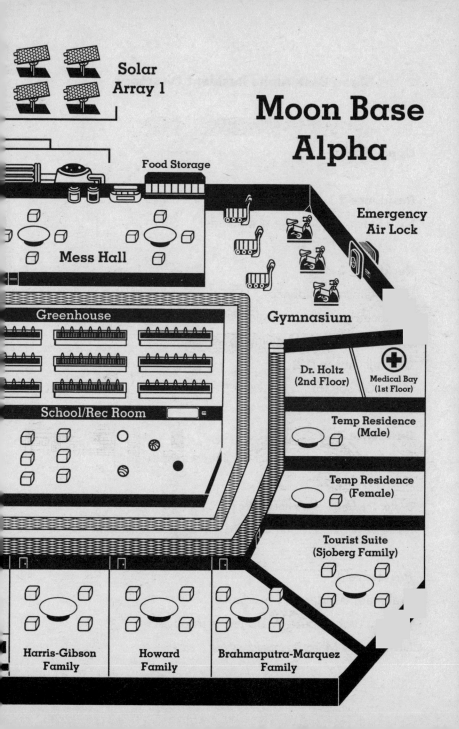

Moon Base Alpha Resident Directory

Upper floor:

Residence 1 *(base commander's quarters and office)*
Nina Stack, moon-base commander

Residence 2

Harris-Gibson residence
Dr. Rose Harris, lunar geologist
Dr. Stephen Gibson, mining specialist
Dashiell Gibson (12)
Violet Gibson (6)

Residence 3

Dr. Maxwell Howard, lunar-engineering specialist
Kira Howard (12)
(Note: The Howards are not due to arrive until Mission 6. This residence will remain empty until then.)

Residence 4

Brahmaputra-Marquez residence
Dr. Ilina Brahmaputra-Marquez, astrophysicist
Dr. Timothy Marquez, psychiatrist

Cesar Marquez (16)

Rodrigo Marquez (13)

Inez Marquez (7)

Tourist Suite

currently occupied by the Sjoberg family:

Lars Sjoberg, industrialist

Sonja Sjoberg, his wife

Patton Sjoberg (16)

Lily Sjoberg (16)

Residence 5 *reserved for temporary base residents (female)*

Residence 6 *reserved for temporary base residents (male)*

Residence 7

Dr. Ronald Holtz, base physician

Lower floor:

Residence 8

Garth Grisan, maintenance specialist

Residence 9

Dr. Wilbur Janke, astrobiologist

Residence 10

Dr. Daphne Merritt, base roboticist

Residence 11

Dr. Chang Kowalski, geochemist

Residence 12

Goldstein-Iwanyi residence

Dr. Shari Goldstein, lunar-agriculture specialist

Dr. Mfuzi Iwanyi, astronomer

Kamoze Iwanyi (7)

Residence 13

Kim-Alvarez residence

Dr. Jennifer Kim, seismic geologist

Dr. Shenzu Alvarez, water-extraction specialist

(Note: Not due to arrive until Mission 6. This residence will remain empty until then.)

Residence 14

Dr. Viktor Balnikov, astrophysicist

(Note: Not due to arrive until Mission 6. This residence will remain empty until then.)

Residence 15

Chen-Patucket residence

Dr. Jasmine Chen, senior engineering coordinator for Moon Base Beta

Dr. Seth Patucket, astrobiologist

Holly Patucket (13)

(Note: Not due to arrive until Mission 8. This residence will be used as housing for temporary base workers until then.)

space case

Excerpt from *The Official Residents' Guide to Moon Base Alpha*, © 2040 by National Aeronautics and Space Administration:

WELCOME TO MOON BASE ALPHA!

Congratulations on your selection as a resident of the first permanent extraterrestrial human habitat! To ease your transition from earth, Moon Base Alpha (referred to from here on as "MBA") has been designed to feel as comfortable and familiar as any residence on our home planet. Our engineers and designers have spared no expense to provide all MBA residents—or "lunarnauts"—with everything they need for a relaxing, pleasurable existence.

However, life on the moon will not be without challenges. There are obviously many differences between this residence and one on earth—many of which you may be pleasantly surprised by! To that end, please take the necessary time to read this helpful, informative manual in its entirety, as it will likely answer any questions you have about your new home (and perhaps a few questions you hadn't even thought to ask yet)!

Once again, congratulations on your selection. Welcome to the moon. Enjoy your new home!

EVIL PLUMBING

Earth year 2041

Lunar day 188

Smack in the middle of the night

Let's get something straight, right off the bat: Everything the movies have ever taught you about space travel is garbage.

Giant spacecraft that are as comfortable as floating cruise ships? Complete fantasy. Warp-speed travel? Never going to happen. Holodecks? Terraforming? Beaming up? Don't count on any of it.

Life in outer space sucks. Trust me, I know.

My name is Dashiell Gibson. I'm twelve years old and I live on the moon.

On Moon Base Alpha, to be exact.

You know this, of course. Everyone on earth knows this, unless they've been living in the Amazon rain forest for the last few years, and since there's barely anything left of the Amazon rain forest, I'm guessing that's unlikely.

Moon Base Alpha—along with everyone who lives on it—has been the subject of an absolutely staggering amount of hype: The first human outpost in space! The first people to live on a celestial body besides earth! A glorious first step in mankind's ultimate colonization of the galaxy!

The government fed my family all that baloney as well, back when they recruited my parents. And I admit, I completely fell for it. We all did. The recruiters made everything sound so amazing: Moon Base Alpha would have all the comforts of earth—and more. We'd go down in history as one of the first families to live in space. We'd be the newest breed of pioneers, pushing the limits of human achievement.

Like I said: garbage.

Living in Moon Base Alpha is like living in a giant tin can built by government contractors. It's as comfortable as an oil refinery. You can't go outside, the food is horrible, it's always cold—and the toilets might as well be medieval torture devices.

Ever notice how, in all the science-fiction movies and TV shows you've ever seen—*Star Wars* and *Battlestar Galactica* and all 142 versions of *Star Trek*—no one ever goes to the bathroom? That's not because, in the future, everyone has figured out how to metabolize their own feces. It's because going to the bathroom in space is a complete pain in the butt. Literally.

At least the moon-base toilet is better than the one on the spaceship we took here. In zero gravity, you have to take extreme precautions to ensure that whatever comes out of your body doesn't fly up into your face. (There's an old saying in zero-g space travel: If you ever see a piece of chocolate floating around the cabin, don't eat it. It's probably not chocolate.) However, using the toilet on Moon Base Alpha is no picnic. If I'd known how exceptionally complicated and disgusting it would be, I never would have agreed to leave earth.

It was because of one of those evil toilets that I wound up involved in far more trouble and danger than I ever could have imagined.

Now, before you get the idea that I'm some whiny, ungrateful kid who just likes to complain and wouldn't be happy anywhere . . . I'm not. Before my family made the awful decision to come live on the moon, I was happy as any kid you've ever met. Happier, maybe. We lived on the Big Island of Hawaii, which was awesome. Mom worked at the W. M. Keck Observatory, which runs the telescopes on the peak of Mauna Kea.

Although the scopes are thirteen thousand feet up, they're managed remotely from the town of Waimea, which meant we could live down by the beach. So my childhood was pretty idyllic. I had lots of friends. I did well in school and played on every sports team. I surfed every weekend—and when I did, there were usually dolphins in the waves with me.

Then the government came calling.

See, my parents have a very unique set of skills. Mom is a lunar geologist who wrote some landmark papers about the moon and the consistency of its mantle and core. Dad is a mining engineer with a specialty in environmentally sound mineral extraction. And one of the major reasons for the moon base is to explore the possibility of mining precious metals there.

Separately, Mom and Dad would each have been solid candidates for Moon Base Alpha. Together, they were an impossible combination to beat. Space is limited on the moon. With them, NASA got two scientists without having to send two separate families. So they wanted my folks badly. We got the full-court press. Politicians called us. The chairman of NASA came to visit. We were all flown to Washington, DC, first class for lunch with the vice president. And every last one of them lied to our faces about how great it would be to live on the moon.

They made it sound like MBA was going to be incredible.

Like our lives there would be nonstop thrills and amazement. Imagine hearing that you've just won a free three-year stay in the most luxurious hotel in the most insane location imaginable. Oh, and you get to be famous, too. Not flash-in-the-pan, one-hit-wonder, reality-TV famous. Have-kids-learn-about-you-in-school-a-hundred-years-from-now famous. We were going to be lumped in with the greatest explorers of all time, maybe even score our own chapter in the history books: Columbus. Magellan. Neil Armstrong. The Harris-Gibson Family of Moon Base Alpha.

It all sounded too good to pass up. So we said yes.

We spent the next year training—but then, you know that. All the families who were headed for MBA became celebrities right off the bat. (NASA tried to get everyone to refer to us as lunarnauts, but the public ended up calling us "Moonies" instead.) The whole world watched all our preparations for life on the moon, our multiple aborted launch attempts, and finally our successful blastoff into space and our triumphant arrival at our new home. And now that we're on the moon, millions of people are still following our lives via webcams and ComLinks and beam-feeds.

And yet, despite all that, you earthlings never get to see the whole story. Instead you see the edited and sanitized version. There's too much at stake to allow anything else through. We Moonies are barred from broadcasting, texting, or transmitting anything to the public that might be "detrimental to the success of Moon Base Alpha." (And if we try, NASA has censors who'll delete it before it goes public.) We can't complain about the toilets or the food or the malfunctioning equipment. We can't mention that anything has ever gone wrong. We have to constantly present a positive face to the public, even when there is nothing to be positive about.

Which is why no one on earth has ever heard about the murder.

I only got involved because I had to use the space toilet at two fifteen in the morning. On the moon this is a major endeavor, because we don't have a toilet in our private living quarters. (Something else the government neglected to mention when talking up the moon base.) Space toilets cost more than thirty million bucks a piece. So instead of springing for one for each family, the moon-base designers only bought six and placed them all in the communal bathrooms, three for the girls and three for the guys.

The living quarters are all in one section of the base, but the geniuses who designed MBA put the bathrooms on the opposite side. The "logical" explanation for this was that the bathrooms would be closer to the work and dining areas, where we—in theory—would spend most of our awake time. Unfortunately, this means that when the urge to purge strikes in the middle of the night, you have to get dressed, leave your quarters, cross the base, use the complicated toilet, and then head back again. It can take fifteen minutes—or more if the toilet jams, which happens far more often than anyone predicted. Everyone at MBA loathes the entire process.

Sometimes I can resist the call of nature and go back to sleep, but on that night I knew it was useless. I'd had chicken parmigiana for dinner. Sort of. Like all our meals, it was a shrink-wrapped block of precooked food that had been irradiated, thermostabilized, dehydrated, and compacted, which meant it didn't taste anything like chicken parm back home. In fairness, a few space foods are actually pretty good— shrimp cocktail and chocolate pudding, for example—but for the most part they all taste like wet sawdust. Some of the other moon kids and I once did a blind taste test of three theoretically different space foods: beef stroganoff, blueberry pancakes, and chicken tikka masala. No one was able to tell the difference.

While almost everything tastes the same going in, though, it all has drastically different effects on my digestive tract. Chicken parm is the worst. It had sent me racing to the john in the middle of the night twice before, so I had avoided it like the plague ever since. But on that night, I screwed up.

All the meals don't merely taste alike. They also *look*

alike. Once you've irradiated, thermostabilized, dehydrated, and compacted a meal, it doesn't look like food anymore; it looks like toy blocks. For this reason, the meals all have identification stickers to tell them apart, but the stickers often come off. (And sometimes things just get labeled wrong.) I had rehydrated what I *thought* was beef teriyaki for dinner, but due to the blandness I was halfway through it before I realized my mistake. By then it was too late. I chucked the remnants in the trash compactor—a flagrant violation of the moon base's food-conservation directives—and hoped for the best.

Instead I found myself running for the toilets at two fifteen. My bowels were rumbling so loudly I was surprised they didn't wake everyone else at MBA.

Actually, what I really did was *bound* for the toilets. The moon's gravity is only one-sixth that of earth's. Zero gravity, which we experienced on the spaceship, could be fun, but one-sixth gravity is disorienting. For the first few days at MBA, everyone essentially had to learn how to walk again and spent a lot of time crashing into walls. We eventually got the hang of it, though we still made mistakes at times. I covered a dozen feet with each leap as I hurried through the base, doing my best not to wipe out en route.

At first glance, the men's bathroom looks like any normal communal bathroom on earth: tiled floor, three stalls, even a bit of graffiti on the walls. (*For a good time, call Princess Leia.*) However, there are no sinks. And no urinals. And the toilets look as though some sadistic plumber mated a vacuum cleaner with an octopus.

The big problem with going to the bathroom on the moon is the scarcity of water. NASA found some ice near the north pole, but it's difficult to extract and there isn't much of it, which means every last drop of H_2O we have is incredibly precious. Therefore, you don't flush your poop at MBA. Instead you essentially do your business in a plastic bag, which is then hermetically sealed, dehydrated, and sucked into a composter. As for pee, you have to use a suction hose, which whisks everything away to a processor that filters out the impurities and sends the rest back into the main reservoir tank.

Yes, we drink our own urine in space. They left that out of *Star Trek* too.

The sitting-on-the-toilet part of the process usually takes about five minutes, but thanks to the chicken parm, I was there for the long haul that night. Thankfully, there was a SlimScreen monitor on the inside of the stall door so I could catch up on the latest news from earth. (In game two of the World Series, the Charlotte Gladiators had beaten the Vegas Mustangs 6–3.) Once I was done, I hit the evacuate button.

To my dismay, the toilet jammed. It made a loud gagging noise, like a cat with a hairball. Then a message on the

SlimScreen informed me that the separator had failed and wouldn't evacuate my poop until it was replaced. Unfortunately, I had no idea what a separator was.

"Help," I said.

"How may I be of assistance?" the base computer asked, speaking through the SlimScreen. The base computer always speaks in an attractive female voice. (That's one thing the movies got right, although I think the computer might have been programmed with a female voice *because* the movies had conditioned us to expect one.) Most of the time it's rather soothing, but when you're a twelve-year-old boy on the toilet with your pants around your ankles, a sexy female voice can be a bit unnerving.

"How do I replace the separator on the toilet?" I asked, and then thought to add, "Quickly."

"I would be delighted to process your request," the computer replied. A second later, instructions appeared on the screen. Thankfully, they weren't too complicated and there were several spare separators stored in a bin above the toilet. Replacing it still wasn't *easy*, though. It took another fifteen minutes, which was why I was still in the bathroom when Dr. Holtz walked in.

Ronald Holtz was one of the most brilliant men I'd ever met. He was an expert in low-gravity human physiology—essentially, how the body holds up in space—and was his own best guinea pig. He had done three extended tours on the International Space Station and thus had spent more time in space than virtually anyone alive. He was now almost seventy, though he was in better shape than most men half his age. Plus everyone liked him: He was always cheerful and friendly, and he knew thousands of jokes. When the time had come to select a physician for the base, there hadn't been any other choice.

I was almost done replacing the separator when I heard Dr. Holtz enter. I knew it was him because he was humming. Dr. Holtz hummed whenever he was in a good mood. He was doing an upbeat tune that night, one my parents liked by some old-time singer named Lady Gaga. He didn't have any idea I was there and I didn't try to tell him. I liked Dr. Holtz a lot, but I didn't want to startle him—and I didn't want to reveal that I'd busted the toilet. I listened to him enter the first stall, pee, evacuate it, and sanitize his hands, humming the whole time. He was walking out when I heard him stop suddenly.

"Hey," he said, as though he was greeting someone.

I hadn't heard anyone else enter, so I assumed Dr. Holtz had just answered a phone call. He didn't seem very surprised to be doing this at two thirty in the morning, so I figured he'd been expecting the call.

I felt guilty eavesdropping, but I also didn't want to burst out of the stall and suddenly reveal my presence. I couldn't think of a third option, so I stayed put and listened.

"Yes," Dr. Holtz said, "I think the time has come to reveal the truth."

The other person must have asked why.

"Because I don't see any point in keeping it a secret anymore," Dr. Holtz replied. "It's too important. I know you have reservations, but I assure you, this is for the best."

There was a pause while he listened to the other person talking.

The space toilet chose this moment to belch some gas that had built up in the system. Luckily, it wasn't loud, and Dr. Holtz was too distracted to notice. However, since I was perched right over the bowl, the gust of space-sewage fumes hit me full on. It was like having an elephant break wind in my face. I almost heaved up the rest of my chicken parm.

"No, I don't think so," Dr. Holtz said, out in the bathroom. "This could be the most important discovery in all of human history. I've kept it under wraps for far longer than I expected, as is. People need to know—"

Another pause.

"Well, no, I can't tell *everyone*," Holtz said. "Not yet. I don't have the authority to inform the general public. But NASA should know about this. And the government. And the National Institute of Science. There are far better scientists than I who ought to be privy to this."

Another pause.

While I was fascinated by what Dr. Holtz was saying, wondering what he could possibly be talking about, I was also desperately trying to control my queasy stomach. The nausea was passing, but it was taking its time. If the toilet released any more gas, I'd puke for sure.

When Dr. Holtz spoke again, he sounded thrilled. Giddy with excitement. "Then you agree? That's fantastic! I promise, you won't regret this. Everything's going to be fine. Better than fine. It's going to be wonderful!"

The other person evidently asked when the news was going to be revealed.

"First thing in the morning," Dr. Holtz replied. "I'd wake everyone here and tell them *now* if I could. We've waited long enough."

A final pause.

"All right. Let's say breakfast, then. Seven o'clock. Tomorrow we're going to make history!"

Dr. Holtz then broke into laughter. Deliriously happy, uncontrolled laughter. Although I'd found his entire conversation intriguing, this was the most startling thing of all. I'd never heard Dr. Holtz laugh like that before. In fact I'd never heard *anyone* laugh like that before. It was like he'd just snorted a whole tank of laughing gas. I listened to it fade away as Dr. Holtz left the bathroom and headed back toward the living quarters.

My stomach was feeling better, so I thought about running after Dr. Holtz and asking what was up, but I had my hands full with the toilet repairs. In retrospect, I wish I'd said to heck with the toilet. Because Dr. Holtz didn't end up revealing his amazing news to anyone the next morning after all.

Instead, at five thirty a.m., in a direct violation of official Moon Base Alpha rules, he made an unauthorized trip through the air lock onto the surface of the moon.

Two minutes later he was dead.

Excerpt from *The Official Residents' Guide to Moon Base Alpha,*
© 2040 by National Aeronautics and Space Administration:

LODGING

Each individual family at Moon Base Alpha has its own separate residence, which has been designed to provide extreme comfort and maximum living space. (In fact, if you have come to MBA from New York City or Beijing, you may even find your residence surprisingly large compared to what you're used to!)

All units are equipped with multiple SlimScreens (enough for the whole family!), direct ComLink connections to earth, ample storage space, and relaxing sleeping quarters. And with SlimScreen's MagicPortal technology, your private "view" can be personalized to any of three million earth locations, allowing you a reminder of home—or a taste of adventure!

RED ALERT

Lunar day 188

Morning

I didn't hear about Dr. Holtz's death until well after it happened.

I hadn't been able to go back to sleep after overhearing his conversation in the bathroom. This was partly because I was excited to learn what he'd discovered—but mostly because our lunar sleeping quarters are horrible. Sleeping in low gravity is difficult to begin with; it's been a major problem with human spaceflight since day one. However, the idiots who designed MBA worked overtime to make the problem even worse. Due to space and weight considerations, no beds were brought to the moon. Instead we all sleep on air mattresses that were specifically designed for minimum weight rather than comfort. They're stiff, they smell like burning tires, and they often leak—so it's common to wake up in the middle of the night to find yourself on the hard floor, surrounded by deflated rubber.

In addition, it's always daytime at Moon Base Alpha. All our power comes from the sun, generated by two massive arrays of solar panels, so MBA is situated near the moon's north pole, where the sun never sets. (Anywhere else on the moon we would have had 354 hours of night at a time, followed by 354 hours of day.) To stay sane, all Moonies are directed to follow a twenty-four hour earth day, synced to the USA's central time zone via Mission Control in Houston, Texas. But I've had a hard time adapting to life without regular phases of night and day.

Finally, we don't have bedrooms. Space is too valuable at MBA for those. Instead we all sleep in "personal sleep pods," which are claustrophobically small chambers built into the wall of our one-room apartment. Each has a sliding door so you can close yourself inside, but no one uses it because that makes the claustrophobia even worse. The sleep pods are stacked two by two like bunk beds, so I have to climb into mine. It's more like a tomb than a bedroom.

With all of that, it was hard enough to sleep on a normal night, let alone when I knew one of the most important discoveries in human history was about to be revealed.

I tossed and turned for hours, then finally gave up and dragged myself from bed at six a.m., figuring I could at least check the SlimScreen for the latest news from earth. However, as I clambered out of my pod, my six-year-old sister, Violet, popped her head out of hers.

"Morning, Dash!" she chirped. "Is it breakfast time?"

"Not quite yet," I whispered, trying not to wake our parents. "Go back to sleep."

"I hope there's bacon this morning!" she said, ignoring me. "D'you think there's bacon?"

"No," I sighed. "There has never been bacon here, and as far as I know, there never will be."

Violet frowned for a split second, then returned to her usual perky self. "Okay. I guess I'll have waffles, then!" She scrambled out of her pod and drifted down to the floor next to me. On earth Violet barely weighed forty pounds; in the moon's weak gravity, she might as well have been a leaf. She was wearing bright pink Hello Kitty pajamas, and her dark hair was sticking out every which way, making her look like Thing One from *The Cat in the Hat*. "Is the rocket here yet?"

I turned to her, surprised. In my excitement about Dr. Holtz, I'd completely forgotten that a rocket was due that day, bringing new Moonies and supplies. The rockets only come every few weeks, which makes their arrivals one of the rare breaks from the dull routine of lunar life. "No. It's not due for another few hours. If it doesn't get delayed."

"Oh. Maybe *they'll* have bacon!"

"I wouldn't get your hopes up."

"Too late! They're up! Want to play chess?"

"You don't know how to play chess."

"I know what all the pieces do!"

"That's not the same thing," I said.

"Did someone mention chess?" My mother slipped out of her own sleep pod. In the one next to hers I caught a glimpse of Dad, who groaned at the early hour and yanked the covers back over his head. Obviously, Violet's refusal to whisper had woken both of them, although Mom, as usual, did her best not to show any annoyance.

"I've got time for a little chess before breakfast," she said, tousling Violet's hair. The two of them look so much alike, with their frizzy hair, dark skin, and green eyes, that people often teasingly ask if Mom just cloned herself. Mom looked to me. "Unless *you* want to play something too? Then I could pick a game for all three of us."

"Ooh! Like Monopoly!" Violet exclaimed. "We can play the Moon Base Alpha version!"

"No, thanks," I said.

"You sure?" Mom asked.

"Definitely." I was too keyed up to spend the next few

hours playing a game—and I certainly wasn't about to play one that took place at Moon Base Alpha. I felt trapped there enough as it was.

"Your loss," Mom chided. Then she turned to the Slim-Screen. "Computer: Chess, please."

Although computers have been able to control everything in homes on earth for years, Mom and Dad always hated the idea. They never installed a control system back in Hawaii. But at MBA the base computer is hardwired into every room, eternally ready to do anything we ask. Fortunately, we can adjust its personality in our private quarters. So Mom and Dad selected the funniest voice they could find: an outrageous, high-pitched German accent.

"It vould be my pleasure!" the computer squealed. "Vhat version of chess do you desire?"

Mom stifled a laugh. "Surprise us," she said.

"I vill do my best, *meine Frau*." On our only table, the SlimScreen surface shifted from the standard simulated-marble screen saver to a three-dimensional, holographic chess game. The computer had selected an extremely ornate version, with pieces that looked like they'd been molded from pure gold and silver and studded with precious gems.

"Ooh!" Violet gasped. "Can you make my pieces pink?"

"I'm afraid I don't have ze ability to emit odors," the computer replied. "Zerefore, I cannot make zem stink."

"Not stink!" Mom snapped. "*Pink!* Can you make her pieces *pink*?"

The computer makes this sort of mistake a lot. Despite billions of dollars in research and development, no tech company has perfected voice-recognition software yet. Even the most state-of-the-art systems screw up. (There's a rumor that World War III almost started when the computer in charge of the North American nuclear missile system misinterpreted a commander saying "I hate syrup" as "annihilate Europe.")

"I'm terribly sorry for ze mistake, *Fraulein*," our computer replied. "I vill correct zis right away." All the golden chess pieces instantly became neon pink.

Violet clapped her hands with delight and sat at the table.

Like the beds, all our chairs at MBA are inflatable: uncomfortable, unwieldy cubes of cheap, squeaky rubber. Whenever you sit on one, it sounds as though you just passed gas.

Mom pulled up an InflatiCube across from Violet. "All right, pumpkin. You go first."

Just so you know, chess isn't Mom's standard pastime. Usually when people hear my parents are scientists, they assume they're awkward, unathletic nerds whose idea of fun is doing long division. That drives me nuts. My parents are the least nerdy people you've ever met. Mom swam competitively in college and competed in triathlons up until we left earth. Dad is a rugged outdoorsman; he's summited dozens of mountains and once free-climbed El Capitan in Yosemite in a day. They met on a Class 5 rafting trip down the Snake River.

But more important, my parents aren't unusual. I've met hundreds of scientists, and most are almost as athletic and adventurous as my parents. I'm not sure how the whole idea that scientists are nerds ever got started. On Moon Base Alpha, the residents aren't merely brilliant; they are also incredibly physically fit. The MBA gym at peak hours looks more like the locker room of a pro soccer team.

Unable to focus on the chess game, I turned to the main SlimScreen in our room. This one is enormous, taking up an entire wall. We don't have a window—almost no one at MBA does, as windows are insanely expensive to deliver and install in space—so we use the screen saver to give ourselves a view. It was currently displaying Hapuna Beach on the Big Island at sunrise, waves lapping on the sand. Frankly, I prefer this to a window. We can project anything we want, while the surface of the moon is dull and gray and, since there is no atmosphere, never changes.

"Computer, bring up the home page on the big screen," I said.

"Ja, mein Herr." Hapuna Beach vanished and the MBA home page took its place.

I scanned it quickly, hoping to see that Dr. Holtz had

called an important meeting for all residents. But there was nothing. In fact the page hadn't even been updated recently: The previous night's Lunar Book Club meeting was still listed as the next "upcoming event" in the calendar.

I couldn't wait in the room any longer. It was feeling even smaller than usual to me. Although Dr. Holtz had said he wouldn't be revealing his discovery until seven o'clock, I figured he might be too excited to sit tight as well. Maybe he was already down in the communal kitchen, holding court. I went to our bureau to grab some clothes.

"Going out already?" Mom asked. "What's the hurry?"

"I'm hungry," I said.

"You didn't even check the World Series scores." Mom sounded slightly suspicious.

"I checked them in the middle of the night," I said. "Charlotte beat Vegas, six to three."

Dad groaned from his sleep pod. "You're kidding."

"No. William Higgins hit a grand slam in the eighth off Jed Bynum."

"What were you doing up in the middle of the night?" Mom asked.

"Bathroom. Revenge of the chicken parmigiana." It didn't take long for me to pick out clothes. Since the moon base is kept sterile, our clothes don't get very dirty—which is good, as we have limited storage space and only one laundry machine at MBA. (Luckily, even if you work out hard, your clothes don't end up smelly, as it's the dirt and grime mixing with your sweat that makes the stink on earth.) Each pair of clothes can be worn multiple times before needing a wash, so we Moonies brought only ten outfits each for our three-year stay. This was fine with me, as I had basically worn a T-shirt and shorts every day back on earth, though some Moonies found life with only ten outfits as awful as I found life without decent food. I pulled on my Waimea Middle School surf team tee and yanked board shorts over the boxers I'd slept in.

As I strapped on my smartwatch, I noticed a message on its tiny video screen: I'd missed a call from Riley Bock, my best friend back on earth, the night before. I texted Riley that I'd call her later; she was probably still asleep—it was one a.m. in Hawaii—and besides, there was too much else to focus on that morning. I slipped into my sneakers and headed for the door.

Violet abandoned her chess game and ran after me. "I'm hungry too! I want waffles! Waffles waffles waffles!"

"Dash, can you wait for your sister to get ready?" Mom asked.

"No." I didn't even slow down on my way out. "It always takes her fifteen minutes to get dressed. I could eat and be back by then."

"I don't need to get dressed!" Violet announced. "I'll just wear my pajamas!"

"I thought you wanted to play chess," I said.

"I want waffles more!"

We don't have real waffles on the moon, of course. We only have reconstituted waffle-flavored substance. It tastes like coagulated maple syrup, but Violet loves it. She's the only one at MBA who eats it.

I grabbed the doorknob, ready to walk out anyhow.

"Dash. Wait for your sister," Mom ordered.

I stopped, knowing better than to disobey my mother. The last thing I needed was to be sent to my sleeping pod. "Let's move it, squirt," I told Violet.

"Let me get my slippers!" Violet scurried back to her pod, singing a song about waffles.

Violet could make up a song about anything. She once performed practically an entire opera about clipping her toenails. Now she was happily crooning, "I love waffles! They're not awful! They taste so good!"

A strange, urgent beeping suddenly filled the room. It sounded like a giant microwave announcing that the popcorn was done. It took me a moment to figure out it was coming from both SlimScreens at once. On the wall and the tabletop, the home page and the chess game vanished and were replaced with a message in blinking red letters:

Urgent communication for Dr. Rose Harris & Dr. Steven Gibson. Log in to the secure portal immediately.

I hadn't even known information could be delivered this way. I turned to my mother, who looked as surprised by it as I was. Violet danced around, excited by the noise, and added her own whooping to it. Dad still hadn't emerged from his sleeping pod. At the sound of the alarm he had jammed his fingers in his ears and burrowed under the covers.

Dad had never been a morning person.

"Steven," Mom called to him. "You'd better take a look at this."

Dad stuck his head out of the pod and glanced at the big SlimScreen. He looked like a squirrel peeking out of its nest. "What the heck is that about?" he grumbled.

Mom shrugged. She was already using the tabletop Slim-Screen to log in to the portal.

I was humming with excitement, figuring the emergency message had to do with Dr. Holtz's discovery. Maybe he hadn't been able to wait until seven and had already revealed his amazing news to the top brass at MBA, who were now getting the word out. Or maybe he was calling a big meeting to share the news with everyone at once.

I opened our door to see if anything was happening. There are two tiers of residences at Moon Base Alpha. Ours is on the second floor, one down from the end. The door opens onto an iron catwalk. (Catwalks are easier to ship and install than real floors.) Over the railing I could see the first-floor hallway below. No one was moving on either level, though the same urgent beeping was coming through the other residence doors. Two residences to the right of mine I could hear the muffled sounds of the Brahmaputra-Marquez family groggily waking.

Voices echoed through the base to my left, in the direction of the main air lock. There was an edge to them, as though the speakers were worried—or panicked—but I couldn't hear what anyone was saying. Their words were all drowned out by my sister, who was still singing about breakfast foods at the top of her voice.

Directly to my left was the residence of the base commander, Nina Stack. It is the closest residence to the air lock. Nina's door hung open, which was unusual. Since there is so much common space at MBA, the residents take their privacy seriously. No one ever leaves their door open. Nina must have left in such a hurry she'd forgotten to shut it behind her.

I started down the catwalk toward the air lock, but a horrified shriek from my mother stopped me in my tracks.

I rushed back into our room. "What's wrong?"

Mom had gone pale. She stared at the tabletop Slim-Screen, eyes wide in astonishment. Dad stood behind her, equally stunned, having read the same message over her shoulder. Mom started to answer me, then noticed Violet.

She looked to Dad and something unspoken passed between them.

"Violet," Dad said. "Want to watch TV before you have your waffles?"

"Now?" Violet's face lit up. Even in the confines of MBA my folks tried to limit our screen time. Offering TV before breakfast was like telling Violet she could have a pony. "Can I watch *Squirrel Force?*"

"Sure." Dad quickly clapped headphones over Violet's ears, ensuring that she wouldn't hear what my mother was about to say, then switched the big SlimScreen to TV mode. The emergency alert vanished and was replaced by animated squirrels battling evil land developers. Violet sat, riveted to it, ignoring us completely. If the base ever catches fire while *Squirrel Force* is on, Violet will probably roast alive rather than stop watching.

Mom turned back to me. She was still so shocked; it took her a while to find her voice. "It's . . . well, you see . . . it's about Dr. Holtz. He . . . he's dead."

I'd been girding myself for bad news, but even this caught me off guard. It simply didn't seem possible. I was so dumbfounded, it felt kind of like my brain had popped inside my head, leaving nothing but air. "How?" I managed to ask.

Dad put an arm around my shoulders. "He went out the air lock this morning. Alone."

I turned to him, almost as startled by this as by Dr. Holtz's death. There are strict rules against anyone ever going out onto the lunar surface alone. "Why?"

Mom wiped tears from her eyes. "We don't know. The report doesn't say."

"Anyhow," Dad went on, "it seems he didn't put on his space suit properly and . . ." He trailed off, not wanting to finish the thought.

I knew how it would end anyhow. Space suits are almost impossible to put on properly by yourself—and if you make a mistake, the air can leak out. If that happens, there isn't any oxygen on the surface of the moon. Without oxygen, the human body can only survive two minutes, at most. Which is exactly why solo moonwalks are forbidden.

I shook my head. "This doesn't make sense. Dr. Holtz would never do anything that risky. . . ."

"He did." Mom placed a hand on mine. "I know this is hard to process. I'm as surprised as you are. We all have questions, and it may be a while before we get answers."

"Where's Dr. Holtz now?" I asked.

"They're still bringing him back inside," Dad told me.

I snapped to my feet and bolted back out the door, racing toward the air lock. Mom and Dad called after me, but I didn't listen. I wasn't sure why, but I desperately wanted to see Dr. Holtz's body for myself.

I ran past Nina Stack's open door. Ahead the catwalk banked left around a corner, where a set of stairs descended into the staging area by the air lock. As I reached the corner, however, Nina came around it. I slammed right into her.

If I'd run into almost anyone else at MBA like that, I probably would have bowled them down the stairs. But running into Nina was like hitting an oak tree. She's the toughest woman I've ever met in my life. Maybe even the toughest person. She was in the Marines before joining NASA and has kept up her physical training ever since. She doesn't *look* that tough—in fact she looks kind of dainty, like a lot of my friends' moms back in Hawaii—but I'd pity anyone who challenged her to a fight. Nina can mop the floor with anyone. And she has an advanced degree in rocket science to boot.

I bounced off her and went down on my butt. "Sorry," I mumbled, then tried to slip past her.

Nina blocked my path. "Go back to your residence, Dash." It wasn't a request. It was an order. If Nina was upset about Dr. Holtz, it didn't show. But I wouldn't have expected that anyhow. I've seen moon rocks that expressed more emotion than Nina. She's so robotic the Moonie kids call her "Nina the Machina" behind her back.

"I have to use the bathroom," I lied.

Nina didn't buy it for a second. "There's nothing to see," she told me.

Which was also a lie, of course. I managed to catch a glimpse of the air lock over her shoulder.

There was plenty to see.

Nina hooked her hands under my arms, hoisted me off the floor, and forcibly carried me ten steps back toward my apartment. Then she set me down and got in my face. "This isn't a game, Dashiell. Go home for now. You'll be able to leave soon."

"When?"

"When I say so." Nina pointed toward my door. I looked back to see both my parents standing there, waiting for me.

I obediently retreated. The fact was, I'd already seen everything I needed to. The brief glimpse I'd gotten was more than enough.

Two Moonies had been emerging from the air lock with Dr. Holtz, carrying him back inside, one holding his heels, the other his arms. Others had been crowded around them. I hadn't even noticed who any of them were. I was too focused on Dr. Holtz. They'd taken him out of his space suit in the air lock, so I could see his face. The color had already drained from him. He was obviously dead.

My parents ushered me back into our residence, seeming very concerned about me. I probably looked terrible after seeing Dr. Holtz. I certainly *felt* terrible.

Dad shut the door. Mom steered me to an InflatiCube. My sister was still watching TV with the headphones clapped over her ears, singing the *Squirrel Force* theme song at full volume, unaware that anything bad had happened.

"This is all wrong," I said.

Dad knelt beside me and put his arm around my shoulders. "I know, pal. It seems wrong to us, too."

I shook my head. "That's not what I meant. I . . . I don't think this was an accident."

Mom and Dad shared a slightly concerned look. Neither seemed sure what to say.

"You mean you think he did this on purpose?" Mom asked.

"No!" I said. "Not at all. I overheard Dr. Holtz in the bathroom last night. He was talking to someone about a discovery he'd made. A discovery he was going to reveal to all of us this morning. He was so excited about it. I've never heard anyone so happy. He couldn't wait to tell everyone. So why would he go outside—*alone*—this morning without checking to make sure his suit was on right? That doesn't make any sense."

Once again Mom and Dad shared a look. This one was considerably more concerned. Although I couldn't tell whether they were worried about me or about something else.

"Dash," Dad said gravely. "Are you saying you think Dr. Holtz was murdered?"

"Yes," I told him. "That's exactly what I'm saying."

Excerpt from *The Official Residents' Guide to Moon Base Alpha*,
© 2040 by National Aeronautics and Space Administration:

EDUCATION

For the benefit of families with children living at MBA, school will take place Monday through Friday, just as on earth. Age-specific classes will be conducted via ComLink with terrestrial instructors to provide the highest-quality education possible. In fact, your children will probably receive an even better education on the moon than they did on earth! NASA has recruited the finest, most effective teachers to lead classes—and your children's education will regularly be supplemented with lectures by NASA specialists in dozens of different fields, ranging from mathematics to biology to engineering. Since your children will be living on the moon, they'll be at the forefront of scientific research—so there's a chance they might even learn some groundbreaking information *before* anyone on earth does!

BLOODTHIRSTY GELATIN

Lunar day 188
Breakfast time

School was canceled because of the crisis.

Back on earth I would have been thrilled for a sudden day off. But on the moon a day without school is even worse than a day *with* it. This isn't because I really love school; I don't. It's because at MBA there is nothing else to do. I couldn't use my newfound freedom to go surfing or mountain biking. Instead I was cooped up in the same place I always was, but now without anything to occupy my time. Which placed me in the bizarre situation of begging my parents to let me attend school.

"Please," I pleaded. "I don't have to go all day. Only a few hours."

"I'm sorry," Dad said. "Nina gave a direct order."

"Come on! Can't I take just one class?"

"No. You're not going to school today and that's final."

"My teachers all work out of their homes," I argued. "And I'm not doing anything. So why can't I just ComLink them and take my classes?"

"Nina wants all Links left open for communication with NASA," Mom replied.

My whole family was now in the mess hall, having breakfast. Or rather, Violet was having breakfast. The rest of us were still too shaken up. I had tried to eat a rehydrated cinnamon bun, which is one of the best space foods we have, but my stomach was so jumpy I'd only managed a few bites. Many of our fellow Moonies seemed to be having the same problem. Most everyone was passing on the solids and simply drinking their reclaimed-urine coffees. Violet, however, was happily scarfing down reconstituted waffles. Mom and Dad were letting her listen to music so she wouldn't notice what else was going on; she had her earbuds in and was happily rocking out to her favorite band, a retro-ska dance group called Coronal Mass Ejection. Between the waffles, the music, and the fact that school had been canceled, it might as well have been Christmas for Violet.

"There are two hundred fifty-six ComLinks," I told my

parents. "That's more than ten for every person here. What could Nina possibly need all of them for?"

"I think it's standard emergency procedure," Dad said.

"I know," I countered, "but the emergency procedures were designed for something like an asteroid strike or an oxygen leak, weren't they? Technically, this isn't even an emergency anymore. It's not like Dr. Holtz can get more dead."

My mother glanced at Violet to see if she'd overheard this, but Violet had her earbuds firmly jammed in her ears. Mom then fixed me with a hard stare. "I don't think that sort of talk is appropriate."

"Sorry," I said. "It's just that, without the Links, I can't talk to my friends on earth. Or download a book. Or watch a movie."

"It's only temporary." Dad looked to the other tables to make sure no one was within eavesdropping range, then lowered his voice. "Things are going to be a little unsettled here for a bit. No one ever expected Dr. Holtz to have an accident like this."

"That's because it *wasn't* an accident," I said under my breath. "Someone forced him to walk out that air lock with his suit on wrong."

Mom sighed. "Dashiell, we've already discussed this. You have no proof of that."

"Dr. Holtz would never have gone out the air lock without a partner," I protested. "He was always warning us that it's almost impossible to put a space suit on right by yourself. He was the one who came up with the buddy system for going out on the surface in the first place!"

"That doesn't mean it was a murder," Dad countered. "There are plenty of reasons he might have decided to ignore the rules. Maybe it had something to do with this big discovery of his. Maybe he had to get something off the lunar surface."

"And risk almost certain death?" I asked. "No way. Dr. Holtz was the most cautious person I ever met. He wore a helmet to ride the stationary bike!"

"Even the most cautious people make mistakes," Mom told me. "And furthermore, there doesn't appear to be any evidence of foul play."

"It's only been an hour," I muttered. "I'm sure some will turn up."

Mom and Dad exchanged one of their concerned looks. They'd been doing this a great deal that morning, like they were far more worried about me than they were about Dr. Holtz.

Dad said, "Dash, you're a smart kid. You're very mature and precocious for your age, and we love that about you. But sometimes that brain of yours works a little too hard to see patterns where there might not be any."

"Dealing with the death of someone close to you is always difficult," Mom added. "We all have our different mechanisms for confronting a tragedy like this—"

"I'm not making this up!" I snapped, way too loud. Everyone in the mess turned toward us, so I had to lower my voice again. "You didn't hear Dr. Holtz in the bathroom last night. If you had, you'd be just as sure as me that this wasn't an accident."

My parents recoiled from me. My outburst had caught them by surprise—but I think it convinced them I wasn't merely having problems dealing. "Well, if this *was* a murder," Dad said, "then you're right, some evidence ought to turn up. But if none does . . ."

"I'll drop it," I finished.

"There's something else you should know about Dr. Holtz that's important . . . ," Mom began, but she didn't get to finish. Dr. Timothy Marquez was approaching our table; Mom fell silent so he wouldn't overhear her.

Dr. Marquez is the Moon Base Alpha psychiatrist. NASA is very concerned about our mental health—living in an enclosed space far from earth is a good recipe for going nuts—so we all have mandatory evaluation sessions once a week. Dr. Marquez is the only Moonie who was really famous *before* being selected to come to MBA. He wrote a bestselling self-help book called *Turn That Frown Upside*

Down and appeared on tons of talk shows. Despite this, I've always found him a little weird. He has a lot of nervous tics and is a little too intense for me. He takes his job way too seriously and is always sticking his nose in everyone else's business, like he was doing right then.

"Is everything all right over here?" he asked, obviously having overheard my outburst. He had a cup of coffee and was compulsively stirring it with a spoon. Dr. Marquez rarely ever actually drinks his coffee; he simply stirs it for hours at a time.

"Yes," Dad said dismissively. "Everything's fine."

Dr. Marquez made a high-pitched giggle. He sounded like a monkey being tickled. "Oh, I highly doubt that. We have all just experienced a highly traumatic incident. In fact we are *still* experiencing it. So I don't think that everything is fine at all. Not for you. Not for me. Not for any of us." Dr. Marquez sat on the InflatiCube beside me without being invited. "So tell me, how are all of you *really* holding up?"

His arrival grabbed Violet's attention. "There's no school today!" she shouted over her music. "And I'm having waffles!"

"Oh." Dr. Marquez never seemed to know how to deal with Violet's effusive happiness. "That's nice."

"We're doing as well as can be expected," Mom put in. "How is your family, Timothy?"

"Oh, they've gone through the whole gamut of emotions." Dr. Marquez picked a chunk of dehydrated fruit out of his teeth and flicked it away. "Shock, disbelief, grief, anger, you name it." He looked to me. "Roddy's had a tough time himself. He's in the rec room right now. I'm sure he could use a friend to talk to."

"That's a great idea," Mom said.

"Is it really?" I asked, not so convinced.

"I think it'd be good for you to talk to someone your own age right now," Dad said. "Besides, we still have to break the news to your sister, and it might be best if we did that on our own." He nodded to Violet, who had returned to obliviously devouring waffles and listening to her music.

I nodded understanding and got up. Dr. Marquez didn't. "Perhaps I could be of some assistance with young Violet," he said to my parents. "It might be nice to have a professional around to help cushion the emotional blow."

"Thanks, that'd be very helpful," Mom said, although I wasn't sure if she meant it. When you live in an enclosed space with only twenty-two other people, you can't ever really afford to offend anyone.

I went to the drink station, poured myself a cup of reclaimed water, and headed to the rec room. Although it would have been faster to go past the moon-base gym, I looped around the long way instead. In truth, MBA isn't that big—it's only about the size of a soccer pitch—so the long way wasn't really all that long. But more important, it took me past the main air lock.

MBA has a simple design. It consists of two octagons, one large and one small. The large octagon is the residential area: The apartments, gym, kitchen, and communal bathrooms line the outer wall, with the control center, greenhouse, and rec room in the center. The small octagon is the science pod, where experiments in biology, chemistry, geology, and astrophysics are conducted. The science pod is attached to the northwest corner of the main building; from above, MBA looks like a large stop sign with a smaller one growing on it like a tumor.

My route first took me between the science pod and the control center. Almost every adult on the base works in one or the other, so on most days they would have been hives of activity. Today both were almost empty. Only Dr. Janke, one of the biologists, was in the science pod, absently fiddling with one of his experiments. He didn't appear to be working so much as trying to distract himself from Dr. Holtz's death.

Nina was the only one in the control center. She was using the ComLink and had her back to me. Mission Control in Houston was on the SlimScreen. A dozen men and women had gathered to talk to her, all with very grave expressions on their faces. I considered trying to eavesdrop, but Nina turned my way and gave me a hard stare that was basically an order to keep on moving, so that was exactly what I did.

I passed the maintenance room and the operations center for the base robots, crossed through the staging area where all the space suits were stored, and finally came to the air lock. The whole journey had taken twenty-six seconds.

The air lock is one of the rare spots at MBA with a window. Technically there are two windows, as the air lock has two doors: an inner door and an outer door, with a four-foot safety chamber between them. The view through the windows is narrow and obstructed, but then the area outside the air lock isn't much to look at anyhow.

Since there is no atmosphere on the moon, the only thing that ever alters the landscape is us—and humans rarely alter a landscape for the better. What was once a pristine, white blanket of moon dust has now been trampled by a million footprints and flattened by the treads of the moon rovers, which are housed in a garage near MBA. It's like when a fresh, beautiful snowfall gets ruined by boot prints and tire tracks—only instead of eventually melting away, it just stays in that ugly, polluted state forever.

On the ruined lunar surface it was impossible to pick out Dr. Holtz's footprints or pinpoint where he'd collapsed and died. All I knew was, without his space suit on right he couldn't have gone far. There is no oxygen outside. The farthest

I can get holding my breath is about fifty feet. (I've tested this indoors on multiple occasions, just in case of trouble.)

There were still some traces of moon dust on the staging-area floor. At breakfast I'd learned who had recovered Dr. Holtz's body: Daphne Merritt, our base roboticist, and Garth Grisan, who is in charge of maintenance. Normally, for sanitation reasons, there were extreme precautions to prevent tracking moon dust into the base, but it had probably been hard to follow them all when one of the three people coming back inside was dead.

Despite being surrounded by megatons of moon dust, I'd never touched the stuff before.

I'd been out on the lunar surface myself exactly once: when passing from the rocket landing pad to MBA after arriving on the moon. It had taken ten minutes, tops. Because I'm a kid, I'd never been allowed another chance to go outside.

I knelt and dragged my fingers through the dust. It felt like slightly gritty powdered sugar. Moon dust isn't really dust; it's mostly tiny shards of a strange kind of glass formed in the extreme heat of meteor impacts. It smelled faintly of gunpowder, reminding me of fireworks.

"Did you drop something?"

I spun around to find Garth Grisan behind me. Mr. Grisan is in his late fifties, which is older than most of the people at MBA, but running maintenance for everything on the base requires someone with a lot of knowledge and experience. He seemed nice enough, but he tended to keep to himself. Although I'd been living at the base with him for more than six months, we'd almost never spoken.

"No," I said. "I was just . . . um . . . There's some moon dust on the floor."

"Yeah. I'm about to take care of that." Mr. Grisan held up a small vacuum. "With all the excitement this morning, I haven't had a chance yet."

I suddenly felt embarrassed. "I wasn't telling you to clean it up," I said. "I just noticed it and . . . well . . ." I trailed off, not quite sure what else to say.

Mr. Grisan smiled warmly, signaling he hadn't been offended. "It's all right, Dashiell. We're all trying to deal with Dr. Holtz in our own way."

I nodded agreement, then thought to ask, "You went out and got him?"

Mr. Grisan's smile faded. "Yes. With Daphne."

"Did anything seem strange about him?"

"Other than him being dead on the surface of the moon? The whole thing seemed strange. Strange and wrong." Mr. Grisan shuddered at the memory.

"Was he . . . ?" I began, but before I could get another word out, Mr. Grisan cut me off.

"To be honest, I'd prefer to forget all about what it was like. And it's probably better for a kid like you not to know. So if you'll excuse me . . ." Mr. Grisan held up the vacuum again and pointed to the floor.

"Right," I said. "Sorry." I turned to leave—and caught sight of Nina in her office. She was glaring at me, apparently annoyed that I was still within range of her.

I took a last glance out the air lock, then hurried off. Behind me I heard the whine of the vacuum as Mr. Grisan sucked up the moon dust.

Like his father had told me, Rodrigo "Roddy" Marquez was in the rec room. This wasn't much of a surprise. Roddy was almost always in the rec room. That's where the best holographic interfaces are.

As usual, Roddy was seated on an InflatiCube, playing a virtual-reality game. His eyes were covered by thick black hologoggles and his hands were sheathed in sensogloves. Either he hadn't heard that Nina had ordered everyone to stay off the ComLink or—more likely—he'd decided to ignore her.

Roddy was my best friend at MBA, although that really didn't mean much: He was the only other kid my age on the moon. Back on earth we probably wouldn't have been friends at all. Roddy is a decent guy, but our interests are completely different. He's what we called a "veeyar" at my old school, short for "virtual resident"—a kid who spends nearly all his time in the computer-generated world.

I've never spent much time in virtual reality myself. We didn't even have a holographic interface at our house. Meanwhile Roddy logged more than ten hours a day online *before* he came to the moon. For that reason he doesn't hate MBA nearly as much as I do. His life here is almost exactly the same as it was back on earth: He spends as much time as possible jacked in and never goes outdoors.

Roddy was so fixated on his game he had no idea I'd entered the room. He was jerking about wildly, arms extended, his index fingers twitching like worms on a fish-hook. That meant he was probably playing a war game, blasting away with virtual guns.

I tapped him on the shoulder. "Hey, Roddy, how are you doing?"

"I'm in the middle of a raid here," he said curtly. "Jack in if you want to talk."

I sighed. This is one of the problems with veeyars: They find talking in the virtual world more comfortable than doing it face-to-face. Still, I didn't feel like waiting around for Roddy to finish his game; knowing him, that could have taken days.

There were plenty of hologoggles and sensogloves stored on a rack on the wall. I slipped some on, sat on the InflatiCube beside Roddy, and jacked in to his interface. With a whoosh the dull gray walls of the rec room vanished, and I suddenly found myself in one of the most startlingly beautiful landscapes I'd ever seen. I was standing in a meadow full of wildflowers by a pristine, blindingly blue lake, with verdant forest on one side and snowcapped mountains on the other. Six separate waterfalls spilled into the lake, each more breathtaking than the last.

Roddy had no doubt combed through thousands of potential earthscapes to find one this stunning—and then selected it to wage a war in. His enemies were some sort of gelatinous pink alien creatures. Although they all had guns, they didn't appear very menacing. Roddy had probably set the game controls to a beginner level, preferring easy victory to stiff competition. The aliens had stubby little flippers instead of hands, which meant they could barely even hold their weapons, let alone fire them. Meanwhile Roddy was blowing them away with ease. Each time he hit one, it burst into a shower of pink goo, like someone had detonated a bowl of strawberry Jell-O.

Roddy had heavily modified his avatar as well. While the actual Roddy is flabby, uncoordinated, and not particularly handsome, virtual Roddy was built like an Olympic decathlete, with movie-star looks and bulging muscles. This was common for veeyars. Several other avatars were fighting alongside Roddy, representing people back on earth who were also playing. The men all appeared equally Olympian, while all the women looked like professional swimsuit models.

I materialized right in the thick of things, at Roddy's side. Since I'd never bothered to modify my avatar, it looked exactly like me. In real life I'm three inches taller than Roddy. Here I looked like a dwarf beside him. His avatar's biceps were bigger than my head. My gun, some kind of bizarre machine gun–bazooka combo, was half the size that I was. I didn't have a clue how to fire it. But then I didn't have any desire to play pretend war anyhow.

"What are we fighting here?" I asked. "Angry pudding?"

Roddy frowned. "Don't be fooled by the appearance of the Gogolaks," he warned. "What they lack in agility they make up for in cunning and guile. Plus, one bite from them makes your brain dissolve into sludge." With that he blasted three into smithereens. Their defense didn't seem particularly cunning to me. After the first got blown away, the other two simply froze and gibbered in terror, allowing Roddy to pick them off effortlessly.

"We're not supposed to be using the ComLinks," I warned.

"Don't tell me you bought that 'we have to leave them

open for emergencies' garbage. Want to know what the real story is?"

Before I could answer, Roddy told me anyhow. Roddy is prone to rants. He's a smart kid; unfortunately, he likes everyone else to *know* how smart he is. "NASA is freaking out about Holtz kicking the bucket. They've told everyone back on earth that this place is safe as can be—and suddenly our doctor's dead on the surface of the moon. The media will go nuts with that story, so NASA's trying to control it. *That's* why they want us off the Links. They don't want us blabbing the truth to our friends before they can put out a press release with a nice, sanitized version of what happened. They'll say Holtz croaked because of a heart attack or something, not 'cause he went out on the surface solo like a moron."

I frowned, annoyed at how Roddy was talking about Dr. Holtz, then glanced at the avatars of the other players blasting Gogolaks close by. "You're saying all this on an open Link. Any one of these people could be listening."

"They're not paying any attention to us. And they don't have any idea what our real identities are. For all they know, we're two yahoos from Podunk."

"Still, we should watch what we say. If you're right—"

"Of course I'm right."

"—and if we spill the beans, Nina will want our heads."

"I'm not forcing you to stay on here. If you're so worried about breaking the rules, why'd you even jack in?"

"Your father said I should come check on you."

Roddy laughed spitefully. "Of course he did. Rather than come check on me himself." He spun around and blasted four more aliens into oblivion. "Tell him I'm totally fine."

"You sure?" I asked. I tried to pick my words carefully, wary of saying anything classified. Thankfully, the other players all appeared distracted with blasting the enemy into pink smithereens. "You're not upset about Dr. Holtz?"

Roddy's avatar shrugged, unmoved, which meant that real Roddy had just done the same thing. "I didn't really know him all that well."

I stared at Roddy, trying to read his expression, but in the virtual world this was almost impossible. The avatars don't mimic the subtle movements of their players' faces. Instead, everyone always looks like they're posing for a magazine cover. I had no idea if Roddy was telling the truth or not.

"Well, *I'm* upset," I said. "I think the whole thing's kind of weird."

Roddy laid down a carpet of gunfire and took out a dozen Gogolaks in one sweep. "Why's that?"

I decided not to repeat the story of overhearing Dr. Holtz's conversation the night before his death. Knowing

Roddy, he'd be far more interested in my breaking the space toilet—and he'd never let me hear the end of it. Instead I brought up something else that had occurred to me. "Living up here was Dr. Holtz's dream come true," I said. "He worked his whole life to be on this mission. And then, only six months in, he does a solo outside without authorization? I can't believe he'd take a risk like that."

Roddy shrugged again. "He was kind of old. Maybe he was losing his mind. My great-grandpa's nuttier than a granola bar. He wanders away from home all the time. Once, they found him at the zoo in his pajamas. Maybe Holtz was losing it too."

I shook my head. "No way. NASA screened all of us for any kind of mental issues. Especially Dr. Holtz. They wouldn't have sent him up here if they'd found he was getting senile."

No Gogolaks had attacked for a while. They appeared to have retreated.

Roddy's avatar scanned the horizon carefully anyhow. "Maybe Holtz developed something while he was here. Some kind of space madness."

"Space madness?" I repeated, failing to hide my skepticism.

"Yeah," Roddy said. "Like where you go bonkers from being cooped up here for too long."

"I could imagine *me* getting that," I said. "But not Dr. Holtz."

"On your left!" Roddy screamed.

I spun around to find a horde of gelatinous aliens mounting a sneak attack. They hadn't retreated; they'd flanked us. I whipped my gun toward them and blasted away. However, since I wasn't very adept at shooter games, I missed most of them and took out two of my fellow players by accident. They both stared at me as they winked out of existence.

"Smooth move," Roddy groused.

The Gogolaks closed the gap on me with surprising speed for creatures made out of instant dessert. Apparently, they were faster—and craftier—than I'd realized. The closest one leaped at me, opening its mouth wide enough to swallow me whole. Right before I could be plunged into its digestive tract, however, Roddy blew it away. Then he obliterated the rest, whooping with delight as he blasted them to bits. I even managed to get one myself. All around us the aliens burst apart, coating us with droplets of pink goo.

The moment Roddy vaporized the last one, a heavenly chorus swelled. Words appeared in the crystal sky over the mountains: LEVEL ONE CLEARED. PREPARE FOR LEVEL TWO.

"You're gonna have to be way better to survive the next round," Roddy warned me.

"I don't think Dr. Holtz had space madness," I told him. "If he did, your dad would have noticed, right?"

"Maybe my dad *did*. He wouldn't have told *us*. He would have told Nina. And she would have probably kept it quieter than a Bosnakkian Snork."

"A what?"

"A Bosnakkian Snork," Roddy repeated curtly, as though this were something everyone had heard of before. "An alien species from the Andromeda Galaxy renowned for not making any sound at all. Haven't you ever played Warp War?"

"Uh . . . no."

"Really? Well, point is, if the word got out that Holtz—the guy who's supposed to be the world expert on human health in space—had gone psycho up here, it'd be an even bigger story than him dying. A massive black eye for the whole space program. I mean, the only reason they let all us kids come up here was because Holtz said it was safe—and suddenly *he* turns out to be loony? Before you know it, Congress will want to shut this place down."

I had to admit, that was a pretty good argument. While the next level of the game loaded, I thought back to all the times I'd seen Dr. Holtz recently. He'd seemed perfectly fine to me. In fact, the night in the bathroom before he'd died, he'd sounded sane as could be—although he *had* laughed pretty maniacally while walking out. Had that been craziness? Or had he just been really excited?

The landscape around me suddenly vanished and a new one appeared. Now I found myself standing next to Roddy inside the Sistine Chapel. Words flashed across Michelangelo's famous painting on the ceiling: PREPARE FOR INVASION.

I turned to Roddy, stunned. "We're fighting aliens inside the Vatican?"

"Yeah," he said with a grin. "Malicious Freeps. Flesh-eating slugs from Neptune. This is gonna be awesome!"

The slurping sound of something large and viscous came from the galleries ahead. Three eyeballs on turquoise stalks poked around the corner, then narrowed angrily upon spotting us.

Even though the enemy was fake, I felt a very real wave of fear. My fingers tensed on the virtual triggers.

Before the attack could come, however, the image froze. I thought it was a glitch at first, the whole game locking up, but then noticed that Roddy was still moving beside me.

"What the . . . ?" he asked.

"Dashiell and Rodrigo!" Nina's voice boomed throughout the chapel, echoing off the walls. "I thought I'd made it clear that all ComLinks were to remain open."

Roddy gulped, far more frightened by Nina than by the entire army of flesh-eating Freeps. "I didn't hear about that," he lied. "Sorry. Logging off now." His avatar vanished a second later.

"Logging off," I echoed.

"Wait one second, Dashiell," Nina told me. "I want you to come see me. Right now."

"Where?"

"I'm in my quarters. Don't dillydally. This is urgent."

"Okay," I said, then logged out of the game. The Sistine Chapel vanished and all I could see was black.

I pried the hologoggles off my face and blinked in the fluorescent light of the rec room. I always find switching from the virtual world to the real one a little disorienting. The virtual world is so overstimulating that sometimes real life feels strangely unnatural afterward. Veeyars refer to this readjustment as "the letdown."

Roddy was still sitting on the cube next to me, frowning at his goggles. "That's just great," he muttered. "What are we supposed to do now?"

"I have some books you could borrow."

"Books?" Roddy snorted with disgust. "Big whoop."

I started for the door.

"Where are you going?" Roddy asked.

"Nina wants to see me."

"Oooh," Roddy taunted, "you're in trouuuuuble! What'd you do wrong?"

"Nothing," I said.

"C'mon," Roddy told me. "Holtz just bit the big one. It's a major crisis—and Nina wants to see you smack in the middle of it? She's not inviting you over for tea. You're definitely up a creek."

"I'm not," I said, though the truth was, I didn't believe that myself. As I headed out the door, I had the disturbing feeling that Roddy was right. I *was* in trouble. I just didn't know why yet.

Excerpt from *The Official Residents' Guide to Moon Base Alpha*,
© 2040 by National Aeronautics and Space Administration:

GOVERNMENT

According to the International Lunar Treaty of 2036, no country from earth may stake a territorial claim to any part of the moon. Thus, the moon has no official government. Instead, all lunarnauts are technically residents of their sovereign nations, and the laws of each base are dictated by the nations that built them. MBA is therefore governed by the laws of the United States of America.

The system for governing MBA was modeled after the successful system at McMurdo Station, the American scientific outpost in Antarctica. The moon-base commander (or MBC) serves as the de facto mayor, handling all issues to the best of his or her ability. The MBC's decisions should be regarded as the final say in all conflicts and disputes. In the unlikely event that an issue arises that is beyond the capacity of the MBC, then it can be appealed to the city government of Houston, Texas, home of NASA Lunar Command at the Johnson Space Center.

It should be stated, however, that the residents of MBA have all been carefully selected for friendliness and compatibility, and thus there ought to be a minimum of conflict—if there are even any conflicts at all!

VEILED THREATS

Lunar day 188
Midmorning

Even though the moon base isn't big, there are still a lot of places I'm not allowed inside. Many areas are restricted for security or maintenance reasons, while others are merely off-limits to kids. I'm not even supposed to enter the science pod or the greenhouse without an adult (although I do, on occasion, because that's a stupid rule). And, of course, I'd never been to the solar arrays or the lunar rover garage, because you have to go outside to get there, and for a kid, that's simply out of the question.

Nina's quarters were another place I'd never been, even though she lives right next door to me. My route there took me right back through the air lock staging area, then up the metal stairs to the catwalk.

Nina answered the door the moment I knocked on it. She ushered me inside, locked the door, then glanced at her smartwatch. "I thought I told you to get here quickly."

It had been maybe two minutes since I'd talked to her. "I came as fast as I could. I had to log out of the ComLink."

Nina gave an annoyed sigh, then pointed to an Inflati-Cube for me to sit on. It might as well have been an order, so I sat. As usual, the cube made a loud, embarrassing sound beneath my bottom.

"What was so urgent that you had to disobey my order about using the Link?" Nina demanded.

"Roddy's dad asked me to check on him. But Roddy was already jacked in and wouldn't log off, so I had to log in myself."

Nina rolled her eyes at this, but moved on. She had bigger fish to fry. "From now on, when I give an order, you follow it. No exceptions. Understand?"

I nodded, then took in the room. To my surprise, Nina's quarters were significantly larger than my family's, even though she had the place to herself. However, hers also had to serve as an office. On earth she probably would have had a massive, imposing desk and several couches. Here, due to the difficulty of getting any sort of furniture to the moon, she had the same InflatiCubes as everyone else and a spindly desk she'd probably had to assemble herself. Still, it was the only desk at MBA, which made it impressive enough.

There was also an actual window. It faced south, the same way my window would have—if I'd had one. I'd never had the chance to look this direction. While much of MBA is surrounded by ugly man-made things like solar arrays and evaporators, there was nothing but moon outside Nina's window. The dust close to the base was tracked up, but beyond that I could see parts of the lunar surface still in their pristine, prehuman condition. A small crater sat on the horizon, gleaming in the sun. Since there's no atmosphere on the moon to diffuse the sun's light, the sky was dark and filled with stars. It was the most beautiful thing I'd seen in months.

"Why don't you think Dr. Holtz's death was an accident?" Nina asked me.

I swung back to face her, startled by the question and how abruptly she'd asked it. "How'd you know that?"

"I'm the base commander, Dashiell. It's my job to know what's going on here."

I knew from her stone-cold expression that I wasn't going to get any more out of her than that. I wasn't upset about it, though. In fact, I was relieved that someone was asking questions about the death. So I opened up and told the whole story of my late-night run to the bathroom and how I'd overheard Dr. Holtz there.

Nina kept her eyes locked on me the whole time. She didn't show a trace of surprise or shock—or any other emotion, for that matter. She was in full Nina the Machina mode.

When I finished, she asked, "Did anyone else besides you hear this conversation?"

"I don't think so," I said. "I was the only other person in the bathroom. Why?"

"I'd just like some confirmation."

"Why?" I repeated. "Don't you believe me?"

"Look, I'm sure you *think* you heard Dr. Holtz say those things."

"I *know* I heard them."

"It was late," Nina went on. "You were tired. You were embarrassed about breaking the toilet."

"I didn't break it! It just broke."

"Whatever the case, you were nervous and exhausted. You were hiding in the stall, so maybe you couldn't hear the conversation as well as you thought."

"Could you check the security cameras?" I asked. There are cameras in all public spaces at MBA. We'd been told they were there for our safety—to monitor our health and the integrity of the base—although Roddy always claimed the real reason for them was to spy on us. "They must have recorded

Dr. Holtz's conversation. You can hear it for yourself."

Nina shook her head. "I can't. There aren't any camera feeds in the bathrooms. For privacy. And besides, the cameras we have don't record sound."

"Oh." Normally, the news that I wasn't being filmed during my most private moments would have been pleasing. But now it meant there was no way to back up what I'd witnessed. "Would the phone call have been recorded somewhere? Because if you tracked that down . . ."

"I'm not going to do that, Dashiell."

I blinked in surprise. "But it would prove that I'm telling the truth."

"I have enough going on here right now," Nina said coldly. "I'm not about to start digging through the call logs—"

"Well, I'm sure you could ask someone else to do it. I could even help out."

Nina rubbed her temples, as though she had a bad headache. "You don't understand. What I mean is, I'm not about to start conducting an investigation. Dr. Holtz wasn't murdered. And I need you to stop saying that he was."

I sat back on my InflatiCube, stunned. The plastic squeaked loudly under me, sounding like a hippopotamus passing gas. "Do you have proof he wasn't murdered?"

"Yes. I have video of him walking out the air lock by himself."

"That doesn't mean no one forced him to do it."

"How?" Nina demanded.

"I don't know," I admitted. "But this just doesn't make sense."

"Accidental deaths never do. But they happen all the time. I don't know why Dr. Holtz went out the air lock solo. I truly wish he hadn't. I know you liked him a lot. Everyone here did. We're all upset."

Nina *didn't* look upset to me, though. She looked exactly the same as she always did.

"I'm not making this up because I'm having trouble dealing with what happened," I said. "I know what I heard."

"I doubt that very much," Nina told me. I started to protest, but she cut me off. "I don't want to sound callous here, but Dr. Holtz's actions this morning have caused NASA and me a great deal of trouble. There are plenty of politicians back on earth who aren't fans of this base. They think it's a colossal waste of money and are looking for any excuse to shut it down. And now our leading authority on the effects of space travel on the human mind and body— the very man who assured all these politicians that this place was perfectly safe—has just done something reckless and died as a result. I can assure you, that isn't going over very well in Washington."

I tried to hide my surprise; Roddy had been right about

all this. "Then why not investigate? Then you could prove Dr. Holtz wasn't being reckless!"

"And prove that we've got a murderer up here instead?" Nina demanded. "That'd be even worse!"

"But if you don't investigate, then the murderer gets away with it," I argued. "And they're still up here with all of us."

"There is no murderer!" Nina shouted. For a moment she seemed as surprised as I was that she'd lost control of her emotions. Then she took a deep breath and calmed herself down. "I was only being rhetorical. The point is, this event is a serious problem for MBA. It is a crisis from a political, personal, and public-relations stance. Plus we have the social ramifications to deal with." Nina began listing points on her fingers. "Do we do an autopsy? How do we deal with Dr. Holtz's children and grandchildren back on earth? Do we return the body there, or do we keep it here? And if we keep it here, what do we do with it? I have my hands full right now. The last thing I need is some kid running around like Chicken Little, telling everyone there's a murderer on the loose."

I met Nina's stare. She was definitely angry now. Most of her face was as stony as usual, but her eyes told the story. They were blazing hot enough to melt steel. I didn't know if she was angry at Dr. Holtz for putting her into this situation or at me for making it worse—or a little of both—but I knew I shouldn't push my luck. If Nina wanted to punish me, she had the authority. She could probably ship me back to earth if she wanted—or worse, force me to stay at MBA even longer than I was supposed to. So I backed down. "I understand," I said.

"Good," Nina told me. "Now then, not only are you forbidden from talking about this anymore, but you are also not to e-mail anyone about it, video log about it, or communicate it to anyone here or on earth in any way. If you have a problem with that—if you really need to talk to someone—I've already contacted Dr. Marquez. He's willing to schedule some extra sessions with you."

"You mean psychiatric sessions?" I asked warily.

"It's nothing to be ashamed of," Nina said. "Living here can be stressful—and Dr. Holtz's death has added an extra layer of stress on top of that. Dr. Marquez will be seeing lots of base residents more than usual over the next few days."

Before I could say anything else, there was a soft ping from the public-address speakers in Nina's room. The soothing female voice of the base computer came on. "Attention all base residents. The supply rocket is en route. Touchdown estimated in sixty minutes."

I stiffened in surprise. With everything that had happened, I'd completely forgotten—once again—that the rocket was coming in that morning.

Nina checked her watch, then snapped to her feet. "I'm

afraid our time is up. I have a great deal to do in the next hour." She came around from behind her desk, took me by the arm, and led me toward the door.

I didn't resist. Spending time with Nina was no fun at all; it felt like being in a cage with a snake. Before I knew it, I was out on the catwalk and Nina was locking the door behind me.

In the hall below, my fellow Moonies were now scurrying about, prepping for the rocket. Since I'm only a kid, I didn't have an assigned task. So I headed for the shower. My encounter with Nina had left me feeling grimy. Or maybe it was the fact that I hadn't bathed in more than a week. Whatever the case, it was a good time to get clean. There is only one shower on base and, for the moment most everyone else was busy. Plus, once the rocket arrived, there'd be a lot of other people who wanted to use it.

The shower is a three-foot-wide metal tube wedged between the men's and women's bathrooms. You can enter it from either side—though you have to remember to lock the doors once you're in it. It's pretty lame compared to a shower on earth: a thin stream of warm water drizzles on you, and you can't even use soap or shampoo because it all gets recycled back into the reservoir. But it's better than nothing.

Roddy was in the men's room, seated in the first stall. I could tell it was him because he was singing out loud to himself: an old tune from my grandparents' time called "I'm Too Sexy." It isn't exactly rare to find Roddy on the toilet. He doesn't seem to hate the device nearly as much as I do, and he often gets distracted by the SlimScreen on the stall door for up to half an hour. This can be a problem in a place where there are only three toilets for each gender, one of which is often broken.

I slipped past Roddy quietly. I wasn't trying to avoid him, exactly. I simply prefer not to have conversations in the bathroom. Roddy, however, has no such concerns. In fact he seems to enjoy having discussions while seated on the throne.

"That you, Dash?" he asked.

I stifled a groan. "Yeah."

"Thought I recognized your shoes. What are you doing in here?"

"I thought I'd play a little ice hockey," I said sarcastically. "It's the bathroom, Roddy. What do you think I'm doing in here?"

"I meant what are you doing: number one or number two?"

I groaned again. "Really?"

"Okay," Roddy said. "I'll guess. Number two."

"Actually, I'm gonna shower." I pulled my shirt off over my head.

"Want to know what I'm doing?" Roddy asked.

"Not really."

"I'm playing Raid on Titan."

"Here?" I asked. "You're playing a virtual-reality game in the can?"

"Not yet, but I'm about to. I've just about got the access figured out. Nina thinks she can kick me off the main ComLink? I'll show her."

"You do that," I said, doing my best to sound like I meant it. I wasn't sure how playing a virtual-reality game on a communal toilet showed anyone anything except how addicted to virtual reality you were.

"Want to jack in?" Roddy asked.

"I'll pass." I kicked off my shoes.

"Your loss," Roddy told me. "I've got a game saved on level upsilon where I've procured a Whipsaw WarpFighter with prion eliminators. You can be my secondary. I'm gonna SynBlast the Heisenbok Ice Fields."

"I don't even know what any of that means. Besides, I've got some other stuff to do before the rocket gets here."

"Like what?"

I didn't answer right away, in part because I didn't really have other stuff to do—and in part because I'd just thought of something. Rather than hop in the shower, I opened the toilet stall closest to me and glanced at the SlimScreen. It was turned off. As I'd expected, there was a tiny black nub in the center of it. A nanocamera. These are standard for all Slim-Screens. Normally, it's hidden by the video projection when the screen's on. I asked, "Roddy, are the SlimScreen nanos here wired to record?"

"Of course. The tech is built-in. Why wouldn't they wire it?"

"Because the screens are in the toilet."

"I don't mind video chatting from the toilet."

"You broadcast from in here?" I asked, doing my best to hide my disgust. "To who?"

"Everyone. Friends, relatives, girls who think it's cool I live on the moon. I've even posted a few video logs from here. No one can tell you're on the can. The camera only shows your face."

"If the stalls are wired, do you know if there are any other cameras in here?"

"Oh yeah. There's a nano up at the ceiling in each corner, and those are just the ones I've noticed. I'll bet there's some others as well."

I looked up at the corners of the ceiling. I couldn't see any cameras, but cameras are so small that scientists at the Department of Defense are getting houseflies to carry them. Any nanos tucked away in the walls would be practically invisible. "You're sure they're there?"

"Definitely. I've pulled up the feeds on my own computer."

"Why?"

"Just to see what I could see. It's not as hard to crack the base security code as NASA thinks. If you ever want to watch Lily Sjoberg getting ready for the shower, let me know."

I groaned for the third time. Not at the idea of Lily Sjoberg, who is certainly the most attractive girl at the base—or even at the idea of Roddy having access to the security camera system (though I'd have to think twice before scratching my rear end from now on, knowing Roddy could be watching).

What I was *really* disturbed by was the fact that Nina had just told me there weren't any cameras in the bathrooms. If Roddy knew they were there, then Nina had to know as well. She knew Moon Base Alpha down to every last nut and bolt.

Which meant Dr. Holtz *had* been recorded the night before. And Nina Stack had just lied to me about it.

Excerpt from *The Official Residents' Guide to Moon Base Alpha,*
© 2040 by National Aeronautics and Space Administration:

TRANSPORTATION

Your adventure at MBA will start well before you set foot on the moon. Just getting here is the experience of a lifetime!

You'll be heading to the moon aboard the world's fastest, most state-of-the-art rocket: the Odyssey Raptor 12. You'll be able to sit back and relax as you race to our base in a mere fifty-three hours. True, that's over two days, but in the expansive Raptor 12 space cabin it'll seem more like only two hours! You'll have your own personal seat, specially contoured to your body with ComforFoam®, plenty to eat and drink, and more than ten thousand channels of entertainment to choose from—*if* you can pry your eyes from the incredible display of the earth dropping away just outside your window. The Raptor 12 isn't just a rocket: It's the future of space travel.* So get ready for the ride of your life!

---

* In the unlikely event that an Odyssey Raptor 12 is not available for lunar travel, you may be asked to transit to MBA on a Soviet Gagarin-class rocket via the launchpad in Vladivostok, Russia. Be advised that some amenities may not be available on the Gagarin.

NEWBIES

Lunar day 188
Noon

The rocket had originally been scheduled to arrive seventeen days earlier. For getting to the moon, though, seventeen days late counts as being almost on time.

Even though we've been launching rockets for almost a hundred years, things still go wrong all the time. It's not like in the movies, where everyone just jumps into their spaceships and flies off whenever they want. Launching a rocket is immensely complicated. It's, well . . . rocket science. And lots of things can go wrong: Any of the millions of parts can malfunction, a computer can glitch, a storm can move in, a cloud of space junk can drift into the flight path. Plus, heading for the moon isn't something you can do whenever you want. You need a window when the earth and moon are in just the right place relative to each other. Miss that window and you might as well unpack your bags—you're going to be waiting a while. Frankly, you're lucky if your rocket takes off within a week of when it's supposed to. One of the original missions for the construction of MBA was delayed for more than a year.

And to think, my grandparents say they used to get upset when planes on earth were delayed an *hour*.

But now the Raptor was almost here. Despite Dr. Holtz's death, there was excitement in the air. Almost every Moonie was gathered in the rec room to watch the rocket's arrival. Yes, that's right. Even though the Raptor was landing less than a football field away from us, we still had to watch it on TV. This was because the moon has no atmosphere. Therefore, no matter how gently a rocket lands, the retro rockets that slow its descent will still blow away every bit of rock and moon dust below them, shelling everything nearby. NASA built a twenty-foot blast wall around the landing pad to protect MBA, but there isn't a single window oriented in that direction, just in case something makes it over. We don't want our precious glass getting shattered by a rogue moon rock. As it is, we've already lost two panels in Solar Array 2 to blast debris.

Violet was seated on the floor right in front of the Slim-Screen, along with Inez Marquez—Roddy's little sister and her best friend—and Kamoze Iwanyi, the only other little kid on base. The three of them were pleading for someone to switch the TV to cartoons instead of the rocket's arrival. (After hearing about Dr. Holtz's death, Violet had been sad for a few minutes but had quickly returned to her usual effusive self.)

The adults weren't paying much more attention than the kids. The first time a rocket had arrived, we'd all sat riveted to the TV. But by now even this amazing event had become routine. Everyone was socializing, only keeping one eye on the screen while they talked science and gossip. Roddy was AWOL. He must still have been in the bathroom, covertly leading raids on virtual moons from the toilet stall.

The older kids, Cesar Marquez (Roddy's big brother) and the Sjoberg twins, Patton and Lily, were all clustered together as usual. Cesar is usually pretty nice to me, but the Sjobergs are jerks. Due to the Transitive Property of Jerkiness, any time they're around Cesar, he becomes kind of nasty himself.

That was it for other kids at MBA, so I was watching the landing with my parents.

"Looks like Katya's coming in perfect," Dad said, meaning Katya King, the head pilot on the Raptor.

"Like always," Mom agreed.

My parents looked around the room for someone else for me to hang out with. They weren't trying to ditch me; I think they felt bad I had no one else to talk to but them. "Where's Roddy?" Dad asked.

"You don't want to know," I replied.

Dad considered that, then nodded. "You're probably right. I don't."

"Nina told me not to talk about Dr. Holtz anymore," I said.

Mom and Dad both scanned the room to see if anyone was eavesdropping on us. No one was. "When?" Mom asked.

"Not too long ago. She called me into her office. She told me the death was an accident, not a murder, and that if I didn't shut up about it, I'd be causing trouble."

Mom and Dad shared a long look. It seemed as though an entire conversation passed between them, unsaid.

"How did she know you thought he was murdered?" Mom asked, keeping her voice low so no one else would overhear.

"She wouldn't say."

Mom nodded. "Well, I can understand her concern. Back on earth, there are a lot of people paying very close attention to this base. If a rumor spread that Dr. Holtz had been murdered, it could be a disaster."

"Well, what if it's not a rumor? What if there's really a

killer on the loose? Shouldn't someone at least investigate?"

"I'm sure they will," Dad replied. "There's no way a death up here wouldn't be looked into. But they're probably only thinking of it as an accident."

"But what if it really is a murder?" I asked. "If no one's looking for the killer, then the killer won't just get away— they'll still be living with us! How long do you think it'll be before someone else gets bumped off?"

Both my parents signaled me to keep my voice down. Before either one could come up with an answer, Chang Hi-Tech came along.

Chang's real last name is Kowalski, but no one calls him that. He's MBA's resident genius. Officially he came to the moon as a geochemist, but he's really a jack-of-all-trades, able to handle everything from computer glitches to leaky rehydrators. It's always easy to find him at MBA, because even on earth he'd stand out in a crowd. He's a tall, muscular Polish-Samoan, he has a Mohawk, and his arms are covered with tattoos. All his favorite scientists' likenesses are inked on his skin—Albert Einstein, Marie Curie, Niels Bohr, Isaac Newton—but they're all drawn as superheroes, clad in spandex, battling enemies like Hitler and Godzilla. Chang designed the art himself.

I was worried Chang had overheard me talking about the possible lunar serial killer, but he showed no sign of it. Instead he was focused on the TV screen, watching the rocket. "Man, that Katya's an ace," he said. "I'll bet you a thou she parks that Raptor dead center on the pad."

Dad shook his head. "Bet against Katya? Forget it."

"Okay," Chang said. "Then let's bet on which of the newbies pukes during the landing."

Dad laughed. Mom rolled her eyes.

Rocket travel isn't for everyone. Almost everybody feels motion sick the first time they go into space. It takes a while to adjust to being weightless. Some people manage to do this quickly. Others spend the trip on very intimate terms with the zero-g toilet.

My parents and Chang knew plenty about the newbies already. NASA had sent them biography files well ahead of time, and all the adults had video chatted several times. It's better to start life on the moon as friends than strangers.

"I'll put a hundred on Maxwell Howard," Dad said.

"The engineer?" Chang laughed. "You're backing the wrong horse, pal. I hear that guy's steady as they come."

Dad shrugged. "I've got a hunch. Some of these stoic guys turn out to have the weakest stomachs."

"My money's on the Russian," Chang said. "What's his name, Balnikov? I read the guy's file. Trust me, the guy's a vomit volcano."

"I don't know what to do with you two," Mom said

with a sigh. "Dashiell, don't pay one bit of attention to these so-called scientists."

"They're only having some fun," I said.

"Yes," Mom agreed. "And they have no idea how to pick a potential puker. If anyone blows chunks, it'll be Jennifer Kim. The geologists are always the first to go."

On the TV there was a sudden blaze of light as the Raptor's retro rockets fired. And yet, even though this was happening almost right over our heads, we didn't hear a thing. There was no atmosphere for the sound to travel through. What would have been deafening on earth was bizarrely silent on the moon.

All conversation ceased. Everyone directed their full attention to the TV. Even the little kids.

The Raptor was lowering slowly toward the pad, the flare from the retros so bright it almost bleached out the screen. Just as Chang had predicted, it was coming in perfectly. Commander Katya King was at the helm. Not only was she the best pilot at NASA, but she'd done this run so many times it was probably routine to her by now.

Nina Stack was suddenly at my side. Without so much as a hello she told me, "I need you to do something for me. There's a girl your age coming in on that rocket."

"Kira Howard," I said. "I've heard."

"You're going to be the welcome wagon for her."

I was so surprised I took my eyes off the TV. "I thought Cesar was assigned to do that."

"I changed my mind." Nina didn't even look at me. She kept her gaze locked on the descending rocket. "Cesar has other duties, and, frankly, you're probably a better representative for Kira anyway, seeing as you're only a few months older than she is."

"But I'm not prepared—" I began.

"I'm sure you can handle it." Nina walked away before I could raise another protest.

Not that I could think of one. Truthfully, I was happy for the assignment. Kira was twelve, like me, and I was kind of excited to meet her. Plus, showing her the ropes at MBA would give me something to do for once.

Of course, I knew the *real* reason for my new assignment. Nina was trying to distract me from raising questions about Dr. Holtz's death.

On TV the second round of retros fired. Katya gently guided the Raptor to the landing pad. Below the rocket, dust and rock exploded out in all directions, scouring the blast wall. The Raptor hovered over the pad for a few moments, then set down in the dead center.

Everyone cheered.

"Now that's how you land a rocket!" Chang whooped. "Way to go, Katya!"

Nina whistled shrilly, interrupting the celebration. "All right, everyone! We all have work to do. Those of you on cargo transfer duty, suit up. Those of you on the welcoming committee, be ready to meet your assignments. Everyone else, stay clear of the staging area. We're going to have enough bodies there as it is." She strode out, having masterfully destroyed any sense of joy within seconds. All the adults dutifully filed after her. So did I. The other kids remained in the rec room. The moment the last adult was out the door, I heard Cesar switch off the rocket feed and turn on *Squirrel Force* for Violet and her friends.

I'd never been assigned a duty for the arrival of a rocket before, so I'd never had a reason to be in the staging area when one came in. It was far more exciting than being asked to make myself scarce. Dad, Chang, Mr. Grisan, and a few others piled into their space suits, prepping for cargo duty. Mom, who'd been assigned to greet Dr. Kim, and I clustered near the main air lock with the others on the welcome wagon. I ended up in the back of the crowd, but I could still get a glimpse outdoors through the air lock window.

After a few minutes, seven people in space suits rounded the blast wall.

Katya King and her copilot, Buster Reisman, were easy to pick out, even though I couldn't see their faces through the reflective visors of their space helmets. They bounded along with the confident, easy grace of people who had been to the lunar surface many times before, covering several yards with each step in the low gravity.

Their fellow travelers moved differently. None had ever been on the lunar surface before, and all were having significant trouble figuring out the low gravity. They wobbled, stumbled, and bounded too far. One tripped and face-planted in a pile of moon dust.

Only five of the new arrivals were officially Moonies, who'd be staying for years. The rest were temps: people who only came for brief stays. Temps might be contractors who installed new equipment, mechanics who repaired broken machinery, or engineers surveying the construction site for Moon Base Beta. In a few days they'd hop on the return rocket and head back home to earth. I wasn't even sure how many temps were scheduled to arrive at MBA this time. Besides the seven people en route to the air lock, I knew there were other passengers I couldn't see, ones who'd remained at the landing pad to unload the rocket.

Dad, Chang, and the other Moonies who had cargo duty were suited up by the time the new arrivals reached the air lock. The cargo team passed through first, emerging onto the surface of the moon, where they did their best to greet the new arrivals. (Space suits are far less bulky than they used to be, but it's still almost impossible to shake hands in them.)

The cargo crew then headed for the landing pad. The new arrivals passed through the air lock into the base and the celebration began.

Greeting new arrivals is always one of the happiest times at MBA. All of us at the base are thrilled to have new people there. And all the new arrivals are thrilled to have finally made it. (Despite all you've heard about how modern space-ships are so elegant and spacious, they're not; after a few hours on board, you still feel like a sardine in a can.) The moment the newbies popped their space helmets off, the base was alive with excitement. All the adults cheered and hugged one another.

I was the only greeter who'd never spoken to my assigned newbie. I'd seen some things about her on the news, but since that was vetted by NASA's PR department, I knew it might not be reliable. (News reports about Roddy had often referred to him as an "impressive athlete".) Other than know-ing what Kira looked like, I wasn't quite sure what to expect.

I wormed my way through the crowd, pausing to say a quick hello to Katya and Buster, and finally found Kira by the air lock. She was standing with her father, Dr. Maxwell Howard. Both had removed their helmets but still wore the rest of their space suits. Dr. Marquez, who was Dr. Howard's official greeter, was talking to them animatedly, though Dr. Howard wasn't paying much attention to him. Instead he was looking all around MBA, taking in his surroundings. He didn't seem to be either amazed or disappointed. His gaze was very clinical, like he was studying the place.

Kira, on the other hand, seemed a bit overwhelmed. Her eyes were nervously darting back and forth. She didn't look very much like her father, who was tall and black. She looked far more like her mother, who'd been Asian. (According to Kira's bio, her mother had died from cancer four years earlier.)

"Hi," I said, trying to sound as cheerful and friendly as possible. "I'm Dashiell. Welcome to Moon Base Alpha."

Kira didn't appear surprised that I had replaced Cesar. In fact, she seemed relieved there was someone her age to talk to. "Hey, Dash. Nice to meet you."

"I know Cesar was supposed to greet you, but—"

"Oh, they let me know about the change as we were landing. It's probably better this way. I know all about you. I've seen all your video logs."

"Really?" All Moonies have to post videos to the MBA website once a week so people back on earth can follow our lives. It's a big public-relations deal. I do my best to make mine interesting, but since NASA policy states I can't say anything bad about the moon base, there isn't much to talk about. So I usually goof around, making up stories that are obviously ridiculous, about meeting martians and fighting moondragons and such. I knew I had followers, but I'd never met one before.

"Yeah," Kira said. "Well, I haven't seen *all* of them. But most of them. They're more fun than anyone else's. Although your sister's can be pretty hilarious."

That was true. Violet has no idea what the point of the video logs is. The week before, she had simply danced around with a pair of underpants on her head while singing the *Squirrel Force* theme song.

"Need any help getting out of your suit?" I asked.

"Definitely." Kira turned to her father. "Hey, Dad, this is Dash. He's gonna help me get settled."

Dr. Howard turned to her, still somewhat distracted, as though he'd forgotten she was even there. "Oh. All right, hon. Have fun."

He didn't even bother introducing himself to me. I'd stuck out my arm to shake hands, but he didn't seem to notice.

"Daddy's a bit monofocused," Kira explained. "He's probably already thinking of ways to improve the base."

"If he needs any help, I have a few thousand suggestions," I said, then winced. I probably wasn't supposed to bad-mouth the station to the newbies. Not right away, anyhow. I tried to cover. "Not that this place isn't great, of course."

Kira laughed. "I know it isn't exactly paradise," she whispered. "Dad's always going off about all the mistakes they've made."

I looked at her, surprised. "And you still wanted to come?"

"It's not like I had any more choice than you did." Kira spun around, exposing the back of her suit to me. "Can you undo this?"

Space suits are really more like suits of armor than clothing; they're designed to protect you from danger rather than provide any comfort at all. And like suits of armor, they're very hard to put on or take off without help. There were several Velcro strips and latches in the back of Kira's suit. I undid everything and Kira wriggled backward out of it, emerging like a butterfly from a cocoon.

Without her suit on she seemed three times smaller. That's true for everyone, but it seemed more evident in Kira's case because she's small to begin with. She was wearing a vintage *Star Wars* T-shirt and warm-up pants.

Kira shook her arms, getting the blood flowing after being in the constricting space suit. "Ahhh. Much better," she sighed, then turned to me. "So where should we start the tour?"

"Are you hungry?" I asked.

"Starving," Kira admitted.

"Then let's start with the mess hall."

"That'd be great. They told us not to eat anything in the hours before landing because it makes people nauseous and they didn't want anyone blowing chunks all over the rocket."

"Did anyone?"

"Dr. Kim, the geologist. Have you ever seen puke in zero gravity? It's disgusting."

I glanced at my mother and Dr. Kim as we passed. Mom had called it right. Dr. Kim's clothes were stained with vomit.

I picked up Kira's space suit and carried it toward the storage area. "Mess is this way."

Kira started to follow me—and bounded way too high in the low gravity, soaring past me and slamming face-first into the wall.

I winced. "Sorry! I forgot to warn you: It takes a while to figure out how to walk around here."

Kira flushed, embarrassed. "I didn't realize how much lighter I'd be without the space suit."

"Yeah. These things double your weight." I slipped Kira's suit and helmet into their racks. "You shouldn't be embarrassed. When I first got here, I did exactly the same thing."

Kira shot me a distrusting glance. "You're only saying that to make me feel better."

"Yes," I admitted. "But I still had plenty of trouble. Everyone does." I pointed to the other newbies.

They were all having problems moving about. Dr. Kim's husband, Dr. Alvarez, had flown into a wall himself, while Viktor Balnikov had bounded so high he'd cracked his head on the bottom of the catwalk. Kira's father was the only one who hadn't wiped out yet—and that was only because he hadn't taken a step.

Kira tentatively gave it another go—and still used too much force. She sailed high in the air and then crashed back to the floor. "Dang it!" she snapped. "Back on earth they said this would be easy!"

I felt terrible, hearing the frustration in her voice. It reminded me of my own, six months earlier. The realization that MBA was far worse than everyone had led her to believe was already setting in. In just a few weeks she'd be as bitter about the whole place as I was.

Only I didn't want that to happen. Maybe I couldn't make the moon base itself better, but I could certainly try to make life there more bearable for Kira.

I extended a hand to her. "It'll get easier. I promise."

The anger faded from Kira's eyes. She took my hand. "I hope so."

I helped her to her feet. "The trick is to barely even use your muscles. Pretend like you're walking on eggshells."

"All right." Kira gingerly took a step. This time she didn't go flying. So she took another. And another.

"There you go," I said.

"Yeah. Three whole steps. Amazing."

I finished storing Kira's suit and then helped her work her way toward the mess. Normally I wouldn't be in any hurry to eat at MBA, but whenever a rocket arrives, a small amount of fresh food comes on it. This is an incredibly transparent tactic by NASA to boost our spirits at MBA—and it always works like a charm. By the time we got to the mess, almost every Moonie had already descended on it, desperate to taste something that wasn't freeze-dried and dehydrated.

Most of the fresh food was still on the rocket, but Katya and Buster had carried in a sack of tangerines. The fruits hadn't weathered the trip that well—back on earth we'd have turned our noses up at them—but I would have eagerly traded a pound of gold for one.

Buster tossed two to me and Kira as we entered the mess. I held hers out to her.

To my surprise, she shook her head. "You can have it. I don't really like tangerines."

"Don't pass this up," I warned her. "You'll regret it. Before I came here, I didn't like tomatoes. Now if someone showed up here with a fresh one, I'd kill for it."

Kira shrugged. "I still pass. It's all yours."

I wasn't going to argue myself out of a second tangerine. I

quickly slipped it into my pocket, then walked Kira through the basics of how to prepare food. Since she'd just done me a good turn, I warned her about the chicken parmigiana and tracked down a shrimp cocktail for her. Kira still wanted to practice her low-gravity walking, so rather than sit and eat, I led her around the base, trying to point out everything of interest, though I was far more focused on my tangerine than on delivering a decent tour.

There are two ways people eat fresh food at MBA. Roddy represents the first: Having no self-control whatsoever, he devours his food as quickly as possible, like a dog that's been given a steak. I represent the second: I try to savor every last molecule. From the moment I tore off the first bit of tangerine peel, I inhaled deeply, relishing the smell. Then I ate one section at a time, resting it on my tongue, slowly sucking the juice out of it, and finally methodically chewing the pulp.

I'd only eaten half my tangerine by the time I'd taken Kira past the gym, the greenhouse, and the rec room and wound back past the residences to the main air lock. "There you go," I said. "You've seen everything."

Kira frowned. I could recognize the disillusionment setting in again. I'd felt it myself after my first tour. "That's it? It's a lot smaller than I expected."

"It's actually just the right size," I said, trying my best to be upbeat. "Trust me, when you're heading to the bathroom in the middle of the night, you'll be thankful this place isn't any bigger."

Kira turned to me, startled. "You mean we don't have our own bathrooms?"

"Er . . . no," I said, then quickly tried to change the subject. "How long are you supposed to be here for?"

"Three years, same as you." Kira frowned, then looked to me hopefully. "It won't be that bad, right? I mean, on your video logs you look like you're having fun up here."

"I am," I told her, hoping it sounded like I meant it. "It's not perfect, but it's still pretty cool to be one of the first people to live on the moon."

"Yeah. It is." Kira nodded, then seemed to shrug off her doubts. "Hey, I haven't seen my room yet."

"You're in Residence Three, right next door to my family." I led the way to the staircase. "Careful coming up, though. Stairs are the trickiest part of low gravity."

Kira followed. She'd already gotten much better at low-g walking on our tour, but the moment she set foot on the stairs, she stumbled. She grabbed the handrail and tried again, but wobbled and had to steady herself. "Whoa," she said. "Why is this so hard?"

"I don't know," I admitted. "Something about how we perceive our own weight gets all messed up. It happens to everyone. NASA considered building a ramp instead of stairs because they can be so much trouble, but the stairs took up less space."

"Why were they so concerned about space?" Kira snapped. "That's all there is up here. We're on the freaking moon, for Pete's sake!"

"It's just expensive to build here, I guess. My folks say Moon Base Beta's going to be a lot bigger."

"When's that gonna be finished?"

"In ten years. If we're lucky."

Kira sighed, then focused on the stairs. Slowly she managed to work her way up them. When she finally arrived at the top, she threw her arms in the air. "Ta-da!" she crowed sarcastically. "A whole flight of stairs in a mere five minutes."

"Just so you know, it's even harder going down," I warned.

"You're kidding."

"No. I usually just jump over the railing." I pointed at the floor fifteen feet below. "In low gravity you barely feel the landing. But don't ever do it when Nina's around. It's against the rules, and she'll have a fit."

Kira grinned. "Thanks for the advice. Nina's a tough nut, huh?"

"Yeah, but she's . . ." I tried to think of something nice

to say about Nina but couldn't. "She's . . . uh . . . very organized."

"Sounds like a real winner." Kira carefully walked down
the catwalk to Residence 3, which is between my family's
quarters and the Brahmaputra-Marquez family's. The door
hung open, as keys hadn't been issued yet.

The room looked exactly like ours. The furnishings
were identical. There were even four sleep pods, because all
residences had been built that way. (Inez Marquez, being
the fifth member of that family, has to sleep on a pad on
the floor.) The SlimScreens were off, so the walls were all
moon-dust gray and dull.

"It's much nicer once you personalize your habitat," I
said reassuringly. "We've got our screen set for Hawaii."

"Right, that's where you're from. Must have been nice."

Way nicer than this, I thought, but I held my tongue. "It
was. Where are you from?"

"Philadelphia," Kira said. "Although now I guess I should
say I'm from the moon. Sounds cooler."

"I can help you do the habitat settings if you'd like," I
offered. "You can even personalize the base computer's personality for your room—"

Kira cut me off. "Thanks. But this is fine for now." She
suddenly yawned. "I'm pretty beat from the landing and all.
If you don't mind, I'd like to take a nap."

"Sure. I understand," I said. My own landing had taken a lot out of me. I'd been jacked up on adrenaline, worried that we were going to crash on the moon. And learning how to walk in low g was pretty exhausting as well. "Take it easy, and if you need anything, well . . . it's not like I'm leaving here anytime soon. I shouldn't be that hard to find."

"Thanks," Kira said. "Catch you later."

I backed out of the room, feeling better than I had all day. I liked Kira a lot. It was nice to have someone my own age around who wasn't a veeyar freak like Roddy. Someone operating on the same wavelength as me.

Plus she'd given me her tangerine.

I'd originally planned to save it until the next day. That way I could extend the enjoyment. But I couldn't wait. The last one had been too good. And if I left it in our room, Violet would probably eat it. So I unlocked my residence and slipped inside, hoping to have the whole thing to myself in peace.

To my surprise, there was a stranger inside the room.

It was a woman, around thirty or so, wearing a NASA security uniform. She was tall and beautiful, with olive skin and long dark hair.

Startled by her presence, I turned away, reaching for the door.

"Dashiell, wait!" she cried. "I need to talk to you in private. It's about Dr. Holtz."

I froze in surprise and turned back to her. "Who are you?"

"My name's Zan Perfonic," she said. "I just arrived on the rocket—and I think you're right about Dr. Holtz. He *was* murdered . . . but I need your help to prove it."

Excerpt from *The Official Residents' Guide to Moon Base Alpha*, © 2040 by National Aeronautics and Space Administration:

SAFETY

Even though Moon Base Alpha is located in a hostile environment, it is one of the safest buildings ever constructed. It has been designed to withstand everything from meteor strikes to moonquakes (even though a large one hasn't been detected in centuries), and all life-support systems have multiple backups. To further ensure the residents' peace of mind, the entire habitat will be constantly monitored at Mission Control in Houston. This will range from computerized analysis of oxygen and carbon dioxide levels to physical observation via cameras installed in all rooms. In the extremely unlikely event that something should go wrong, Mission Control will instantly address the problem, either by fixing the issues remotely (such as computer glitches) or providing technical support for anything that must be handled on-site.

Of course, the monitoring systems can also be used to address issues of a criminal nature. But given the exceedingly careful selection process for the lunarnaut program, there is virtually no chance of any such events arising at all. MBA isn't just the safest colony on the moon—it's one of the safest human colonies, period!

SECRET MISSION

Lunar day 188

Afternoon

I was so startled, I forgot all about the tangerine in my pocket. I reflexively locked the door and asked, "How did you get in here?"

"Everyone in security has a master key," Zan explained. "I know coming in here like this was wrong, but I didn't know what else to do. It's of great importance that no one see me talking to you."

"Why?" I asked.

Zan waved to the InflatiCubes arranged around our SlimScreen table. "Sit down. Eat your tangerine. This might take a while to explain."

I sat and Zan sat across from me. "How'd you know I had a tangerine?"

"I can smell it."

I pulled it out of my pocket. "Do you want any?"

Zan smiled. When she did, her whole face seemed to light up. "That's very nice of you to offer, but it's yours. I had several on the rocket."

I started to peel the fruit. "Why do you think Dr. Holtz was murdered?"

Zan stared at me, as though trying to decide where to begin. Now that I was close to her, I noticed that her eyes were extremely unusual. They were an amazingly brilliant blue that reminded me of the shallow water above the coral reefs in Hawaii. Just looking at them made me feel homesick.

"Before I get into that, there's something you ought to know," Zan told me. "Although I work for the security division, I'm not here as an investigator. My official duty is to upgrade and assess the base security systems."

"You're a temp," I said.

"Right. When the rocket returns to earth in two days, I'll be on it. And I don't have any authority to investigate crimes here. That's Nina's jurisdiction."

"But Nina says there wasn't a crime at all," I pointed out.

"So I've gathered. Which is unfortunate, because I think she's wrong." Zan suddenly locked her bright blue eyes on mine. "There's something very suspicious about Dr. Holtz's death."

I hesitated before responding. After all, I'd just met Zan and wasn't completely sure whether or not to trust her. I wondered if this was all a trick of some sort, something Nina had cooked up with NASA to see if I was going to disobey a direct order from her. So I tried to be as cautious as possible. "Why do you say that?"

"I knew Ronald," Zan replied. "Quite well, in fact. He would never have done something so risky as a solo moon-walk. Not when death was a possibility. Living at this base was his dream, the culmination of his life's work. . . ."

"Maybe he was going crazy," I said, echoing Roddy. "Maybe he got some sort of space madness."

"If that had been the case, he wouldn't have kept it a secret. And there were no indications that he was losing his mind. In fact, according to his most recent medical reports Dr. Holtz was in complete control of his mental faculties. He wouldn't have gone out that air lock alone on purpose. Especially not right now. Not with what he was working on." Zan suddenly lowered her eyes and bit her lip. It looked like she was about to cry.

I decided this wasn't a trick Nina had cooked up. Zan was genuinely upset about Dr. Holtz's death. "You know about that?" I asked.

"I know he was on the verge of revealing something exciting, but that's it."

"How?"

"Like I said, we were friends. We've been talking a lot lately."

I sat up, struck by a thought. "I overheard Dr. Holtz in the bathroom the night before he died. He was speaking to someone on the phone about a new discovery. Was that you?"

Zan met my eyes again, surprised by this piece of information. "No, I wasn't on the phone with him. Did you hear what the discovery was?"

I shook my head. "Dr. Holtz didn't say. But he was extremely excited about it. He said it would make history. He and whoever he was talking to planned to announce it first thing this morning. That's why I don't think his death was an accident. Why would he do something so dangerous *before* the announcement?"

"I don't know." Zan held my gaze. "But I want to find out."

I nodded, pleased that someone with authority was finally willing to listen to me, but then I thought of something. "If you didn't know I'd overheard Dr. Holtz's call, how did you know to come to me?"

"Nina reported you were making waves," Zan said.

"Asking too many questions about Dr. Holtz's death. She thought maybe I could keep an eye on you while I was here."

"But she didn't ever think you might agree with me." I smiled, pleased by the idea of Nina's plan backfiring.

"No, she didn't," Zan said. "Unfortunately, Nina isn't the only one who's concerned that a murder investigation would be bad press for MBA. My superiors agree with her."

"Even though they run security and we're talking about a murder here?"

"None of them knew Ronald like I did. And since they were responsible for vetting the Moonies, they don't think it's possible that one of you committed murder. Instead they think the *real* problem here is you saying there was a murder at all."

I put another piece of tangerine on my tongue. Somehow it didn't taste as good anymore. "So . . . they don't want you to investigate?"

Zan turned away, as though ashamed. "My official orders are, if anything, to make sure that there *isn't* an investigation. I'm to quash any suggestion that there was a murder."

"That's why you're here?" I asked, upset.

"No. Those are my *official* orders. But as a member of the security division, I feel it'd be a dereliction of duty to not look into this matter."

I relaxed, feeling better.

"However," Zan continued, "given that my superiors—and *their* superiors—don't want me to do this, any investigation will have to be conducted secretly. Which is where *you* come in."

"Why?"

"I can only do so much. As a temp, I don't have all the privileges you do. Therefore, I need your help."

"Sure." I was surprised by how quickly I agreed, given that there was certainly some potential for trouble. But then I figured that if there *was* a murderer on the loose at MBA, someone ought to be trying to find them. I would have preferred that somebody else do it—but at least I wouldn't be working alone. If trouble cropped up, Zan would be there for me.

And, truth be told, I was out for more than justice—or my own safety. I was bored out of my skull at MBA. Being asked to aid in a murder investigation was the most exciting thing that had happened to me since I'd arrived on the moon.

"What do you need me to do?" I asked.

Zan smiled, pleased by my response. "If Dr. Holtz didn't walk out that air lock on purpose, then someone forced him to do it. I need to see the security footage of that event."

"But that footage is exactly what Nina says *proves* he

wasn't murdered," I countered. "She says it's just him, going out the air lock solo."

"How well do you think you can trust Nina on this?" Zan asked.

I frowned. "Not much."

"Exactly," Zan agreed. "I'm not saying Nina had anything to do with Dr. Holtz's death. But I'm well aware that she'd rather sweep this whole mess under the rug than look into it. I'll bet there's far more in that footage than she says there is."

I set another piece of tangerine in my mouth. "Since you're in security, why can't *you* get the footage?"

"Because this is way out of my jurisdiction. In fact, my being in security actually works against us. I made the mistake of raising the issue en route here and was shot down by my superiors. Now I have direct orders not to get involved, and I guarantee you, they're keeping a very close eye on me. If I try to access the footage, they'll know." Embarrassment reddened Zan's cheeks. "That's why I've been forced to make the . . . well, let's say 'unorthodox' decision to come to *you* for help, rather than anyone else. I suspect NASA is far less likely to be monitoring your computer activity than that of any adult."

"Even though I already told Nina I was suspicious?"

"Nina's given you an order to back off. You've never disobeyed her before. Your reputation around here is sterling.

I'll bet she's already forgotten about you. She has a lot of other things to deal with right now."

"There's only one problem," I admitted. "I don't have the slightest idea how to access the security footage."

Zan laughed. It caught me by surprise. It was a light, infectious laugh that brightened the whole room like a ray of sunshine. "I figured as much. However, I can be of some help there. And I suspect your friend Roddy might be as well."

I thought back to my recent conversation with Roddy in the toilet stall. "Maybe. He knows how to hack the base computer, but that doesn't mean he'll help *me* do it."

"Well, see what you can do. Once you can access the computers, it shouldn't be too hard to find the footage we need."

I started to peel off another tangerine section, then noticed that my palms were sweaty. It was all well and good to *talk* about hacking the base computers to conduct an unauthorized murder investigation; *doing it* was an entirely different story. "I'll try my best," I said.

"I appreciate that," Zan told me. "I truly do. I know I'm asking you to take a big risk here."

"Maybe not," I said, trying to lighten things up. "If I get caught, maybe they'll be so upset, they'll ship me back to earth again."

"I wouldn't count on it. I think your parents are too vital up here."

"Then maybe I ought to break the rules more often."

Zan smiled, but quickly grew serious again. "Just so you know, we don't have much time to do this. The rocket returns to earth in two days. If we haven't caught the murderer by then, you'll be stuck here with whoever it is for another month. Or more, if the next rocket is delayed."

I hadn't thought of that. "Is there even any way to lock someone up here?"

"Not that I'm aware of." Zan sighed. "I don't think it ever occurred to anyone. I suppose there's a way to barricade someone in their room, but you'd have to let them out anytime they needed the bathroom. On the whole it'd be much better if I could escort our killer back to earth."

"But if you're not supposed to investigate, won't NASA flip when you suddenly arrest one of the Moonies?"

"If and when we have proof, I think they'll change their tune—no matter how bad the PR is." Zan glanced at her watch and stood. "Sorry, but I've spent too much time here as it is. People are going to start wondering where I am."

I got to my feet and met her by the door. "Thanks," I said.

"For what?"

"Wanting to find out what happened to Dr. Holtz."

"I should be thanking *you* for that." Zan reached for the

door, then seemed to think of something and turned back to face me. "I hate that I have to say this, but for your safety we need to keep our alliance a secret. You can't let *anyone* know we're working together—or that I've even come to you. In fact, it's probably best if you don't even let on that we've met at all. Don't mention my name to anyone. If anyone asks you about me, say you haven't met me yet."

"Even my parents?"

"Even your parents. This is a very small community, and gossip will travel through it quickly. If there is a murderer, I don't want them having any idea you're involved in this. To that end, don't come to me with anything. I'll come to you."

"But what if I find something important?" I asked.

"I'll be keeping a close eye on you," Zan told me. "It won't be hard to do in quarters as tight as this. Though be aware, our target will be able to keep a close eye on everyone as well. Both of us need to exercise extreme caution. Speaking of which, no one should see me leaving your room."

"Right." I opened the door and checked the catwalk. No one was outside. "Coast is clear."

"I'll be in touch." Zan gave me a wink, then slipped out and quickly ducked around the corner.

I closed the door behind her, wondering what I'd gotten myself into.

Excerpt from *The Official Residents' Guide to Moon Base Alpha*,
© 2040 by National Aeronautics and Space Administration:

VISITORS

As a lunarnaut, you are probably aware that there will occasion-
ally be visitors at Moon Base Alpha. In fact, there would be no
MBA without the funds provided by space tourism!* Be aware,
our visitors' commitment to MBA is just as strong as yours. So
don't think of them as tourists; consider them investors in the
international space program. And though our guests are not
official employees of NASA or their families, remember: They
still have undergone a rigorous selection process and exten-
sive training for their visit, just like you.

The visitors have strict instructions not to get involved
in—or interfere with—the day-to-day workings of MBA. It is
requested that all lunarnauts return the favor and provide our
guests with the highest-quality lunar experience possible. To
that end, please do not:

- Bother, harass or pester the visitors in any way
- Ask the visitors for money or employment after your stint
  at MBA ends
- Enter the visitors' quarters without their express permission
- Spread gossip, rumors, or idle hearsay about the visitors

Thank you for your cooperation!

---

* Currently, tourism is slated to provide 51.2 percent of the working budget
for MBA. That adds up to billions of dollars a year coming from the private
sector—rather than taxes.

SPACE JERKS

Lunar day 188
Afternoon

I had to find Roddy. I didn't know how to hack the computer and dig up the security footage on my own.

Now that Nina and everyone else were distracted by the arrival of the new Moonies, I figured Roddy would probably have returned to the rec room to play veeyar games. Sure enough, I found him there, jacked in as usual.

Unfortunately, I also found Patton and Lily Sjoberg.

The Sjobergs and their parents were the first lunar tourists. Since Moon Base Alpha ended up costing more than five times what NASA had originally projected, the agency was forced to get additional financing from space tourism.

Maximum Adventure Travel ponied up the money in return for two concessions: 1) A residence at MBA would be converted into a "deluxe lunar hotel suite." 2) Maximum Adventure had the exclusive rights to charge incredibly wealthy people staggering sums of money to come stay at Moon Base Alpha.

In truth, the "deluxe lunar hotel suite" isn't that deluxe. There was no way to deliver anything particularly fancy to MBA, like nice mattresses or Jacuzzi tubs. The suite has an actual window, and the SlimScreens are slightly higher quality than ours, but other than that it's as lame as every other room at MBA. The tourists still have to eat the same awful food we do and use the same sadistic toilets. And yet MBA is the only place for tourists to stay on the moon, so incredibly rich suckers are lining up to shell out big bucks to come here. The Sjobergs outbid hundreds of other elite families in a silent auction, spending what's rumored to be more than half a billion dollars to be the first lunar tourist family. The money bought them a four-month stay at MBA, which they were already four weeks into.

Hard as it is to believe, half a billion isn't much money for the Sjobergs. They are some of the richest people on earth. Lars, the father, made his fortune in deep-sea oil drilling. Sonja, the mother, inherited half of Norway. Together they have so much money, they've run out of ways to spend it. They have more homes in more countries than anyone can count, a fleet of private jets, a solid gold bathtub, and a pet snow leopard named Schatzi. They've already visited every place on earth, so when the chance came to go to the moon, they jumped at it.

Unfortunately, just like the rest of us, they discovered Moon Base Alpha wasn't what they'd hoped. But even if MBA had been absolutely incredible, with fancy suites and gourmet meals, I still doubt the Sjobergs would have been happy. They're spoiled rotten. Back on earth, servants did everything for them. And I mean *everything*. They had cooks, gardeners, butlers, dog walkers, maids, doormen, barbers, decorators, masseuses, stablemen, pool boys, and art curators. But since there were only four seats available on the rocket, there was no way for them to bring even a single butler to MBA. So, for the first time in their lives, the Sjobergs have to do things for themselves. And they hate it. They've been so pampered; none of them has the slightest idea how to work anything, no matter how simple. On the first night at MBA, Lars Sjoberg nearly lost a finger trying to use a can opener.

Once they learned they were incompetent without servants, the Sjobergs came up with a new plan: Try to make everyone else at MBA do things for them. This didn't work out so well either. In the first place, they never *asked* us to do anything. They ordered us to do it. Second, all the adults had plenty to do already. They couldn't just drop everything to make breakfast for a bunch of helpless rich people. So everyone told the Sjobergs they'd have to handle things on their own. (Except Chang Hi-Tech, who bluntly informed Lars Sjoberg that he should get off his lazy butt before Chang drove his foot up it.)

From there things only got worse. None of the Sjobergs had been very nice to begin with. Now, realizing they'd spent more than some entire countries made in a year to end up in their own private hell, they turned on us, becoming even nastier than before. Any encounter with them was a bad one. The only Moonie any of them remotely got along with was Cesar Marquez, and that's only because Lily Sjoberg had a crush on him. And since Cesar didn't like his little brother much, the Sjoberg kids were worse to Roddy than to anyone else.

When I found them in the rec room, Patton and Lily had just swiped Roddy's hologoggles and were playing keep-away.

"Come on! Give them back!" Roddy whined as he haplessly ran back and forth between the twins. "I was just about to liberate Titan from the Pernicious Skrinks!"

"Ooh!" Patton Sjoberg taunted. "If you're such a big hero, why can't you get your goggles back?"

"Why do you guys have to be such jerks?" Roddy mewled.

"Why do you have to be such a loser?" Lily shot back.

Normally I might have hustled off before anyone noticed me. I didn't like the idea of being on Patton Sjoberg's bad side. In addition to being as mean as a rabid badger, he was also quite strong. He spent most of his time at MBA in the gym, bulking up his muscles. His biceps had grown by an inch in the last four weeks. And Lily was pretty strong herself, surprisingly tall and broad for a girl.

But I needed a favor from Roddy, and Roddy wasn't much for helping anyone but himself. So I figured I'd get on his good side.

Roddy made a desperate lunge for Patton, who flipped the goggles over his head. Given the low gravity, they sailed high into the air.

I cocked my legs and launched myself as hard as I could. On earth my vertical jump was about two feet. On the moon it's four times that. I flew over Lily's head and snatched the goggles before she could.

Unfortunately, even after six months I was still mastering low gravity. I flew much farther than I'd expected, crashed into the wall, and tumbled back down to the floor. Still, I managed to keep a hold on the goggles. When I got to my feet, the Sjobergs were flanking me, glaring hatefully with their beady blue eyes.

"Look who thinks he's a hero now," Patton scoffed. "Give them back, Dash."

He reached for the goggles, but I yanked them away. "They're not yours."

"They're not yours, either," Lily said. "We're trying to have some fun here and you're ruining it. So why don't you blast off and leave us alone?"

"Why don't you go instead?" I asked. "I'll bet Roddy was here first."

Patton scowled. His muscles flexed, stretching the fabric of his shirt. "Hand over the goggles," he said. "Trust me. You do not want to make enemies with me."

I turned to face him, and as I did, I caught a glimpse of my reflection in the SlimScreen. Behind my back, Lily Sjoberg was coiling to strike. "You're right," I said. "I don't. But that shouldn't mean I have to give you whatever you want."

"Then we'll just take it." Patton sprang at me. At the same time, in the reflection, I saw his sister do the same.

I was ready for them, though. As they both came at me, I launched myself again. I soared out of Patton and Lily's path and they slammed into each other, clocking heads so hard that I could practically hear their tiny brains rattle around in their skulls.

This time I stuck the landing, alighting perfectly by Roddy. "Here you go," I said, valiantly handing over his goggles.

He didn't even say thanks. He was too busy watching the Sjobergs.

Patton and Lily staggered a moment before regaining their balance, then wheeled on me. Lily's nose had gotten bloodied in their collision, while Patton now had a fat lip. Patton put his fingers to his mouth, then pulled them away bloody. A tiny shard of white sat on one fingertip. "You chipped my tooth!" he yelled. Although with his fat lip it sounded like "toof."

"I didn't do anything," I countered. "You attacked *me*."

"You two are going to pay for this," Patton growled.

"Me?" Roddy gulped. "I didn't have anything to do with this! Dash is the one you want!" And then, even though I'd just come to his aid, the weasel scurried out of the rec room, leaving me on my own with the Nordic nightmares.

Neither Patton nor Lily went after him. Instead they both marched toward me.

"You break my tooth," Patton said, "I break your head."

I stared at them, unable to believe things had come to this. The Sjobergs were doing their best to look menacing, but with blood trickling from Lily's nose and smeared over Patton's broken teeth, they both looked even stranger than usual.

You see, Patton and Lily are virtually the only pure white people my age I've ever met. Everyone else I know is a blend.

Me and Violet for example (black mom, white dad). Or the Brahmaputra-Marquez family (Indian mom, Latino dad). Or Kira (Asian mom, black dad). Or Riley Bock, back on earth (Korean-Italian mom, Irish–Sri Lankan–Peruvian-Choctaw dad). The Sjobergs, however, are pure northern European Caucasian stock, with blond hair and blue eyes and skin so pale it looks like the belly of a fish. Mom and Dad have some friends like that from their generation, and my grandparents say it was pretty common when they were young, and I've been told that back when my great-grandparents were kids, people of different races couldn't even marry each other in America. I know that's true, but it still seems impossible.

Every kid I'd ever known was some shade of brown. So to me, on a normal day, the snow-white Sjobergs were strange. Now, with their sneering, blood-smeared faces, they looked like things from one of Roddy's intergalactic virtual reality games.

I held out my hands, signaling Patton and Lily to calm down. "Hold on now. Can we talk about this?"

To my surprise, the Sjobergs stopped right in front of me. "Sure," Patton said. "Let's talk."

"Really?" I asked. "Okay. Look, I'm very sorry you got hurt—"

I almost didn't see Lily's fist coming. The Sjobergs hadn't stopped out of any sense of kindness. They'd only done it so

I'd let my guard down. Plus I was focused on Patton, thinking that if anyone threw a punch, it'd be him. While Lily looked gentler, however, she could be just as nasty.

I ducked to the side. Lily's knuckles grazed my ear. She sailed past me, and instead of connecting with my face, her fist slammed into the doorjamb. Lily howled in pain.

Patton dove for me. I sprang out of his way, once again sailing higher than I would have on earth, and landed in the hall, where I took off, bounding as fast as I could. Patton tumbled to the floor, but quickly righted himself and came after me. Lily followed us, cradling her wounded fist, yelling, "Get him, Patton! Smash his stupid face in!"

You can't really run in low gravity. Running requires keeping your feet on the ground, which is impossible to do when every step sends you flying through the air. Patton and I were still trying, though, which meant we ended up looking ridiculous, pinwheeling our legs in the air like cartoon characters that had just run off a cliff. Patton actually had the advantage, though; because he was bigger, he hit the ground more, which meant he was closing the gap on me.

We reached the main air lock. Even now, more than an hour after the Raptor's arrival, the adults were still hard at work unloading the rocket. The outdoor crew had delivered a new load of cargo to the air lock and other people were moving it into the station. The staging area was full of shrink-wrapped bales of new supplies: dehydrated food packets, robot replacement parts, medical supplies, sanitary wipes, toilet paper, and the highly anticipated fresh fruit and vegetables. Half a dozen adults were shuttling the cargo about.

Dr. Janke stepped right in my path, holding a huge block of food.

It was three feet square, the kind of thing you'd normally see on a forklift. On earth it would have probably weighed two hundred pounds. On the moon it was less than forty, so Dr. Janke could lift it by himself. Still, because it was so big, it nearly blocked the entire hall.

I didn't have time to stop.

But I could go over it. In low gravity, you can run along walls. You can't do it for long, but I didn't have to. I sprang up, hit the wall with my feet, and charged a few steps, clearing the bale before dropping to the floor again.

Behind me Patton—whose brain was more dense than his muscles—tried to stop instead. But his inertia carried him forward, and he slammed right into the bale. His legs went out from under him, he landed flat on his back—and then the huge bale, knocked free from Dr. Janke's hands, landed right on top of him. There was a sickening crunch, followed by a scream of disgust from Patton.

All the adults rushed to his aid, lifting the crate off him.

I'd thought the crunch might have come from Patton's nose breaking; instead it turned out to be three cartons of fresh eggs cracking on his head. By the time Patton wriggled free, the smashed yolks had already oozed through the shrink-wrap, coating his head in yellow goo. A bag of dried coconut had also burst open on impact, and the shavings were now stuck in the eggs, making Patton look like a mangy poodle.

The adults gasped in horror. Not because of how Patton appeared—but because we'd just lost our only fresh eggs. And a good bit of coconut.

Patton staggered to his feet, blinded by the raw egg that had oozed into his eyes. "Dash!" he bellowed. "I'm gonna kill you!"

I tried to slip away before he regained his sight, only to feel a sudden viselike grip on my arm. "What have you done?" Nina demanded.

"Me?" I asked. "I didn't do anything! You heard Patton. He was trying to kill me!"

"I was not!" Patton blubbered in his defense. Since he couldn't see Nina, he mistakenly faced the wrong way, delivering his argument to a wall. "First that little freak breaks my tooth! Then he does this!"

Lily hurried to her brother's side. "Look at him, Nina! He's covered in egg!"

"He started this!" I argued. "I was only defending myself!"

Nina spun me around to face her. "You're on probation as of this moment."

"Only me?" I asked. "Why isn't Patton in trouble too?"

"Because your parents didn't shell out half a billion dollars to come here," Dr. Janke muttered.

Everyone else laughed, except Nina. Instead she grew even angrier and directed it at me. "I thought my orders were clear. Anyone who doesn't have cargo duty is to stay out of this area so things like this don't happen." She stabbed a finger at the mess on the floor. "So I'm going to give you another order, Dashiell. And I expect you to follow it this time. Go to my quarters. *Now.*"

I had no choice but to obey. I slunk back through the staging area, feeling everyone's eyes on me. I got the sense they all knew I wasn't really to blame, but no one wanted to get on Nina's bad side—or the Sjobergs'—by sticking up for me at the moment. Only Patton seemed pleased. "Sucks to be you," he chuckled as I passed him.

"At least I don't look like an omelet," I shot back.

Patton stopped laughing. "You'd better watch your back," he growled.

"I'll be up there soon," Nina told me. "Right after I take care of the mess you've made."

I didn't bother to look back. I continued past the air lock, then climbed the stairs to Nina's residence. Once I got there, however, I found her door was locked. I had no choice but to sit on the catwalk and wait. Below me everyone in the staging area went back to their business.

At the end of the hall, behind them all, I caught a glimpse of Zan Perfonic by the science pod. She shot a quick glance in my direction. I couldn't quite read it from that distance, but I got the idea she was trying to comfort me somehow.

I still felt lousy, though. I'd failed miserably at my first assignment. I'd gone to ask for Roddy's help hacking into the computer and had ended up on probation. Of course, that wasn't entirely my fault. I hoped Roddy might come by, looking to thank me for helping him out, but there was no sign of him. I figured he was probably in the mess hall, waiting for fresh food to arrive.

"Hey," Kira said.

I glanced toward her voice. She was standing in the doorway of her residence. It was only a few feet away, but it was far enough so that Nina, who was still in the staging area, couldn't see her.

"What was all that about?" she asked.

"The Sjobergs were picking on Roddy Marquez," I reported. "I tried to help him and they came after me instead."

"They're the tourists?"

"Yeah. You'll learn to hate them soon enough."

Kira laughed. "That was nice of you, standing up for Roddy."

I shrugged, not feeling like getting into the reasons *why* I'd stood up for Roddy. For the moment I wanted to look like a good guy. "I guess."

"So . . . is he going to hack the computer for you?"

I spun toward Kira, surprised. She instantly turned away, her cheeks flushing red, as though embarrassed she'd made a mistake. "How did you . . . ?" I began.

"I didn't mean to overhear," Kira said quickly. "Really. I was trying to nap like I said I was going to. Only . . . the wall between your room and ours isn't very thick. I could hear your conversation through it."

I frowned, concerned. It had never occurred to me that anyone could hear through our walls. Kira's room had been empty the whole time my family had been at MBA—and Nina had never said anything. Although it now occurred to me that Nina had been heading to her room that morning right before I told my parents I thought Dr. Holtz had been murdered. If Nina had been eavesdropping on us, that would explain how she'd known about my suspicions. "How much did you hear?"

"Not everything," Kira admitted. "I was trying not to listen. Honest. In fact I could only hear you. Maybe you were closer to that wall than the other person. . . ."

"I was," I said, feeling relieved. Kira hadn't heard Zan at all.

"But a few parts came through anyway," Kira went on.

"Which parts?" I asked.

"That Dr. Holtz's death wasn't an accident. And that you need to hack the computer to get some evidence."

I glanced back toward the staging area. Thankfully, no one was close enough to overhear us. In fact no one was even looking our way. They were busily moving cargo while Nina supervised cleanup of the eggs. "Please don't tell anyone," I pleaded.

"Oh, I won't," Kira said quickly. "Under one condition."

I looked back toward her. "What's that?"

"You let me help."

Excerpt from *The Official Residents' Guide to Moon Base Alpha,*
© 2040 by National Aeronautics and Space Administration:

VIDEO LOGS

As a lunarnaut, you will serve as an ambassador between MBA and earth. Your selection as one of the lucky few to live on the moon has no doubt already brought you plenty of attention, and as you serve at MBA, millions of earthlings will be eager to hear what you are doing. To that end, it is required that each lunarnaut keep a video log to update his or her fans as to the goings-on at MBA. It is suggested that this be done once a week at minimum (although you are certainly free to update yours far more often!).

Have fun with this. Don't merely give a dull recitation of the week's events. Instead, spice it up! Let your fans get to see the *real* you. Tell stories, show off your low-gravity juggling skills, or do karaoke. As long as it's fun to watch, we don't care what you do!*

---

* With a few exceptions. Lunarnauts are prohibited from insulting, disparaging, slandering, or otherwise saying negative things about MBA or any of its inhabitants.

8

UNEXPECTED HELP

Lunar day 188
Afternoon

"I knew Dr. Holtz," Kira told me. "Back on earth. He and my father worked on some projects together. They told us about his death as we were landing. They said it was an accident, that he made an unauthorized moonwalk—but that doesn't sound right to me."

I ran my fingers through my hair, worried. Nina had warned me not to tell people Dr. Holtz had been murdered—and I'd already done it. Of course, it wasn't exactly my fault. How was I supposed to know the lousy lunar contractors had made the walls too thin? But still, if Nina found out about this, on top of all the other things she was upset at me about . . . for all I knew, she'd sentence me to remain on the moon until I was sixty. "Look," I said. "I'm not really supposed to be investigating this at all. . . ."

"Who were you talking to in your room, then?" Kira asked. "I got the idea it was someone in security."

"It's hard to explain." From where I sat on the catwalk, I was still visible to everyone down by the air lock—including Nina—so I faced forward, away from Kira, and templed my fingers in front of my mouth, trying to give the impression that I wasn't talking to anyone at all.

"But it was an adult, right?"

"Er . . . right."

"So then, you've been asked to do it. It's not like we'd be snooping around on our own."

"Well, we'd still be in trouble if we got caught."

"Let's not get caught, then." Kira grinned.

"I'm serious," I told her. "You just got here. You don't want to get off on the wrong foot with Nina."

"I'll be careful. I can handle this. I've done worse."

I was about to ask, "Like what?" but before I could, down in the staging area, Nina turned toward me—as though she had sensed I was talking about her. She couldn't see Kira—but the sight of me simply sitting on the catwalk was enough to get her angry. "I told you to wait in my office!" she yelled.

"It's locked!" I called back.

Nina scowled and kept staring at me.

Kira took a step back, making sure she was out of Nina's eye line, then mused, "I wonder if *she* had something to do with Dr. Holtz's death. It's kind of suspicious, ordering everyone *not* to investigate a murder, isn't it?"

I started to deny this, but then thought about it. I put my hand over my mouth, trying to look thoughtful as I covered my lips. "You're right. It is."

"So let me help, then. I'm pretty good with computers myself."

"Can you hack?"

"Yeah, a bit. What do you need?"

"The security tapes of Dr. Holtz going out the air lock this morning."

Kira frowned. "Oh. That's not going to be easy."

"I know. I'm not sure if even Roddy can do it."

In the staging area, Nina started heading my way.

"Nina's coming!" I warned. "Better go before she sees you."

Kira didn't question this. She quickly ducked back into her room. "I'll see what I can get you." There was a gleam of excitement in her eye as she closed the door.

Nina reached the base of the stairs. If Kira had been a half second slower, Nina would have seen her. Instead Nina only saw me, sitting by myself. She came up the steps to the catwalk. I hopped to my feet to meet her.

"Who were you talking to?" Nina asked.

Apparently, covering my mouth with my hand hadn't fooled her. "Violet," I lied, pointing down to the rec room. "She was down there. She came out into the hall and wanted to know where our parents were. I told her and she went back in."

Nina cased both levels of the hallway, trying to determine if I was lying. The halls were empty; there was no one else around for her to presume I'd been talking to.

Nina shifted her attention back to me. "I want you to go into your room and stay there. You're grounded until I say otherwise."

"What?" I asked. "You can't do that! You're not my mom!"

"At this base I have the authority to delegate any punishment I see fit. I gave you a direct order to stay out of the staging area and you disobeyed it."

"What was I supposed to do? Let the Sjobergs beat me up?"

"Do you know how difficult it was to requisition those eggs?" Nina demanded. "NASA didn't want to send them. I spent hours working every angle I could. They were going to be a treat for everyone up here. A special reward for their hard work. And now that's not going to happen. Every last egg is broken, and after this disaster NASA will never agree to ship any more. Which means it will be three years until I taste a fresh egg again!"

Oh, I thought, *so that's what all this is about.* For all her posturing that I had disobeyed orders, Nina was really upset that she'd lost her precious eggs. Sure, she was claiming she'd requested them for everyone, but she wouldn't have spent hours on it unless she'd really wanted them herself. I understood where she was coming from, though. We all have our own food obsessions at MBA. You have no idea what you'll *really* miss until you get here. Personally, I'd have thought I would want ice cream more than anything else. But now that I'm on the moon, for some reason I always find myself craving picante sauce. I couldn't imagine what would happen if a jar had been shipped up for me and then ended up broken. I might have been desperate enough to lick everything up off the floor.

And yet I was still ticked off that I was getting punished for this—while the Sjobergs were getting off scot-free because they were rich. "What am I supposed to do in my room all day?" I asked.

"You haven't updated your video log in over a week," Nina told me. "Start with that."

"That'll only take five minutes," I protested.

"No," Nina said, "I want you to take your time with this. Think about it very carefully. Don't say one word about Dr. Holtz's death being suspicious—"

"You mean, I can't say anything about his death?"

"You're welcome to talk about it. In fact, I encourage you to. The public knows about the death by now and they're eager to hear what we all have to say. So tell them what a great man Dr. Holtz was. Let them know you're upset he's gone. But do not, under any circumstances, even *hint* that there might have been foul play. I'm going to review your video before you post it, and if I don't like it, I'll have you do it again. So don't take this lightly. No crazy stories about moondragons or finding hoards of green cheese today. Is that clear?"

"Crystal," I muttered, then headed into my room and slammed the door behind me.

Nina might have been upset about her eggs, but she'd used the incident to manipulate me in a big way. By grounding me, she was shutting down any chance I had to investigate Dr. Holtz's death—or to recruit anyone else to help me. And by demanding that I compose a video log about Dr. Holtz, Nina was forcing me to publicly back her side of the story. If I decided to push the murder angle later, I'd come across as fickle.

I found myself thinking about Kira's suggestion. If Nina truly had been involved in Dr. Holtz's death, she was certainly in a great position to cover her tracks. She was doing everything in her power to muzzle me and derail any investigation.

I sat at the SlimScreen table. Instead of starting my video log, I said, "Computer, get me all information you can on Nina Stack."

"It vould be my pleasure!" the computer exclaimed. It instantly opened a ComLink and brought up a dozen web pages about Nina. I figured there was no harm in using a ComLink now. It wasn't like Nina could punish me any more than she had already.

Now that the Link was open, I discovered that I had hundreds of messages as well. Virtually everyone I knew on earth had reached out to me after hearing about Dr. Holtz's death. I read a few. They all said basically the same thing: *Heard the news. Thinking about you. Let me know how you are.*

Riley Bock had left a dozen messages herself. With all the excitement, I'd forgotten that I'd promised to call her that day. It would have to wait a little longer, though; I had investigating to do.

I scanned through the web pages about Nina, but there was nothing I didn't already know. Either Nina had never done anything wrong in her life, or NASA had completely whitewashed her history. Whatever the case, every biography of Nina was glowing. She was a decorated soldier, a clever scientist, a highly respected employee, and the top choice to command MBA: competent, straitlaced, and honest as could be.

But then all of our official bios read like that. First, NASA truly had sought out extremely well-behaved people to serve at MBA, not wanting any chance of scandal. And then, if we had ever misbehaved, even a bit, NASA had scrubbed any mention of that from our records. For example, at school on earth I'd been sent to the principal's office plenty of times, but according to my bio I'd been a model student. It made me sound like a Boy Scout.

However, someone at MBA obviously wasn't as moral as their bio claimed, because they'd murdered Dr. Holtz. Either they'd hidden their true nature or NASA had hidden it for them. Whatever the case, I probably wasn't going to find any dirt on them online.

"Has anyone at MBA ever done anything wrong?" I sighed.

"Your sister once put chewing gum in ze rehydrator," the computer replied.

"Right." I'd forgotten about that. Violet had broken the machine, forcing us all to eat nonhydrated food cubes for two days until Mr. Grisan could fix it. "I meant the adults."

"Lars Sjoberg is rumored to have done some shady things in his business dealings."

I straightened up, annoyed at myself for not thinking of the Sjobergs first. "Show me what you've got."

Hundreds of web pages popped open, so quickly I worried they might overwhelm the ComLink. I spent the next hour reading through them.

In his business Lars had been accused of everything from ignoring environmental laws to bribing government officials to violating oil embargoes. However, none of the charges had ever stuck. Inevitably, someone below Lars at his company ended up taking the fall, while Lars himself came out unscathed. He was known to say, "When you're on the top of the heap, lots of people will try to drag you down to their level"—and yet it was hard to believe that a fundamentally good person would have been accused of so many bad things. Instead Lars came across as someone who'd behaved badly time and time again, but who had the wealth and power to avoid getting in trouble.

Could Lars Sjoberg have killed Dr. Holtz? It wasn't hard to imagine him committing murder. He was basically the worst person I'd ever met. Plus he had a volcanic temper and was prone to fits of rage that shook the entire base.

And now that I thought about it, Patton and Lily Sjoberg were also volatile and violent. I wondered if either one of them was capable of murder too.

I rubbed my eyes, which were bleary from reading. "Computer, can you bring up the news?" I asked.

"Of course, *mein Herr.*" The web page for the *New York Times* appeared. (When my parents were kids, there were lots of newspapers, one for almost every city. Now in America only the *Times* is left.) As I'd suspected, Dr. Holtz's death was the lead story. I tapped on the headline, which instantly linked to a video report.

Footage of Dr. Holtz training for his mission to MBA appeared, while a reporter began, "Dr. Ronald Holtz, a lunarnaut on Moon Base Alpha and a highly respected professor, died this morning during a routine moonwalk at the base."

"Routine?" I repeated, surprised. Obviously NASA was covering up the real details of the death. Or maybe Nina had hidden the details from NASA.

A telephone's ring interrupted the news report. Then a message flashed: INCOMING CALL. RILEY BOCK.

After so much time focusing on the Sjobergs, I was ready for a friendly face. I accepted the call.

The news story automatically muted and shifted to the background while Riley's face popped up in a central window. Her sister, Eliza, who is two years younger than us, was right next to her. They were speaking to me on Riley's smartwatch while their car automatically drove them someplace—probably the beach, knowing the Bocks. (Ever since cars started driving themselves, parents have been letting them chaperone kids.) It was gorgeously sunny, as usual; the girls were wearing bikini tops, board shorts, and sunglasses.

The phone service on the moon isn't bad. In fact I can get a better connection from MBA than I could from a lot of places in Hawaii. However, the signal has to travel 238,900 miles between earth and the moon, so it takes a few seconds between the time you speak and the time the other person hears it. Then there are another few seconds after they speak until you hear them. Originally this was difficult to deal with; we ended up talking over each other all the time. But after a while we got used to it. Since I speak to Riley every few days, she knows the routine.

"Hey," she said. "Is everything all right? I left you a ton of messages."

"Sorry. I didn't get them until an hour ago. They wanted us off the ComLink."

"Oh. Guess it's been an exciting day up there."

"Yeah, for once." NASA usually has censors eavesdrop on our personal calls, but I've learned I can get away with insulting the base if I make it sound like sarcasm.

"I'm serious," Riley said. "Are you doing okay? Did you know the guy?"

"There are only twenty-two people here. Of course I knew him."

"You know what she means!" Eliza said. "Did you hang out with him or was he just some old coot who never paid attention to you?"

My eyes flicked to the news footage of Dr. Holtz. It was now showing him boarding the rocket for the launch to the moon. He looked as happy as anyone could be, beaming in his space suit, waving cheerfully to the cameras.

"Somewhere in between," I admitted. "Since he was a lot older, he hung out more with the other adults than any of us kids. But he was always really nice to me. Everyone really liked him."

"Oh," Riley said. "Well, I'm sorry he's gone. Are you guys gonna have a funeral for him?"

"To be honest, I have no idea. I don't know if anyone's even thought about that yet."

"Are you gonna bury him there?" Eliza asked. "Is he gonna be, like, the first dead guy laid to rest on the moon?"

"I don't think so," I said.

"So what are you gonna do?" Eliza demanded. "Shoot him into space?"

"I doubt it. Though I think Dr. Holtz might have liked that idea."

"Well, it's all over the news down here," Riley reported. "Like being the first human to die on the moon makes you a hero somehow. So we figured we'd check in."

"Thanks," I said. "What are you up to? Surfing?"

"You know it. Kohala. Looks like an epic break today. Check it." Riley turned her smartwatch so I could see they were arriving at the beach. On cue a perfect wave came in, a beautiful blue curl.

I groaned, missing earth terribly. "Come on. Don't rub it in like that."

"Rub it in?" Eliza asked. "Dude, you're on the moon!"

"You hit six g's on a rocket," Riley added. "Kohala's probably as exciting as riding a merry-go-round compared to that."

"Yeah," I said, trying to sell it to the censors. "You're right. But I still miss that place."

"Ha," Riley said, not believing me at all. "You're famous and you're having the adventure of a lifetime. I get to go surfing every once in a while. Trust me, my life blows compared to yours."

I desperately wanted to tell them the truth, that I wasn't lucky at all, that all the amazing stories they'd heard about life on the moon (none of which had come from me, by the way) were merely hype and public relations. Instead I could only say, "Your life's not so bad."

"Mr. Cochran's gonna flunk me in English and Dad wants me to work in his office this summer," Riley shot back. "What's good about that?"

She still had her smartwatch aimed toward the beach. I noticed several friends from school there, pulling on wetsuits and waxing their boards, feeling the sand on their toes and the warm sun on their faces. In the distance a surfer shot through the tunnel of a wave.

"It's all good," I told her. "Trust me."

The Bock girls' car pulled into the sand lot by the beach and self-parked. Lori Yee-Cohen, one of my classmates, set down her surfboard and waved hello to them. "Check it out!" Riley said, pointing to her watch. "I'm talking to Dash Gibson—in space!"

"Awesome!" Lori exclaimed, then waved to me. "Hey, Dash! How's the moon?"

"Great," I lied. "How's earth?"

"All right, I guess. We miss you!"

This from a girl who hadn't even known I went to her school until my family got tapped for MBA. Then I got famous and everyone suddenly started acting like we'd been friends our whole lives. I don't mind when Riley milks her friendship with me for social status—we really are friends, and I'd do the same if she were the one on the moon—but it bugs me when other people do it.

"I miss all you guys too," I said, just to be polite.

"Take it easy!" Lori picked up her board again and continued to the water's edge.

Riley turned the watch back so I could see her. She now looked slightly concerned; I probably hadn't done a great job of hiding my homesickness. "You sure you're all right?"

"Yeah," I said, forcing a smile. "I'm fine."

"Hey, some new girl came up there today, right?" Eliza asked. "Did you meet her yet?"

"Yeah, I've met her. I'm her official welcomer."

"What's she like?" asked Riley.

"She's nice."

"Ooooh!" Eliza crooned. "You like her! Are you gonna kiss her?"

"Don't be such a dork." Riley shoved her sister out of the frame.

"Dash has a girlfriend!" Eliza sang, unfazed. "On the mooooon!"

Something suddenly caught my eye in the news report on Dr. Holtz, which was still running in the background on the SlimScreen. I wasn't quite sure what it was, as I'd been focused on the beach instead. But it was enough to make me sit up, aware I'd just missed something important.

Riley must have noticed my expression change. "What's wrong?"

I tapped the SlimScreen, pausing the news report on an image of a somewhat younger Dr. Holtz dressed for a fancy party. "Nothing," I said. "I just have to jump."

"Oh. Well, I've gotta go myself," Riley told me. "The waves are calling. Take it easy up there. If you start freaking out or anything, you know where to find me."

"Have a good ride for me," I said.

"You know I will. Aloha, Moonie."

"Have fun with your girlfriend!" Eliza shouted.

Riley clicked off. I stared at her final image—sand, sun, and beach—feeling desperately homesick for a few more moments.

I was about to return to the news report when a thought occurred to me.

When I'd overheard Dr. Holtz's phone call, there hadn't been any two-second gaps in the conversation. True, I hadn't been able to hear the person on the other end of the call, but still, you can tell. Talking to someone when you have to wait a few seconds for an answer always sounds a little stilted. But Dr. Holtz's conversation hadn't been that way at all.

Which meant he hadn't been talking to someone on earth. He'd been talking to someone on the moon.

I wondered who it could be. Who else had been up at that time of night? And why had they used the phone, rather than meeting somewhere on the base?

I sighed. Trapped in my room, there was no way I could pursue that line of investigation any further.

So I returned my attention to the news report, rewinding it thirty seconds to see what I'd missed.

The report was recapping Dr. Holtz's life and, judging

from the photos of him, was somewhere near the last decade. Dr. Holtz's hair was graying, but not white like it had ultimately become. Various shots of him working at NASA flashed by, while the reporter said, "In more recent years, Dr. Holtz was a key player in designing Moon Base Alpha, drawing upon his research and his own experiences in space to help create the best lunar living environment for humans."

The video then shifted to the party I'd glimpsed, which turned out to be an event in Dr. Holtz's honor. "Dr. Holtz was widely respected for his work," the reporter continued, "garnering such awards as the National Medal of Science and NASA's Exceptional Scientific Achievement Medal for his work on the effects of low gravity on the human body."

"Pause," I told the computer. The same thing that had caught my eye before had done so again. It was so fleeting I didn't even know what it was, but this time I'd been alert enough to stop the news report in the right place, giving me time to examine the scene.

Dr. Holtz was up on a podium, wearing a nice suit, while Caroline Lesser, the chief administrator of NASA, draped a medal around his neck. In the room around them, hundreds of fellow NASA employees were also dressed to the nines, seated at dinner tables and applauding enthusiastically.

Well, not everyone was applauding enthusiastically.

While all the other guests looked pleased, one person

seated at a front table didn't seem happy at all. I might never have noticed him, but he stood out because he had a Mohawk.

I tapped on the image. "Enlarge," I told the computer.

The computer zoomed in on Chang Hi-Tech, enhancing and adjusting the resolution until Chang's face was as bright and clear as if I had been sitting right next to him.

Close up, he didn't seem merely unhappy.

He was glaring at Dr. Holtz with complete and total hatred.

Excerpt from *The Official Residents' Guide to Moon Base Alpha*, © 2040 by National Aeronautics and Space Administration:

DINING

Dining at MBA is a communal affair, so every meal is like a party! You'll join all your fellow lunarnauts in the mess hall, where you'll be able to select any of hundreds of possible meals. NASA chefs have been perfecting recipes for more than eighty years now, so whatever your taste, there will be plenty of options for you. Choose from old favorites like chicken parmigiana, cheese enchiladas, or classic shrimp cocktail—or try one of our new, exciting culinary fusions like Korean duck tacos, lamb-curry lasagna, or Peruvian spring rolls!* Simply pick your convenient, premade dining packet, insert it in the rehydrator for thirty seconds—and *bon appetit!* Best of all, it's free, courtesy of NASA.† Eating at MBA is so easy and delicious, you'll be disappointed when you return to earth!

---

* To respect the dietary restrictions of our lunarnauts, before launch you can also request personally designed meals if you keep kosher or halal, are vegetarian or vegan, or have any other food restrictions.

† In order to prevent food shortages, please limit yourself to only one meal per dining period.

FRESH MEAT

Lunar day 188
Dinnertime

My parents sprang me for dinner.

They had been so busy with their various duties that day that it wasn't till evening that they heard I'd been grounded. Once they did, they were livid at Nina. First, everyone who'd witnessed the raw-egg incident had made it clear that Patton Sjoberg was as much to blame as me—if not more. And neither Mom nor Dad felt it was Nina's right to ground me. So come dinnertime I was seated in the mess with everyone else.

Normally I would consider dining at MBA to be as big a punishment as being grounded, but since fresh food had arrived that day, I was actually excited to eat for once. Everyone else was too. Most nights the Moonies dribble in at random times to scarf something down as quickly as possible. (It's the general theory at MBA that the faster you eat your freeze-dried crud, the less chance you have of actually tasting it.) But tonight the mess was full, everyone gathered together and eager for their meal.

On a normal night we all prepare our own food. (Even Violet can work the rehydrator, so long as she doesn't stick chewing gum in it.) But the fresh food took a bit more care. So Nina, Chang, and Mr. Grisan had the honor of prepping it while the rest of us waited. It was too crowded for my family to have a table to ourselves; Kira's father and Daphne Merritt sat with us. Kira was the only person at MBA who hadn't shown up for dinner.

"Where's your daughter?" Violet asked Dr. Howard bluntly.

"Hmm?" asked Dr. Howard, who'd been staring off into space. He looked around and seemed to notice for the first time that Kira was missing. However, he didn't seem concerned about this. "Oh, she's off exploring her new home, I suppose."

"That shouldn't take long," I muttered. "This place isn't big."

"That's one of the things I like about it," Daphne said cheerfully. Other than Violet, Daphne is the only person who seems continually thrilled to be at the moon base.

Unlike Violet, though, Daphne is fully aware of all the base's faults; she simply doesn't care. "It's cozy here, don't you think? Much nicer than a big, empty moon base."

"Yeah!" Violet said. "I like it here too!"

No one else seconded the thought.

I wondered if Kira was off trying to hack the computer somewhere. This was probably the best chance she'd have. With everyone in the mess, she had the rest of MBA to herself.

Across the room I caught sight of Zan, sitting at a table with some of the other temps who'd come in that day: two solar-panel contractors and a woman who I hadn't been introduced to yet. While the others chatted, Zan caught my eye and gave me a quick wink, letting me know we were still in this together.

Dad turned to Dr. Howard. "You ought to track Kira down. There won't be another meal like this for a while. She really shouldn't miss it." He pointed toward the kitchen, where Nina, Chang, and Mr. Grisan were busily preparing dinner: actual, honest-to-goodness hamburgers.

They couldn't grill the burgers at MBA, of course. We can't have any open flames, as they'd suck up all our precious oxygen. And if the base catches fire, there isn't anywhere else for us to go. So the burgers were all cooked back in Houston (where they really know their grilling) and then vacuum-sealed in plastic sheets. These look weird, like huge meaty button candies, but the plastic preserves the flavor amazingly well. Now our chefs were microwaving the burgers as quickly as they could—and serving them up with sides of relatively fresh carrots, pickles, and coleslaw. The Sjobergs had selfishly demanded to be served first, even before the kids. They'd just received their dinner, and the smell of cooked meat was intoxicating. My mouth was watering so much I was worried I'd drool on the table.

Virtually everyone else in the mess was equally mesmerized, eagerly waiting the moment when they'd get their food. Dr. Howard, however, had already checked out mentally again. "Hmm?" he asked once more. "Kira? Oh, I think she's a vegetarian."

"You're not sure?" Mom asked, surprised.

Dr. Howard shook his head, smiling vacantly. "Who can keep track of what a twelve-year-old girl likes and doesn't like?"

There was a soft ping and then my smartwatch displayed a text. It was from Eliza Bock: How's your new girlfriend?

"Dash, no messaging at dinner," Mom said.

"I know." I didn't feel like responding to Eliza anyhow. I pretended to turn my watch off, while actually setting it to silent mode.

I glanced toward the Sjobergs, my stomach grumbling. The entire family was making a disgusting show of enjoying their food, groaning with delight at each bite and smacking their lips. "This is absolutely exquisite!" Sonja announced. Her lips, which had been overinflated by a plastic surgeon back on earth, were now painted red with barbecue sauce, making her look like a tropical fish. Lars Sjoberg and his children only grunted in response, not even lifting their heads from their plates.

A microwave dinged. Everyone else in the mess turned toward it expectantly, like dogs who'd seen a squirrel. Now that the Sjobergs had claimed their burgers, the base children got priority on the next round. Mr. Grisan set the burgers and slaw out on plates, and then Nina and Chang delivered the goods. Nina brought two plates to our table, acting nice and friendly, as though she hadn't spent the entire day chastising me. "Here you go!" she announced to Violet and me. "Enjoy!"

She took a step away, then looked back and asked, "By the way, Dash, have you done your video log yet?"

I'd forgotten all about it, but I stayed calm and lied convincingly. "I'm still working on it. I'm taking my time to give you exactly what you asked for."

Nina's eyes narrowed briefly, like she knew I was lying and wanted to bust me, but then she smiled and said, "Thanks. I'm looking forward to seeing it."

As annoyed as I was with Nina, I still could have hugged her for bringing me that burger. I'd never seen anything as delicious in my life. My salivary glands immediately went into overdrive.

Mom, still angry at Nina herself, glared after the base commander as she headed back to get more burgers. "Look at her. Acting like she's Mary Poppins after the way she treated Dash today. I ought to report her to NASA for overstepping her bounds—"

"Now, now," Dad cautioned, "This has been a rough day for all of us. And I'm sure Nina is under far more stress than everyone else put together."

"She didn't have to take it out on our son," Mom groused.

Before eating my burger, I looked to everyone else at the table. So did Violet. Unlike the Sjobergs, even she had manners. "Can I start eating?" she asked.

"Sure," Dad said. "Both of you, dig in."

"Oh boy!" Violet cried. She snatched her burger off the plate and took a huge bite.

"Anyone want a bite of mine?" I offered.

"Well, aren't you the gentleman," Daphne said. "Go on ahead now. I've been waiting weeks for this. Another few minutes won't kill me." She then winced, embarrassed. "Ooh. Bad choice of words, right? Given the events of today. I didn't mean to be so callous. . . ."

"We know you didn't," Mom said.

I launched into my standard procedure for eating fresh

food, trying to make it last as long as possible. I sliced off a thin sliver of burger and rolled it around in my mouth. It was incredible. The flavor was so overwhelming it almost made me woozy.

Across the room, Chang Hi-Tech placed burgers in front of the Marquez kids. Roddy pounced on his before it even hit the table and crammed half of it into his mouth in a single bite.

"Did Chang ever work with Dr. Holtz before they both came here?" I asked.

"Yes," Dad said. "They collaborated on a project at NASA a few years back."

I slipped another sliver of hamburger into my mouth. "Did they like each other?"

Mom looked at me curiously. "Why do you ask?"

I shrugged, trying to appear as though the thought had only popped into my head that moment. "I don't know. Chang hasn't seemed that upset about Dr. Holtz."

"That doesn't mean he *isn't* upset," Mom informed me. "You know how macho Chang is. He's probably afraid of letting his guard down. But I can assure you, he liked Ronald as much as anyone here."

"Er . . . not quite," Dad said.

Mom and Daphne turned to him, surprised. Dr. Howard didn't; he was staring at something on the ceiling.

"What do you mean?" Daphne asked.

Dad lowered his voice so no one at the surrounding tables could overhear us. "Chang claims Dr. Holtz stole an idea of his."

"When?" Mom asked.

"About five years ago," Dad replied. "Chang had some idea about how to improve human oxygen consumption in space. Don't ask me to explain it. I can't. It's way too complicated. Anyhow, since Chang isn't a biologist, he approached Dr. Holtz with the idea—and the next thing he knew, Dr. Holtz was presenting the idea as his own."

Daphne gasped. "I can't believe Dr. Holtz would ever do something like that!"

Dad shrugged. "I'm only telling you what Chang said. I can't imagine Dr. Holtz stealing someone's idea either, but I have just as much trouble imagining Chang making up the story."

"It must have been a misunderstanding," Mom said.

"That's my guess too," Dad agreed. "Whatever the case, though, I'm sure it's all water under the bridge. I don't think NASA would have brought both Dr. Holtz and Chang up here if there was still bad blood between them."

I wondered if that was true. Maybe Chang had simply pretended to have forgiven Dr. Holtz, not wanting it to prevent him from going to the moon. But was a stolen idea really worth killing a man over? That seemed ridiculous, but then people were doubtlessly killed for ridiculous reasons all the time.

"I'm sure it's all forgotten," Daphne suggested cheerfully. "How could anyone stay angry at Dr. Holtz? He was such a sweetheart!"

"Maybe, but he still had his share of people who didn't like him," Dad said.

Daphne looked like a child who'd just been told there was no Easter Bunny. "No!"

"I'm not saying he deserved any of it," Dad went on. "But no matter how good a person you are, when you work in academics or at a big, political place like NASA, there are going to be people who don't like you. Even Dr. Holtz had enemies."

"Like who?" I asked, trying to sound as casual as possible.

Before Dad could answer, there was a commotion across the room. Roddy Marquez was choking. In his attempt to devour his burger as quickly as possible, he had apparently forgotten to chew. Now he was red-faced and wheezing, desperately signaling that something was jammed in his gullet.

"Ooh!" Violet cried happily. "Charades!"

"He's choking!" Mom corrected, and then she and Dad rushed to Roddy's aid.

Half the room was doing the same thing. Every single person at MBA had to take courses in basic first aid. (Even Violet, though she mostly just played house with the CPR dummy.) There is probably no better place to nearly choke to death.

Chang got there first. He snaked his tattooed arms around Roddy's waist from behind and gave him a quick, sharp jab in the solar plexus.

A hunk of meat the size of an egg rocketed out of Roddy's mouth, sailed halfway across the room, and nailed Lars Sjoberg in the face.

Lars had been too busy gobbling his own meal to pay attention to anything else, even the near death of another person, so he didn't even see the partly chewed burger coming until it hit his forehead with a wet splat. Startled, Lars shrieked and toppled backward off his inflatable chair, upending the dinner table en route. All the Sjoberg family's food—including the entire tub of coleslaw Patton had demanded—pitched into the air and then landed on Lars.

If this had happened to anyone else at MBA, the rest of us might have reacted with concern. But since Lars Sjoberg had spent the last few weeks coming up with new ways to prove he was the biggest jerk in the universe, we all burst into laughter instead. Even Nina, who I'd never seen laugh before.

Lars scrambled to his feet, flushed in embarrassment, coated in coleslaw, Roddy's hacked-up hamburger still clinging to his face like a meat barnacle. "This is not funny!" he screamed at us, which just made the whole thing even funnier. Everyone laughed harder, and Lars seethed so angrily I thought the meat on his head might start frying. "That does it!" he roared, then wheeled on Nina. "I've had it with this horrible place! I want my money back!"

Nina stifled her laughter in surprise. "Er . . . I have no authorization to do that. As far as I'm aware, Mr. Sjoberg, your contract said there would be no refunds."

"The contract also said this would be the adventure of a lifetime!" Lars pried the hunk of masticated meat off his head and threw it against the wall, where it stuck fast. "Instead it's been torture! Our accommodations are hideous, the food is repulsive, and you have all been terrible hosts! I've had enough. When the rocket returns to earth in two days, I demand that my family and I be on it!"

Back at the Marquez table Roddy had quickly recovered from his near-death experience—and was currently throwing a fit, as he'd hocked up a good portion of his hamburger and now wanted a new one. His mother was trying to calm him. "There's only one hamburger per person," she told him.

"That's not fair!" Roddy wailed. "I only got to eat half of mine!"

"Next time try chewing your food," Cesar told him. "Like this." He took a bite of his own hamburger and made a show of enjoying it to his brother.

Roddy screamed with frustration and dove across the table, grabbing for Cesar's burger. Cesar casually slammed Roddy's face into the table and pinned him there, then continued to eat while his brother squirmed helplessly.

"Lots of entertainment here tonight," Dad said to us.

Across the room Nina was facing down Lars Sjoberg. "You know I can't send you back," she said. "All available seats on that rocket are filled. You're not scheduled to leave for another three months."

"Then bump some people!" Lars demanded.

"Yes, Nina!" Chang cried. "Please, bump someone. The sooner we get rid of the Sjobergs the better."

Everyone in the room chimed agreement—except for the temps scheduled to go back on the rocket, who looked horrified by the idea that they might end up stuck at the station for another three months.

This embarrassed and enraged Lars Sjoberg even more. "You can't keep me here against my will!" he told Nina. "I am one of the most influential men on earth!"

"I hate to break it to you," Chang taunted, "but you're not on earth anymore."

At the Marquez table, Roddy squirmed loose from Cesar's

grasp and—aware he wasn't going to get any of his brother's burger—ran for his pre-chewed chunk of meat, which was still stuck to the wall.

"Roddy, no!" his mother cried, grabbing him by the collar. "Don't you dare eat that!"

Meanwhile Lars was staring Nina down. "I want to be on the next rocket home," he told her. "Make it happen—or I can make your life very, very difficult from now on. Not just here, but back on earth as well. I have many friends in high places." With that he spun on his heel and stormed out of the mess, his family right behind him.

There was a moment of stunned silence, and then everyone who didn't have a hamburger yet began clamoring for one. Maybe they all felt that Lars's threat had been an empty one. Or maybe their desire for fresh meat trumped any concerns about Nina. But with the Sjobergs gone, the atmosphere in the mess became even more festive than before. Only Nina seemed concerned.

And me. I was concerned too. If Lars Sjoberg had murdered Dr. Holtz, he'd just found an excuse to get himself off the moon quickly. Or at least he was trying. I could understand why. If Lars Sjoberg was guilty, as long as he stayed on the moon he was trapped. But if he could get back to earth, he was so rich and powerful that his lawyers could probably fight off any attempt to bring him to justice.

Across the room Roddy wriggled free of his mother's grasp and snatched the chewed burger off the wall. He was about to cram it into his mouth again when his mother tackled him. The two of them rolled around on the floor, grappling for the ball of half-eaten meat. "For goodness sake, Rodrigo, have some dignity!" Dr. Brahmaputra-Marquez yelled.

"No!" Roddy cried. "I'm too hungry!"

My smartwatch vibrated. I was so on edge that I jumped, startled by the sensation. I checked it and found a text from Kira.

Found what you were looking for. Come see. My room. Now.

Excerpt from *The Official Residents' Guide to Moon Base Alpha*,
© 2040 by National Aeronautics and Space Administration:

AIR LOCKS

There are two exit points at MBA: the main air lock and the emergency backup air lock. The main air lock is the primary access to and from the lunar surface, whereas the emergency backup air lock should never, ever be used unless 1) immediate evacuation from MBA is necessary and 2) the main air lock is blocked and/or nonfunctional.*

Use of the main air lock is limited to those lunarnauts with official, sanctioned duties upon the lunar surface (i.e., maintenance, research, or transit to and from the launchpad). If you do not have sanctioned duties on the lunar surface, please stay away from the main air lock. The main air lock is not a toy! Tampering with it could jeopardize your life—as well as the lives of your family and friends at MBA.

---

* Rest assured, however, that such an occurrence is extremely unlikely. The Hamilton XP-50 air lock at MBA has been subjected to years of stress testing at NASA and during that time has had a 99.9995 percent success rate!

LAST WORDS

Lunar day 188
After dinner

Kira opened the door to her residence the moment after I knocked on it, then yanked me inside and locked it behind us.

"What took you so long?" she asked suspiciously.

"I came as soon as I got your message," I said.

"I texted you five minutes ago."

"I had to excuse myself from dinner. And . . . there was pie."

Kira arched an eyebrow. "Pie?"

"I haven't had pie in months," I told her. "And this was apple. My favorite." I produced a plate with a slice from behind my back. "I brought you some as well. I figured you'd be hungry, seeing as you skipped dinner."

"I was working on our project." Kira accepted the pie from me and eagerly took a bite. Then she made a face.

"What's wrong?" I asked.

"This pie isn't very good," she said.

"It's not?" I was genuinely surprised. To me the pie had tasted incredible. "Wow. My taste buds must have really deteriorated up here. If you don't want the pie, I'll eat it—"

"No," Kira said quickly. "You were right. I'm starving. I got all wrapped up in this and totally lost track of time." She pointed toward her SlimScreen table with her fork.

I quickly sat down there. "So you found the footage of Dr. Holtz?"

"I did." Kira pulled up an InflatiCube beside me, her eyes wide with excitement.

"That's amazing. You must be some kind of computer genius."

"Not exactly. I kind of cheated."

"What do you mean?"

"Well, you told me Roddy had already figured out how to hack the system . . . so I tracked him down this afternoon and asked him how to do it."

"And he told you? You just met him."

"I just met *you*," Kira countered. "And you trusted me to do this investigation with you."

"That's different," I said defensively, knowing it really wasn't. "You overheard me talking about this. I had no choice but to let you help."

"Whatever." Kira shrugged. "Point is, Roddy told me how to do it. I didn't tell him the real reason *why* I wanted to, of course. I just said I didn't like NASA having control of everything I did online here."

"And he bought that?"

"Yeah. Although, to be honest, I think he might have a bit of a crush on me. He was a little *too* excited to help me hack the system. And then he kept asking if I wanted to eat dinner with him and his family tonight. Or to see his room."

I considered things from Roddy's point of view. There he was, on the moon, cut off from any girls his age for months, and the first one who showed up was cute and seemed to like computers as much as he did. "He's got a crush on you all right."

"Ick. So now, by helping you with this, I could end up in trouble with Nina *and* I've got the virtual-reality fiend crushing on me?"

"Hey, you *asked* to help me. And besides, you said you'd done plenty of worse things."

Kira cast a wary glance at me. "Yeah. I have."

I really wanted to see what Kira had found on the computer, but I couldn't help asking, "Like what?"

Kira sized me up for a moment, then said, "I like going places I'm not supposed to go."

"You mean, like trespassing?"

"Yeah. But not like in a bad way, really." Kira now looked embarrassed that I'd brought this up. "It's just that, a lot of the time, there are rules telling you you can't go someplace for no good reason. And so I just kind of ignore them."

"So where have you gone?"

"All sorts of cool places. The storage area where they keep all the paintings at the Philadelphia Museum of Art. The places where they keep the animals at the zoo. The tunnels underneath the Eagles' football stadium."

"Really?" I asked. "How do you get in there?"

"I just walk in."

"And your dad doesn't freak out?"

"Have you met my dad? He's usually not paying much attention to me. I've wandered off for an hour without him noticing."

"So he's *never* realized?"

"No, he has. And he wasn't happy, of course. But I'm not a criminal. I don't steal anything or vandalize stuff. I'm just curious. Especially about places that people think should be off-limits. Which might be why I was so interested to come up here. How much more off-limits can you get than the moon, right?"

"Did you ever get caught?"

"Not really. Most people didn't even seem to notice me. But if security did come, I'd just pretend to be a lost little kid and cry a bit and they'd take pity on me. Half the time they'd even give me candy. Dad told me to knock it off when NASA started vetting us, though. He didn't want them to ding us because I was a troublemaker."

I started to ask something else, but before I could, Kira said, "Do you want to see what I found about Dr. Holtz or not?"

"Of course I do."

"Okay then. Computer, bring up the footage."

"Yes, ma'am." The computer spoke in the standard factory-setting female voice; Kira and her father obviously hadn't bothered to customize it yet. A frozen image of security footage appeared on the SlimScreen. It was the staging area for the main air lock, viewed from a high angle.

Kira explained, "Even though getting into the system was easy after Roddy told me how, it still took a while to track all this down. And then, after I figured out how to access the camera feeds, I still had to figure out which ones to look at. Do you have any idea how many cameras there are at this place?"

"A few hundred?" I ventured.

"Two thousand and twenty six," Kira corrected.

I sat back in surprise. "Really?"

Kira nodded. "They're *everywhere*. There are at least a dozen in every room—except for our residences. Even the exterior is covered with them. They're on the roof, in the walls, out by the solar arrays . . ."

"They're supposed to be for safety," I said. "In case a meteor takes out a solar panel or something. We can see what happened without having to go outside."

"I get that," Kira told me. "But how do you explain having sixteen cameras in the bathrooms? Does NASA think there are going to be a lot of meteor strikes in there?"

"I know," I said. "It's creepy."

"Anyway," Kira went on, "there were a ton of camera feeds to sort through. And each one of them has months of footage logged. But I finally tracked down what you need." She pointed at the frozen frame on the SlimScreen. "This is the widest angle I could find of the staging area. So if Dr. Holtz was with anyone, you ought to be able to see them, right?"

"Right," I agreed. Indeed this particular footage had been shot with a wide-angle fish-eye lens, so that frame showed not just the staging area and the main air lock, but significant portions of the hallways on either side.

"Okay, then," Kira said. "Watch what happens. Computer, run it!"

"Yes, ma'am." The camera feed began running. There was a time stamp at the bottom indicating it was 5:23 in the morning.

After a few seconds Dr. Holtz entered the staging area, coming from the direction of the mess and the science pod. He plodded along slowly, his face drawn and sad.

"Whoa," I said.

"What?" Kira asked.

"That hardly seems like Dr. Holtz," I told her. "Usually he was incredibly happy. He loved being here. You could even see it in how he walked. He always had this kind of bounce to his step. But look at him here." I pointed to the screen.

"He looks miserable," Kira said. "Like he *knows* he's about to die."

"Yes," I agreed, struck by the thought. "But when I overheard him in the bathroom three hours before this, he was even happier than usual. Delirious, really."

"Wait." Kira paused the footage. "What's this about the bathroom?"

I recounted what I'd overheard as quickly as I could, desperately wanting to see the rest of the security footage but aware that Kira ought to be up to speed on everything I knew. When I got to the part about Dr. Holtz's discovery, her jaw dropped.

"Whoa," she said. "Do you have *any* idea what he'd found?"

"No," I told her. "But that's what's so strange. How do you go from being on top of the world like he was at two thirty in the morning, so excited to share his discovery with everyone, to looking as miserable as he does at five thirty?"

"I don't know," Kira admitted. "Computer, let it run."

The tape started up again. Dr. Holtz opened the locker where the space suits were stored, removed his suit, and slowly pulled it on. Kira's words about him knowing he was going to die echoed in my ears. Now Dr. Holtz looked like a man dressing for his own funeral.

"There's something I don't get," Kira said. "If he *knew* he was going to die, why bother suiting up at all? Why not just walk outside in his regular clothes?"

"I guess whoever was behind this wanted it to look like an accident," I suggested.

"Well, that brings us to another problem." Kira turned to me. "If there was someone else behind this, where were they when it was happening?"

"I don't know," I conceded. That had been nagging at me too. In the entire wide sweep shown by the camera angle, not a single other person was visible. Dr. Holtz was entirely on his own.

In the footage he was making a good show of taking the proper precautions for going outside. He sealed his suit. He locked the helmet on. He checked the various gauges and readouts. As far as I could tell, his suit looked like it was on correctly.

Then Dr. Holtz started toward the air lock.

I sighed.

"What's wrong?" Kira asked.

"I thought this was going to be easier," I said. "That there'd be a bad guy forcing him out the air lock with a gun or something. But there's not. This looks exactly like what Nina says it is: an accident, not a murder."

"But what about Dr. Holtz's behavior? You said that was strange."

I shrugged. "That's still not proof anyone forced him to do this. If anything, it might look like *more* evidence that this was an accident. Like maybe he was distracted and not thinking clearly. Or like he was depressed and this was a suicide."

"You're right," Kira agreed. "But there's one more thing you need to see."

"What?" I asked.

"Watch Dr. Holtz closely once he gets into the air lock."

I returned my full attention to the screen. Dr. Holtz was at the air lock now. He typed the access code on a keypad and the inner door slid open. Dr. Holtz stepped into the pressurization chamber and the door slid back, locking him in.

Dr. Holtz then slid his right hand beneath the open palm of his left hand.

"There!" Kira cried, stopping the footage.

"What?" I asked. "All he's doing is moving his hands around."

"Yeah, but why? That's a weird gesture to make, isn't it? Especially if you only have a few seconds left to live."

I thought about it. At first glance the gesture was so small it hadn't even seemed deliberate. But now that Kira mentioned it . . . "It does seem a little strange."

"Yeah," Kira said. "If *I* only had a few seconds left to live, I'd be trying to say something. Especially if I knew there were cameras all around."

"Is there a better angle of what he's doing?" I asked.

"Of course. There are four cameras in the air lock alone. I just started with this angle so you could see there wasn't anyone around. Computer, bring up angle two and run it."

"Yes, ma'am." A new piece of security footage popped up. This one was taken from inside the air lock.

"Okay," Kira said. "We're starting this from right after he enters the air lock. *Before* he moves his hands."

This camera was much closer to Dr. Holtz, set in the wall between the air lock doors. As Dr. Holtz stepped into the air lock, he took up the entire frame. Unfortunately, we couldn't see his face. The moon's atmosphere isn't strong enough to reflect the sun's radiation, so all space helmets have protective shielding built in, which turns them all into big mirrors. (Check out any photos of astronauts on the moon if you want to see what I mean.) Instead of Dr. Holtz, we saw the reflection of the interior of the air lock.

The inner air lock door slid shut behind Dr. Holtz. Then, for only a fraction of a second, he turned toward the camera.

"There!" Kira said. "Did you see that? He knows the camera's there, but he's trying not to look at it."

"Why not?" I asked.

"Maybe because he knew someone was watching him on it," Kira suggested. "Check out his hands . . ."

Once again I watched Dr. Holtz move his hands, this time from the much-closer camera inside the air lock. He'd returned his gaze to the lunar surface, as though he wasn't even aware of what his own hands were doing. In fact the hand gestures he was making were so subtle, I might not have even noticed he was making them had Kira not pointed it out.

From this angle we could see that he was pointing with his right hand as he slid it under the open palm of his left.

Then he balled his right fist and raised it to his chest.

Kira paused the footage again. "What is that? It's not just fidgeting, right? His movements are too deliberate."

"Yeah, they are." I shut my eyes, trying to think. There was something about Dr. Holtz's motions that was familiar to me, only I couldn't recall why. An idea was nagging at me, though, like I'd seen them before, but a long time ago.

"At first I thought they might be some hand exercises," Kira said. "You know, to get his space gloves all flexed out for the moonwalk. But then I thought, 'If he knows he's going to die, what's the point of flexing his gloves?'"

"Hold on," I told her. "I need a minute to figure this out."

"You know what he's doing?" Kira asked, excitedly.

"Maybe." I kept my eyes closed, digging through the recesses of my mind. I knew Kira had a point about the gloves. They were important somehow. Space gloves had always been trouble for astronauts. The issue was, space suits had to be inflated to the right atmospheric pressure or you'd die—but when you inflated them, the gloves filled up with air as well and got stiff, which made them hard to use. It was like having your hands inside balloons. In the early days of moonwalks, even something as simple as making a fist had been incredibly difficult. Over the years NASA had spent billions to improve the gloves—as well as the rest of the suits. Through a combination of space-age fabrics, new pressure systems, and robotics embedded in their exterior, the gloves became far easier to use—but they still aren't perfect. Making any motion with your fingers is work, which meant that, no matter how casual Dr. Holtz was trying to appear, the signs he was making with his hands weren't random.

Signs.

A sudden memory came to me. I was six years old, visiting my great-grandfather in Palm Springs, California. I didn't know it at the time, but it was the last time I was going to see him. My parents knew he was sick, though, and so did he; Mom and Dad had brought me there to say good-bye to him. I remembered being upset that Great-Granddad couldn't play with me the way he normally did when I came to visit. Instead he was staying inside on the couch while I swam in his pool with my father. Dad had been teaching me to do a cannonball, and I wanted Great-Granddad to see, so I looked through the glass doors into the house.

My mother was talking to Great-Granddad, her back to me so that he could watch me through the windows. Only she wasn't talking at all. She was making gestures with her hands—and Great-Granddad was responding in kind.

My eyes snapped open. "It's sign language!" I exclaimed.

My sudden outburst caught Kira by surprise so badly she

tumbled off her InflatiCube. But she sprang right back to her feet. "What's sign language?"

"You know how people are sometimes born without the ability to hear?" I asked.

"Sure. Deafness. My cousin had that. But they gave her a cochlear implant and she could hear right away. It's no big deal."

"Right. But it wasn't always like that. Not so long ago, you couldn't just give an operation to a deaf person, or a blind person, or someone who was paralyzed, and make them like everyone else. Instead, if you were born deaf, or blind, or paraplegic, you stayed that way."

"I know," Kira said, a little indignantly. "I read history."

"Well, how do you think deaf people communicated back then?"

Kira looked at me blankly. It was probably the same look I'd given my parents when they'd asked me to guess how people had ever taken photographs before there were digital cameras. And then I saw the wheels start to turn in her mind. "They used their hands?"

"Exactly," I said. "It was called sign language. Almost no one uses it anymore, because pretty much everyone who's born deaf gets the cochlear operation right away, but Mom once told me that sign language used to be one of the most common languages in the world."

"So Dr. Holtz might have learned it when he was a kid!" Kira suggested.

"Right. Maybe he had a relative who was born deaf. Or who lost their hearing. That's what happened with my great-granddad. His ears went at the end and he was too sick to operate on to fix it, so he and my Mom had to learn signs to communicate."

Kira whooped happily. "You're a genius, Dash! I never would have thought of that in a million years!"

"I'm sure you would have soon enough."

"No. I've never even heard of sign language before. So what's Dr. Holtz saying?"

"I don't know," I admitted. "I never learned it myself. But the base computer is programmed to understand thousands of languages. Maybe this is one of them."

"Of course!" Kira exclaimed. "Computer, can you translate sign language?"

"Which Mayan language?" the computer replied. "I am programmed for Ch'olan, Tzeltalan and Q'anjob'alan."

"Not *Mayan* language!" I snapped. "*Sign* language. Can you translate *sign* language?"

"American Sign Language?" the computer asked.

"Uh . . . I guess." I hadn't known there were other kinds.

"Yes," the computer told me. "I have that capability."

"Great!" Kira said. "I'm going to play a piece of video.

Please analyze it and tell us what Dr. Holtz is saying."

"I will do my best," the computer replied.

Kira rewound the footage to the moment of Dr. Holtz stepping into the air lock, then played it. We watched as he made his hand signals again and let it continue beyond the point where we'd paused the footage before. As Dr. Holtz signed, I felt a terrible sense of fear begin to overwhelm me. Because every moment took us closer to the end of Dr. Holtz's life. I didn't want to watch it—and yet I had to, for Dr. Holtz's sake.

Obviously he'd hoped that someone would watch the footage. That was the whole point of signing. To get a final message across. And yet, at the same time, he was hoping that whoever had forced him out onto the lunar surface wouldn't notice what he was doing.

Save for the one quick glance at the camera, he faced out the window toward the moon. His hands seemed to move completely independently of the rest of him. On occasion he moved his arms, lifting his hands close to his helmet, though he did it with a subtlety that made it look more like stretching than signing.

After about twenty seconds the outer air lock door slid open. Although it wasn't visible, all the precious oxygen in the air lock would have dissipated instantly.

Dr. Holtz didn't cower from his fate. Instead he met it

boldly. He stepped out the door, onto the dusty surface of the moon. He had stopped signing by now. His message was finished. If anything, Dr. Holtz seemed to be relishing his final moments of life. After all, he was spending them on the moon. He bounded twice on the surface, then turned back toward the moon base, tilting his head back as far as he could.

"What do you think he's looking at?" Kira asked.

"Let's find out. Computer, zoom in on Dr. Holtz."

"Yes, sir." The image of Dr. Holtz enlarged, got grainier, and then resolved.

In the visor of Dr. Holtz's space helmet we could see the reflection of a blue-green ball above him.

"It's earth," Kira said. "What do you think he's looking there for?"

I shrugged. "Maybe he wanted to be looking at something beautiful when he died instead of this ugly moon base."

Kira nodded, accepting that. "It happens in only a few more seconds," she told me. "Do you want to see it?"

"No," I said honestly. "I don't." I liked the idea of my last image of Dr. Holtz being one in which he was still upright, staring at earth from the surface of the moon. "Computer, can you translate the signs he made?"

"Yes. Here is what Dr. Holtz signed: 'I am being murdered—'"

"Really?" I looked to Kira, my heart thumping. I was at once thrilled and horrified to have been right. Kira seemed to be struck the same way. "You're sure? He says he was being murdered?"

The computer explained, "Well, in actuality he was simply making the hand signal for 'murder.' In American Sign Language, the verb forms of 'to be' are not signed, but are instead extrapolated from the context. One could also argue that he was saying 'This is a murder,' but 'I am being murdered' seems more appropriate."

Even though I'd suspected there had been foul play, it was stunning to hear it confirmed. Somehow the computer's voice made it worse. The computer, being a computer, was completely emotionless, even when discussing such an awful event. It seemed horribly wrong to me.

"What else does he say?" I asked.

The computer replied, "The full transcript of his statement is: 'I am being murdered. Earth killed me. Find my phone. Tell my family I love them.'"

Kira and I kept our eyes locked on each other, trying to make sense of all that. She was the first to speak. "*Earth killed me?*"

"That's correct," the computer replied.

"How could the earth kill someone?" Kira asked, this time to me.

I could only shake my head in response. "I have no idea. Maybe that's why he wants us to find his phone—"

"You mean that ancient cell phone he had back on earth? He was still using that thing?"

"Yes. He said the smartwatch screens were too small."

"That must have been thirty years old." Kira shook her head. "Boy, what a caveman."

"Dr. Holtz wasn't anti tech," I said defensively. "He lived on the *moon*, for Pete's sake. He just liked using his old phone."

"So what are you thinking? That he left some evidence on it somehow?"

"Yes. Or maybe a longer explanation for why he did this."

"Where do you think it is? His residence?"

"I doubt it. If he was trying to hide his phone, that's the first place anyone would look."

"What makes you think he hid it?" Kira asked.

"If you had evidence proving someone killed you, would you leave it out where anyone could find it?"

"Good point."

"Still, it's probably worth checking his room anyhow," I admitted. "Just in case."

Kira jumped to her feet. "Let's do it now, while everyone else is still at dinner."

"Wait," I said. "I need a copy of those recordings."

"Sure," Kira agreed. "We need to show them to someone, right? I mean, we've got Dr. Holtz stating he's being murdered here."

"By planet earth," I said with a sigh. "Whatever that means."

Kira said, "It's still evidence, though. Who should we give it to? Nina? She won't be able to ignore this."

"She might try," I countered. "This is probably the last thing Nina wants to see."

"So? This is a murder! Someone has to investigate it!"

"Don't worry. Someone will." I touched my watch to the SlimScreen. The computer immediately downloaded the recordings of Dr. Holtz to it. "I know who to show these to."

"Who?" Kira asked.

"I can't tell you right now." I hurried out the door.

Kira did her best to follow me, though she was still having trouble walking in low gravity. "Oh, come on! I got them for you!"

"And I owe you big for this." I led the way down the catwalk. Dr. Holtz also lived on the upper residence level, at the opposite end from Nina. We had to pass the Sjobergs' suite on the way. I could hear Lars raging inside. It sounded like he was on the phone, shouting at someone on earth. "I don't care what it takes! Just get me off this godforsaken rock!"

As we reached Dr. Holtz's residence, my smartwatch pinged, delivering a text.

To my surprise, the text said it was from Kira. Which wasn't possible, as she was standing right in front of me, jostling the knob of Dr. Holtz's door.

Even more unsettling was the text itself.

Dash—Be careful—or you'll end up like Dr. Holtz.

Kira turned back to me, frustrated. "The room's locked. Any idea how to get in?"

"Uh . . . no." My mind was racing after the threatening text. Whoever had sent it must have hacked Kira's account to hide their identity. But the message was still clear: They knew I was investigating and wanted me to stop. But was it from the killer themselves, or someone who didn't want me snooping? And if it was from the killer, was this just a scare tactic—or would they really come for me, too?

"Dash?" Kira asked. "What's wrong?"

I met her gaze and saw the concern in her eyes. I wondered if I looked as scared as I felt. My heart was pounding, and I could feel sweat blossoming on my brow. And now, here I was, with Kira, poking around Dr. Holtz's door right out in the open, meaning whoever had sent the text would know she was helping me out.

"Nothing," I said.

"Oh, please," Kira sighed. "You look like you just got punched in the stomach. What's going on?"

I couldn't bring myself to tell her the truth. Not right then. I didn't want to frighten her. "You ought to get back to your room," I told her. "I have to go find someone."

"Who?"

"Someone who can help us," I said, and then ran off in search of Zan Perfonic.

Excerpt from *The Official Residents' Guide to Moon Base Alpha*, © 2040 by National Aeronautics and Space Administration:

ROBOTICS

As robots are an increasingly important part of life on earth, it should come as no surprise that they are integral to life at MBA as well. Since the lunar surface is so inhospitable to humans, robots will be used to handle as many tasks outside the base as possible, including maintenance, repairs, and research. If a robot can handle the job, please do not send a human outside to do it.

Use of all robotics must be coordinated via the base roboticist. Please do not attempt to work the robots without permission. Even though they are designed to be indestructible, they can still break. Should this happen, they are extremely expensive and very difficult to replace. However, when used properly—with supervision—the robots can make your life at MBA safer, easier, and much more enjoyable.

11

SPACE MADNESS

Lunar day 188
Bedtime

Unfortunately, Zan was nowhere to be found. I circled the entire base three times, but she wasn't in any of the common areas. Lots of people remained in the mess, still savoring their last morsels of fresh pie—a few were even licking their plates clean—although a lot of the temps had retired to their quarters. (Arrival day can be exhausting.) My parents and Violet had left as well.

There were a few folks in the gym, and Roddy had taken his usual place in the rec room, jacked into the ComLink. He's there so often he might as well be a piece of furniture.

The science pod was empty, as were the control rooms,

save for Daphne, who was overseeing the robot arm. The Raptor rocket had brought plenty of heavy cargo that humans couldn't carry: new solar arrays, a lunar rover, and construction materials for Moon Base Beta. All of that had to be moved with the arm, which is half robot, half crane. It's enormous, with a span of one hundred feet, and it looks surprisingly like a real human arm and hand, minus the flesh and with steel instead of bone. There are only two differences: The "hand" has two thumbs in addition to its four fingers, which gives it better grip, while the "arm" has three joints, which gives it greater flexibility. The arm is anchored next to the rover garage outside, where it can reach from MBA to the launchpad and Solar Array 2.

Like most robots, the arm can do its job well without much human input. All it needs is the occasional order from Daphne about what to do next. Therefore, Daphne wasn't working that hard. She was reading an e-book, only glancing at the camera monitors every now and then to make sure everything was going well.

However, when I looped past her on my third sweep of the base, she had stopped reading. Instead she was furiously typing at one of the computers. Lines of code filled the screen. I edged forward, wondering what she was doing.

Daphne suddenly seemed to sense I was there. She spun around quickly, covering the computer screen with her body.

"Hey, Dash!" she called, trying to sound casual, although her voice sounded higher than usual. "Are you doing laps—or looking for someone?"

I almost asked if she'd seen Zan, but then caught myself, remembering that Zan had warned me not to let anyone know we were working together. Daphne was the least threatening adult at the station—I couldn't imagine her squashing a bug, let alone bumping off Dr. Holtz—but Zan still wouldn't want me tipping her off about us. "I'm looking for my folks," I lied.

"I think they took your sister back to your room." Daphne laughed. "That Violet's such a pistol. I love her. She conned three people into giving her an extra slice of pie, then got hopped up on sugar and ran around like a hurricane until she collapsed from exhaustion."

"Sounds like Violet all right." I gave Daphne a wave of thanks and headed home. I figured Zan must have turned in for the night herself, and all the temps shared sleeping quarters. Despite how anxious I was to talk to her, it looked like I'd have to wait for her to come find me.

Daphne didn't resume typing on the computer. At least not while I was in range. Instead she made a show of monitoring the robot arm as I walked away.

Sure enough, my family was back in our room. Violet was almost comatose after her sugar rush, murmuring nonsense while Dad tried to pour her into her Hello Kitty pajamas. Mom was seated at the table, typing on the SlimScreen.

"Hey!" Mom said, nice and chipper. "Did you find Kira?"

"Yes."

"Mmmm," Violet sighed sleepily. "I love pie."

"What was the big emergency?" Dad asked me.

"She was just trying to get everything set up in her room and couldn't figure out the computer." I didn't like lying to my parents, but I knew they wouldn't be pleased with the truth.

"That couldn't have waited until the end of dinner?" Mom inquired.

"What are you writing?" I asked, trying to change the subject.

It worked. "A eulogy for Dr. Holtz," Mom said. "Nina wants to have a ceremony for him tomorrow, and she asked me to speak."

"Only you?" I wanted to know.

"No," Mom said. "A few others will talk too. Nina. Dr. Janke. Maybe Kira's father."

"I want a pony," Violet said dreamily.

Dad slid her into her sleep pod and gave her a kiss on the forehead. A second later she was snoring.

"What's happening to Dr. Holtz's body?" I asked.

"NASA gave permission to bury it on the moon," Mom

said. "And so did Dr. Holtz's daughter. She said it would be the perfect place for her father to end up. Plus Katya and the others didn't like the idea of bringing a corpse back with them on the rocket."

"Who's digging the grave?" I asked.

"No one," Mom explained. "Daphne's sending some robots out to do it tomorrow. It's too dangerous to use humans for this. The crust is so thick they'll have to blast through it."

I sat next to my mother at the table. "Will the body decay here?"

"Ew," Mom said. "What kind of question is that?"

"A legitimate one," Dad told her. "No, the body won't really decay, without an atmosphere or any life forms to break it down. Instead it'll sort of mummify."

I nodded, then turned back to my mother. "What are you going to say?"

"The usual, I guess. What a great person Dr. Holtz was. How he was so committed to human spaceflight. How this place was the realization of his life's work. Blah blah blah." Mom frowned and put her face in her hands. "It's so darn difficult, summing up a man's entire life in one speech."

Dad said, "If anyone can do it, it's you." He came behind Mom and kneaded her shoulders. Mom sighed with relief and closed her eyes.

"Mom," I said, "you were going to tell me something about Dr. Holtz at breakfast. But you never got to because Dr. Marquez interrupted us. Something important I should know about Dr. Holtz."

Mom reluctantly opened her eyes. She looked a little confused, like she was trying to remember the conversation.

I tried to jolt her memory. "I was saying this hadn't been an accident. And you said there was something else I ought to know."

"Oh, right." Mom leaned in close to me. "This is not to be repeated, though. I don't want it leaving this room."

"Sure. What is it?"

Mom said, "I think Dr. Holtz's mind might have been slipping."

I glanced at Dad. He didn't seem surprised by this, so I guess he and Mom had discussed it before. "How so?"

"Well, he didn't seem as sharp as usual over the last few weeks," Mom told me. "He was distracted a lot. Kind of spaced out. And then he'd be manic. Incredibly happy. Unnaturally so."

I thought back to Dr. Holtz in the bathroom the night before he died. "Maybe he was just excited about this big discovery he'd made."

Mom sighed. "Perhaps, but . . . I wonder if Dr. Holtz had even made a discovery at all."

"You mean, he only thought he had?" I asked.

"It's possible," Mom replied, "if he was really suffering from some sort of mental breakdown. There's a lot of precedent with this. A scientist believes they're on the verge of something huge: figuring out some famous unsolved math problem, or developing a new physical theory. They fill up notebooks with ideas and formulas and it all looks very convincing. But when other scientists come in and look everything over . . . they find it's all just nonsense."

I frowned. "But those scientists are dealing with serious mental disorders, right? Like schizophrenia. Dr. Holtz never seemed that bad to me. . . ."

"He was talking to himself too," Mom said.

"Lots of people do that," I countered.

"Not like this," Mom said gravely. "I came across him doing it one night. It wasn't talking like you mean. It was like he was having a conversation with an imaginary person. Someone he actually thought was there. He wasn't just talking. He was *listening* too."

I straightened up, concerned. "So . . . you think he was really going crazy? Like certifiably nuts?"

"I don't know," Mom sighed. "This isn't my specialty. But I brought it up to Nina and she said I wasn't the only one who'd noticed."

"Who else had seen him?" I asked.

"Nina wouldn't say. But she'd asked Dr. Marquez to start keeping a close eye on Dr. Holtz."

"A lot of things can go wrong with the human mind," Dad told me. "Dr. Holtz was getting on in years. This might have been the start of Alzheimer's or some other age-related dementia. Or perhaps it was something triggered by spending so much time here at an advanced age. Maybe due to the lower concentration of oxygen in the air or something like that."

"You mean he might really have had some sort of space madness?" I said. "Roddy suggested that today. I can't believe Roddy actually might have been right about something."

Dad looked surprised as well. "Neither can I," he said. "Although Roddy is the son of our base psychiatrist. I suppose he could learn something now and then."

I looked down at my hands. "So . . . you think this all has something to do with why Dr. Holtz walked out the air lock alone?"

"It might," Mom said. "If he was really losing his mind, it explains why he might have done something so uncharacteristically careless like that."

I thought back to the footage I'd seen of Dr. Holtz in the air lock. If he was really going crazy, could he have simply *imagined* someone was forcing him to go out on the lunar surface to die? It made sense—and yet Dr. Holtz had seemed to me like he was in complete control of his mind. His sign language had been so deliberate. He'd had such focus. But then I was only a kid. I didn't know squat about mental illness.

I considered telling my parents about the footage I'd seen of Dr. Holtz in the air lock—and the cryptic message he'd left. I was tired of keeping it all a secret. But I'd promised Zan not to tell anyone about our investigation. At the very least, it seemed, I should update her first on what I'd learned, before telling anyone else. Certainly I'd be able to find her the next day—if she didn't come find me herself.

"So that's why Nina didn't want me making a stink about Dr. Holtz's death?" I asked. "She thinks he was losing it too?"

"I don't know the specific reasons why Nina told you to keep quiet," Mom answered. "But I'd say that makes sense. I'm sure NASA doesn't want the public—or the press—to have any idea that Dr. Holtz might have been slipping."

"Why not?"

"Because it could make people question the entire manned space program," Dad explained. "What if Dr. Holtz's illness was caused—or hastened—by his living here?

What does that say for the future of human habitation on the moon? Or any long-term space travel?"

"So NASA isn't going to look into any of that?" I asked, concerned. "It seems kind of important, seeing as *we're* living on the moon."

Mom gave Dad a pointed stare, not pleased with him for bringing this issue up. Then she spoke in her most comforting voice. "Your father was only posing a question for the sake of argument. If Dr. Holtz had mental problems, they weren't caused by living up here. These types of health issues are usually genetic—or related to aging. And Dr. Holtz was a lot older than everyone else here."

"Even older than Mr. Grisan?" Violet asked from her sleep pod.

We all turned to her, surprised she was awake again. She seemed to be still partly asleep, cocooned in her blankets, her eyelids drooping.

"How long have you been listening?" Dad asked.

"I don't know." Violet yawned. "Mr. Grisan seems *way* older than Dr. Holtz. Like a hundred years older."

Mom knelt by Violet's pod and stroked her hair to soothe her back to sleep. "He's not."

"He's still not that young," I said thoughtfully. "Is anyone worried about *his* mental health? He acts a lot stranger than Dr. Holtz ever did. He barely ever talks to anyone."

"Mr. Grisan's just quiet," Mom told me. "And perhaps a bit self-conscious. He's the only blue-collar worker in a base filled with scientists. That can't be easy."

"I want to be a ballerina," Violet sighed, and then her eyes slid shut. Mom tickled her nose and got no response.

"She's asleep again," Mom said, keeping her voice lower now.

I asked, "If Dr. Holtz might have gone through the air lock because he was crazy, is NASA going to investigate that?"

"Oh, there's definitely going to be a major inquiry into this," Dad replied. "There's been a death, after all."

"So is NASA going to send investigators up here?"

"No," Dad said. "We're in a very unusual position. If this were a military base on earth, the government would probably send a whole team of people in to find out exactly what happened. But that's just not feasible here. There's no seat available for even one investigator on any of the rockets—and even if there was, they wouldn't be able to get here for weeks. So there's not much NASA can do except rely on Nina for the answers. I know she's been ordered to compile a report on Dr. Holtz's death—and that Dr. Marquez has been asked to help."

I asked, "So if Dr. Marquez said Dr. Holtz went out the air lock because he was going crazy, NASA would buy it?"

"So would I," Mom said pointedly. "It was his job to analyze Dr. Holtz."

I nodded understanding. My parents' stories about Dr. Holtz had shaken me. They seemed to truly believe he might have been going crazy—and that his great discovery might have been a delusion. I now wondered that myself. Could his euphoria that night in the bathroom have been the result of mental illness? Could his signing that he was being murdered have merely been paranoia? Come to think of it, he'd signed that the earth had killed him, which certainly *sounded* crazy.

Or were my parents wrong? Neither one of them was a licensed psychiatrist. Maybe they had misdiagnosed Dr. Holtz's behavior. Maybe Dr. Holtz had seemed paranoid because he had good reason to be: someone was trying to kill him.

Besides, I had one more piece of evidence there might be a killer loose on the base. "Someone texted me a threat tonight."

My parents both reacted with surprise and concern. "When?" they asked at once.

"About an hour ago." I brought the message up on my watch and showed it to them:

Dash—Be careful—or you'll end up like Dr. Holtz.

I figured my parents would grow even more worried. Instead they both got angry.

"Who sent this to you?" Dad demanded.

"Well, according to my watch, it was Kira. But I was with her at the time, so I'm guessing whoever sent it hacked her account."

"I'll bet it's that jerk Patton Sjoberg," Mom said.

"Patton?" I asked. "You don't think it's from the murderer?"

My parents glanced toward each other, then looked back at me. "This text just looks like stupid, senseless bullying," Mom said. "And Patton Sjoberg is a stupid, senseless bully who you greatly embarrassed today."

"If he's so stupid, how'd he know how to send a text from Kira?" I asked.

"It's not so hard to hack someone's account," Dad explained. "Lily Sjoberg's supposed to have all the brains in that family. Maybe she helped him do it."

"Or maybe *Lily* sent it," Mom suggested. "Or either of the parents could have too. Anyone in that family is capable of doing something this insensitive."

"Why would they send it from Kira?" I asked. "Why not just send it directly?"

"Because sending a threat like that is actually a crime,"

Dad told me. "And besides, doing it anonymously like this is probably more frightening."

I was frustrated with my parents for being so quick to discount my murder theory, but then I reconsidered the text. I had assumed it had come from the murderer, but now that I thought about it, it easily could have been a mindless threat from someone who was angry at me. "You don't think there's *any* chance it's the killer telling me to back off?" I asked.

Dad shook his head. "Dash, there's an extremely good chance that Dr. Holtz died by accident, rather than murder. And there's an even better chance that this text was sent by a dumb lout like Patton Sjoberg." He turned to Mom. "We ought to show this to Nina first thing in the morning. Whoever sent it ought to be punished, no matter how rich they are."

Mom nodded agreement. "Absolutely."

I suddenly found myself wondering if my parents were being completely honest with me. If they *did* think the text was from someone dangerous, it made sense that they'd try to calm me with a lie rather than get me even more worried about it.

My parents seemed to sense my unease. They shared a look, and although they didn't say anything, it seemed like they had. Mom nodded, then turned to me. "You know what?" she asked. "This has been a tough day for all of us.

I can finish this speech in the morning. For now let's have some fun. I think we have a game of Risk stored on the computer."

"In fact," Dad said to me, "I think you were kicking our butts."

I laughed. "Yeah. I was."

"Not for long," Mom warned me. "Computer, bring up that Risk game."

"It vould be my pleasure!" the computer squealed.

Mom's eulogy vanished and a hologram of the Risk map appeared before us. Our armies—hundreds of little holographic men, horses, and cannons—were frozen in the midst of battle.

According to my parents, games like Risk used to be played on boards with tiny plastic pieces, and all the battles had to be imagined. I might not be a big fan of virtual reality, but a game of Risk in which you can't watch your armies go to war doesn't seem like nearly as much fun to me.

"All right," Mom told me. "I'm cashing in my cards for thirty armies. Central America, prepare to be overthrown."

Her forces amassed in Venezuela instantly attacked mine. Salvos of cannon fire blasted my men to virtual bits.

Back on earth I might have balked at the idea of playing games with my parents night after night. I certainly have a lot of friends who would consider it lame. But on the moon I don't have many other options. And to be honest, the forced time with my family is one of the best things about living here.

For the next few hours we launched attacks against one another, conquering countries and continents and then losing them again, until finally I wiped both my parents off the globe. I actually forgot about Dr. Holtz, his suspicious death, and the threat that had been made against me.

For a little while, at least.

Excerpt from *The Official Residents' Guide to Moon Base Alpha*,
© 2040 by National Aeronautics and Space Administration:

EXERCISE

Physical activity is an important part of a healthy lifestyle on earth—and on the moon it's even more important. Due to the significantly lower gravity on the moon (only one-sixth that of earth!) your muscles won't have to work nearly as hard at MBA. But while this *sounds* relaxing, it can have serious consequences. Muscles that would normally be worked by moderate exercise—such as walking, lifting objects, or even simply sitting upright—may begin to atrophy on the lunar surface from disuse. If this is allowed to continue unchecked, you might return to earth to find your muscles have weakened to the point where you can't even stand up! In addition, without the usual force of gravity placed on them, your bones can begin to lose density on the moon.

Don't fear, however! There is a simple solution that will prevent both muscle and bone loss and provide plenty of enjoyment: exercise! MBA has a full-service gym equipped with state-of-the-art equipment. To counteract the effects of low gravity, at least two hours of exercise are suggested every day—although even more can't hurt! Exercise should be divided between endurance (treadmills, StairMasters, stationary bikes) and muscle-building (resistance bands) with perhaps a bit more emphasis on resistance to fight that pesky muscular deterioration.

All lunarnauts should keep a detailed record of their exercise so that their health, muscle strength, and bone density can be accurately tracked and measured—but that doesn't mean working out has to be a chore! Watch a movie or read a book while you're on the machines, or better yet, exercise with a friend. At MBA, staying in shape can be just as much fun as it is back on earth—if not more!

PREHISTORIC MOTIVATION

Lunar day 189

Smack in the middle of the night

I couldn't sleep again.

Only this time it wasn't due to the litany of things that normally prevented me from sleeping: claustrophobia, the rancid air mattress, space food making me sick. Instead I was wound up thinking about Dr. Holtz's death—and all the other mysterious things going on at Moon Base Alpha. Was Dr. Holtz losing his mind, or had he really made a great discovery? Why had Nina lied to me about the cameras in the bathrooms? Was she trying to cover up Dr. Holtz's craziness—or something else? Was Chang still mad enough at Dr. Holtz to kill him? Why was Lars

Sjoberg suddenly so desperate to get off the moon? The Sjobergs had hated MBA since they'd arrived, so why hadn't they ever tried to go home *before* Dr. Holtz's death? Had Patton Sjoberg—or someone else in his family—really sent me that threat? And what was Daphne doing on the computer when she was supposed to be operating the robot arm?

Finally, at two in the morning, I couldn't take it anymore. In my cramped sleep pod I was starting to feel like I'd been buried alive. I slipped out, taking care not to wake my family, and headed for the gym.

With everything that had happened the day before, I hadn't done my mandated two hours of exercise to keep my bones and muscles from turning to mush. In truth, missing a day probably doesn't make a difference, but it's better to be safe than sorry. Once you start slacking off, it's hard to get back in the routine. I didn't want to end up like Roddy, who hadn't done a lick of exercise in weeks. He now had the muscle tone of a bowl of pudding. Dad said there was a decent chance that when Roddy eventually got back to earth, the increased gravity would snap his legs like toothpicks.

I'd expected to have the gym to myself, but Chang Hi-Tech was there.

He was working out with the resistance bands. These are

the MBA equivalent of weightlifting. It was too expensive to fly several tons of weights to space—and given the low gravity, we would have needed weights six times heavier than those at an earthbound gym—so the bands had been developed instead. They're like giant rubber bands that you can electronically adjust the elasticity of. You attach them to the floor or wall, then push against them with your legs or arms. It feels the exact same as lifting free weights, only without the fear that you might accidentally drop them and crush your rib cage.

I paused in the doorway. Chang had always been friendly to me and my family, but now, with murder on my mind, I found myself slightly frightened of him. The idea of being alone with *anyone* suddenly seemed like a bad idea. I wavered for a moment, thinking I should hurry back to my room.

But Chang saw me before I could. "Hey!" he called out. "A fellow insomniac! What's keeping you up, Dash?"

"Guess I'm still freaked out about Dr. Holtz."

"I hear you, pal." Chang was only wearing a tank top, revealing all the tattoos on his arms. Every time he flexed against the resistance bands, Albert Einstein and the rest of the great scientists swelled in size. "This thing's been a punch in the gut to all of us. I mean, I knew Holtz was getting on in years, but he always *seemed* so young; it kind of felt like he was gonna live forever. Want to do a race on the Head-to-Head?"

The Head-to-Head is one of the few fun things to do at MBA. It's a virtual-reality system that hooks to any of the workout machines and simulates a race between them. It isn't quite the same thing as a real foot- or bicycle race, but since there's no other outlet for physical competition on the moon, it's quite popular. As much as I enjoy it, though, I looked for an excuse to leave. "No, thanks. You'll crush me."

"I'll set it on a harder level for me." Chang gave one last flex against the resistance bands, then let them snap back to the wall. His muscles were so pumped with blood that Einstein's and Niels Bohr's heads looked ready to explode.

"I probably shouldn't . . . ," I said.

"C'mon! It'll be fun!" Chang waved for me to join him.

By now, making more excuses would only seem suspicious. "Okay."

"Excellent! Treadmills?"

"Sure." While Chang set the Head-to-Head up, I subtly checked out the settings on his resistance bands. He'd had them set to three thousand pounds—equal to five hundred back on earth. I gave one a test flex. It didn't give an inch. I might as well have been trying to stretch concrete.

"All right!" Chang called. "We are ready to rumble!" He waved gallantly to one of two treadmills.

I climbed aboard. There was a belt attached to the tread-mill to hold me down on it, simulating earth gravity so I could actually run. I locked it around my waist, slipped on a pair of hologoggles, and instantly found myself in Yosemite Valley, back on earth. It was a beautiful day with a bright blue, cloudless sky. In the distance Vernal Falls plunged down a sheer rock face into a cloud of mist.

I couldn't see my avatar in this game; the entire race was from my point of view.

Chang materialized next to me a moment later. Unlike Roddy, he hadn't enhanced his avatar at all. It looked exactly like the real Chang. But then real-life Chang is so freakishly athletic he kind of looks like a video-game warrior anyhow.

"Ready?" he asked.

"Yeah."

"On your marks, then."

I tensed reflexively.

A numeric countdown flashed over Half Dome: 3 . . . 2 . . . 1 . . .

A buzzer sounded.

I sprang into action, but Chang was faster, pulling out in front right away. I didn't try to catch him, not wanting to tire myself out right off the bat. Instead I let him set the pace, following him along the wooded trail. It felt good to run in earth gravity again—or at least a simulation of it—rather than bound into the air with every step.

Chang had enabled the sound options on the Head-to-Head as well, so I could hear birds chirping in the trees, water burbling in a nearby stream, and the occasional chitter of a chipmunk. The two of us could also talk to each other as we ran. Now that Chang had roped me into the race, I figured I should take advantage of the opportunity and question him. I probably wouldn't get another chance alone with him for a while. "So you're upset about Dr. Holtz too?"

"Of course," Chang said. "Why wouldn't I be?"

"I heard he stole some ideas from you."

Chang's avatar looked back at me, which meant that the real Chang had just glanced my way as well. Then, to my surprise, he laughed. "Yeah, he did. But that doesn't mean I'm happy that the guy's dead."

A new sound arose from the woods to the side: an eerie guttural croak that made me shiver. "What was that?" I asked.

"A velociraptor, I think," Chang said.

"*What?* There aren't any dinosaurs in Yosemite!"

"There are now. It's a new module I designed for the Head-to-Head. It provides motivation to run faster."

Another guttural croak came from the forest, closer this time. Even though the dinosaurs were imaginary, they provoked a very real fear in me. I felt my adrenaline spike and reflexively picked up the pace.

Ahead of me Chang did too. He said, "I'll admit, I was angry at Dr. Holtz when I first learned he'd stolen my idea. I mean, big ideas don't just come to you every day. Holtz and I were both working at NASA, doing research. I'd thought of a way to increase our metabolism of oxygen in outer space and shared it with him—and a couple months later the guy's taking credit for it. Frankly, I wanted his head on a stick. But that was years ago. There's no point in holding on to that kind of emotion. It'll eat you up inside. So I dealt with it. Talked to my shrink, did some yoga. Eventually I realized that Dr. Holtz wasn't even aware of what he'd done. He hadn't stolen my idea maliciously. In fact I think he'd forgotten all about our conversation and thought he came up with the idea himself. Which happens more than you'd think in science. People are always forgetting where ideas come from. Whoa!"

Chang leaped aside as a six-foot-tall velociraptor lunged out of the trees at him. It shot across the trail in front of me, so close that I had to duck under its tail.

Another roar sounded directly behind me. I looked back and found two more velociraptors in pursuit. I ran even faster, my legs pounding on the treadmill. I didn't like this new motivator. I'd been perfectly happy in regular Yosemite without prehistoric carnivores to worry about. But I didn't want to bother Chang to shut it off. If I did, he might stop talking about Dr. Holtz. As it was, he was eagerly unburdening himself, unconcerned by the dinosaurs.

"And then the chance to come up here presented itself," Chang was saying. "And I wanted it. I knew Holtz was going to be here. He was a lock for this place, the only person guaranteed a trip. So I had to take whatever issues I had with him and chuck them once and for all. There were a lot of hoops to jump through to get up here. A million interviews. Psych reviews. Physical exams. And if there was a part of your body they could probe, they probed it. If anyone thought I had an ax to grind with Holtz, I wouldn't have made it past round one. And believe me, they asked. Over and over again. But like I said, I'm over it. The past is the past. What happened between Holtz and me is long forgotten."

The way Chang said it, it sounded completely honest and convincing, though I was a bit distracted by the velociraptors pursuing me. I wished I could have seen Chang's face as he talked, rather than the back of his avatar's head. In retrospect, deciding to grill a murder suspect in a virtual world hadn't turned out to be such a good idea. But I didn't have a choice now.

I asked, "So, given that, then there's no way that *anyone* who didn't like Dr. Holtz could have gotten up here, right? NASA would have booted them."

"Well, not necessarily," Chang admitted. "That was certainly the case for me, because I was coming here solo and there was a lot of competition for my slot. In the vetting process they were looking for any reason to ding you. But there are others up here who didn't have such a rigorous assessment."

A bear burst through the trees ahead of us and scampered across the trail. Normally, that alone would have been exciting, but now three carnotauruses emerged from the forest in pursuit. They plunged into the trees and disappeared again without so much as a glance at us.

"Who had an easy time getting approved for here?" I asked.

"The whole Sjoberg clan, for starters," Chang replied. "Since they bought their way in here, no one really cared much that they were a bunch of twits."

"Do you think any of them didn't like Dr. Holtz?"

"I wouldn't be surprised. Those Nordic dorkwads don't seem to like anybody. And then there's Dr. Marquez. Holtz tried to block him from even coming up here."

"Really? Why?"

"'Cause Marquez is a lousy psychiatrist."

"What?" I stumbled slightly on the treadmill in surprise. "But he's famous."

"That doesn't mean he's *good*. The guy got his medical

degree from a sixth-rate school in the Bahamas. He couldn't diagnose a baked potato. Holtz thought he'd be a waste of space up here. But NASA trumped him. They wanted Ilina Brahmaputra-Marquez up here for her astrophysics chops—and they figured her celebrity husband would be good for publicity."

"You mean they only wanted Marquez for his name?"

"Absolutely. Think about all the press coverage before we all came up here. Who got the most attention?"

I thought back to the time after all the Moonies had been announced to the public. We had all become famous—but Dr. Marquez had been at a different level. He'd been invited on hundreds of talk shows and been at every NASA press conference. "It was Dr. Marquez."

"Right. The public doesn't care about astrophysicists or geochemists. They care about famous people. NASA probably would have sent up a movie star if it didn't mean bumping a scientist from coming here. Dr. Marquez was the next best thing. He was famous enough to get a lot of attention—and he filled the slot for a psychiatrist."

"But wasn't anyone besides Dr. Holtz concerned that he's not good?"

"I'm sure someone was. But I know there were other people who felt it wasn't that important to have a psychiatrist here at all, so they might as well send a lousy one who could get publicity for the moon base rather than looking for a good one who couldn't."

There was a snort behind me, so close I thought I could feel the exhalation riffle my hair. I'd been so caught up in what Chang was saying that I'd momentarily forgotten about the raptors behind us. Now I spun to find three dozen toothbrush-size teeth ready to clamp down on my head, a strand of drool ominously dangling from them. I sprinted forward, pulling alongside Chang as the jaws snapped shut.

"That was close!" he laughed. "You were almost an appetizer!"

I didn't think it was nearly as funny. My heart was pounding. "Did Dr. Marquez know Dr. Holtz tried to block him?"

"Oh yeah. It wasn't a secret. Holtz wrote a whole report detailing why Marquez was bad at his job. Marquez was livid. And definitely embarrassed. Then when NASA okayed him to come here, he figured that vindicated him. But Holtz kept dissing him. And he refused to ever let Marquez assess him up here. In fact he wouldn't even talk to the guy."

"So . . . if Dr. Holtz had a mental problem, no one would have caught it?"

"I suppose not. Although Holtz probably would have argued that Marquez wouldn't have been able to diagnose it anyhow."

I wondered if a bruised ego was enough motivation to want to kill somebody. "Was there anyone else who didn't like Dr. Holtz?"

Chang's avatar shot me a sidelong glance. "Why are you so interested in this?"

"Up till yesterday, I thought everyone liked him. And then I started hearing that people didn't. It's pretty surprising." This was an understatement. In truth I found the number of potential killers Dr. Holtz was racking up to be extremely disturbing. How could anyone who was so nice have so many enemies? I wondered. Or was Dr. Holtz not quite as nice as I'd believed?

"You're not thinking someone bumped Holtz off, are you?" Chang asked.

"No!" I said, way too fast. "I . . . uh . . . I don't know what I was thinking. It's really hard to concentrate with these dinosaurs chasing us."

"You don't like it?" Chang seemed genuinely surprised. "I think they're cool."

"They creep me out."

"Oh." Chang's avatar frowned. "You know they can't really hurt you, right? Even virtually. It's not like they'll eat your avatar if you don't run fast enough. They're only designed to stay right behind us and push our pace."

"I can think of lots of less scary ways to do that," I

argued. "Like, *we* could chase something. Rabbits. Or squirrels. Something that isn't dangerous."

"You're sure you want me to shut it off?" Chang sounded disappointed. "It gets *really* exciting right about . . . now."

We emerged into a clearing near Yosemite Falls—only we could barely see the cataract because there was a tyrannosaurus standing in front of it. It loomed over us, straddling the trail, and loosed a primal roar that jackhammered my eardrums.

"Yes, shut it off," I said. "I'm done." I snapped off my goggles and stopped running.

To my surprise, the readout said we'd gone almost two miles.

"Look at that!" Chang crowed, his goggles now perched on his forehead. "I *told* you those raptors were good motivators! Nice run!" He held up his hand for a high five.

I held up mine, and Chang slapped it so hard I thought it might come off.

"Could you half-wits shut your stupid mouths for once?"

I knew who'd spoken, even before turning to face him. There was only one person at MBA who was so relentlessly mean-spirited: Lars Sjoberg.

He stood in the doorway of the gym, scowling, wearing pajamas, slippers, and a fluffy robe emblazoned with an MBA logo. (The robe was part of the Sjobergs' deluxe tourist package.) There still appeared to be some dried coleslaw crusted in his white-blond hair. "It's hard enough to sleep in this dung heap without imbeciles carrying on at all hours of the night."

Chang's muscles tensed, though I could tell he was trying hard to restrain his temper. He undid his gravity belt, stepped off the treadmill, and hung his goggles on the wall by the resistance bands. "We weren't carrying on, Mr. Sjoberg. We were simply working out."

"At two o'clock in the morning!" Lars snarled. "A time when normal people are in bed!"

"We couldn't sleep," I told him. "We're too upset about Dr. Holtz."

Lars snorted in disgust. "As if that old fool didn't cause me enough grief when he was alive."

"What's that supposed to mean?" Chang demanded.

"All of you put this man on a pedestal when he deserved no such thing," Lars groused. "He was an adviser on this base. A man who supposedly specialized in improving our quality of life off earth. Well, given that there is no quality of life here at all, I'd say that makes your Dr. Holtz a complete and total failure."

"Dr. Holtz's job was to assess the effects of low gravity and space travel on the human body," Chang said. "Not to run a spa for rich dinks like you. If you're unhappy here, that's your fault, not his. He didn't ask you to come here.

In fact he tried to prevent you from doing it. You came on your own."

"Only because NASA and its so-called scientists assured us this would be the adventure of a lifetime!" Lars stormed toward Chang, his pale blue eyes blazing. He seemed to be itching for a fight, every annoyance he'd felt at MBA now flowing out of him. "They all lied to us, including your precious Dr. Holtz. The man was a quack! A fool who knew nothing except how to shill for NASA."

Lars was now face-to-face with Chang. I'd never realized it before, but Lars was a big man, as tall as Chang. Though he was flabby around the middle, Lars looked like he could handle himself in a fight.

"Take that back," Chang said. "The man just died. He deserves some respect."

Lars poked Chang in the chest with his finger. "Not from me."

"Don't touch me," Chang told him.

"I'll do whatever I want." Lars poked Chang in the chest again. "My family and I are leaving on that rocket, so we'll only be in this godforsaken place a few more days. But during that time, you and your fellow so-called scientists will give us the respect we deserve."

"Oh, I'm happy to give you exactly what you deserve." Chang's hands clenched into fists.

Lars had been waiting for this. He was already swinging his fist. I could see the hatred in his eyes. It seemed he'd been wanting to punch Chang for a long time.

But Chang was ready for it. He sidestepped deftly. Lars's fist grazed Chang's nose and then slammed into the wall.

While Lars howled in pain, Chang grabbed the loose end of a wall-mounted resistance band and yanked the band tight across Lars's face, flinging the trillionaire backward into the wall. Lars's head banged into the cement so hard it staggered him.

Chang released the resistance band. The fight was already over. Lars reeled, struggling to focus on his opponent. "I . . . hate . . . you," he gasped, and then collapsed face-first on the floor.

Chang looked at me. "You're my witness, Dash. This was self-defense—and technically, I never laid a hand on the guy." He stepped over Lars Sjoberg's prone body and left the gym, whistling so cheerfully it was unsettling.

I stared at the unconscious trillionaire, worried. I'd just learned two very disturbing things.

Lars Sjoberg was a dangerous man who'd had a big grudge against Dr. Holtz.

And even though Chang Kowalski *said* he'd forgiven Dr. Holtz, he certainly wasn't someone you wanted angry at you.

Excerpt from *The Official Residents' Guide to Moon Base Alpha*,
© 2040 by National Aeronautics and Space Administration:

SLEEP

Although great care has been taken to provide the highest quality sleeping quarters at MBA, there is a slight chance you might experience some issues with sleep at night, especially immediately after your arrival. Sleep difficulties are not new to the space program, but you will be pleased to know that decades of research have greatly improved your ability to get a good night's rest! With our dark, quiet sleeping spaces, steady oxygen flows, and comfortable mattresses, after a few days' adjustment to life on the moon we guarantee you'll be sleeping just as well as you did on earth—if not better!*

---

* A full night's sleep is actually not guaranteed. If you continue to have difficulties getting rest, please consult with the base doctor and/or psychiatrist for help. If sleeplessness persists, specialized drugs designed to aid sleep in non-earth locations can be prescribed.

POSSIBLE SUSPECTS

Lunar day 189

Much later in the morning than expected

"Wake up, sleepyhead." The words were soft and gentle in my ear.

I groggily pried my eyes open and found Zan Perfonic peering into my sleep pod. "What time is it?" I groaned.

"Nearly lunchtime."

"What?" I sat up, cracking my head on the low ceiling. "Darn it! I overslept!"

"It's all right," Zan said soothingly. "School's been canceled again today. You're not missing anything."

I lay back down, rubbing my head. "I couldn't fall asleep," I explained. "I was up until five in the morning."

"Well, you had an emotionally exhausting day yesterday. And a stressful night in the gym as well."

I groaned again. "You know about that?"

"*Everyone* knows about it. It's all anyone is talking about. Lars Sjoberg is threatening to sue NASA, Chang, and anyone else he can think of. Meanwhile Chang is saying it was self-defense—and that you can back him up. Although Nina has already viewed the security footage from the gym and she says the evidence looks like it's in Chang's favor."

I was starting to feel a little weird, having this conversation while I was still in bed. Under the sheets I was only wearing my boxers. "Do you mind closing your eyes while I get some clothes on?" I asked.

"Oh, of course." Zan ducked away from the entrance to my sleep pod. "Sorry. I didn't want to barge in on you like this, but I really need to see what you've found."

"It's okay. I've wanted to talk to you since yesterday." I peered out of my sleep pod and saw Zan standing at the far end of the room, her back to me. She was watching the big SlimScreen, which was displaying a fictitious landscape full of rainbows and unicorns instead of Hapuna Beach. Violet must have reprogrammed it. I leaped to the floor and scurried over to the bureau. "I even came looking for you—"

"Dash! I told you not to do that! No one can know we're working together."

"I was careful. I didn't *tell* anyone I was looking for you. I just looked."

"You haven't told anyone about me? Or what we're doing?"

"No. I swear. Where were you last night?"

"In the temp quarters. I'm sorry. I was wiped out from the trip here."

I yanked on a T-shirt and shorts. "Okay. I'm dressed."

Zan swung back to face me. "Did you get the footage of the air lock?"

"Yes."

Zan's face lit up in excitement. Her eyes were almost the exact same color as those of the unicorns on the SlimScreen behind her. "Well . . . ?"

"Dr. Holtz might have been forced to go out the air lock against his will."

The news upset Zan—and yet she seemed excited by it too. I could understand why. I'd felt the same way: It proved we were both right about the death being suspicious. "How do you know?"

"It's better if I show it to you." I'd slept with my watch on to protect it. I touched it to our tabletop SlimScreen, transferring the security footage Kira had found, then played it for Zan.

"It doesn't look like anyone's forcing him to do anything," Zan said.

"Just wait." I fast-forwarded to the point where Dr. Holtz started signing with his hands.

"What's he doing?" Zan asked.

"It's sign language," I told her. "The way deaf people used to communicate."

"Oh. Right. Do you speak it?"

"No. I had to have the computer translate it. Dr. Holtz said, 'This is a murder. Earth killed me. Find my phone. Tell my family I love them.'"

Zan took in a sharp breath and turned away. It looked like she was trying not to cry. She bowed her head and rubbed her temples, like she was trying to process everything.

I froze the footage on the image of Dr. Holtz on the moon, staring up at earth. "Do you want to watch it again?"

Zan shook her head. "No. Once was enough. To know that another person was behind this is so . . . so upsetting."

"Well," I said cautiously, "Dr. Holtz doesn't actually say that another *person* is behind this. He says the earth made him do it."

"Yes, that is odd. But I suspect it's some sort of code for the name of whoever forced him onto the moon."

"Isn't the sign language already code enough?"

"Maybe not," Zan replied sadly. "Maybe he was afraid the killer would watch the footage and erase it if they recognized their name. Which would mean the killer would have access to the security system . . ."

"Nina," I said.

"She's the only one with that kind of access here," Zan agreed. "And she's been trying to block any investigation since the beginning."

"But why would she want Dr. Holtz dead?" I asked. "And how did she force him to go out the air lock?"

"I don't know," Zan admitted sadly. "Maybe there's another camera angle that shows her. You might have to grab all the footage from around the staging area that night."

I started to say, "We did," but caught myself at the last second, not wanting to mention Kira. "I did. There's no one else visible in any shot except Dr. Holtz."

Zan sighed. "Then she must have gotten to him earlier somehow. Sometime between his conversation in the bath-room and the time he went out the air lock. Something important transpired in those two and a half hours. Dr. Holtz says, 'Find my phone.' He must have recorded some-thing on it. Do you have any idea where it might be?"

I sat on an InflatiCube, daunted. "No. I tried his room last night, but it was locked."

Zan shook her head and started pacing. "I doubt he would have hidden it there anyway. That's far too obvious. I guarantee you, Nina—or someone else—has already scoured his quarters. And he wouldn't have kept the evidence on him, either, knowing they'd search his body."

"The science pod, then? He had a station there."

"He shared that station with Dr. Janke. And it seems too obvious as well."

"Then where?" I asked, feeling frustrated. "This base isn't huge, but there are still thousands of places to hide something as small as a phone."

"I know." Zan sounded as frustrated as I was. "We'll both just have to think on this."

I hesitated before bringing up my next point, aware Zan wouldn't like hearing it any more than I had. "There's one other thing you should know. According to my parents, there's a possibility that Dr. Holtz was losing his mind."

Zan stopped pacing. She whirled toward me, her eyes wide in surprise. "Why would they say that?"

"They said he'd been acting strange lately. And talking to himself. They think he might have gone out the air lock because he was paranoid or schizophrenic or something. They even think his big discovery might not be real, like a figment of his imagination."

Zan looked very upset by all this for a moment, but then shook it off. "Dr. Holtz might have seemed a bit erratic lately, but I'm sure your parents are wrong. He wasn't crazy. I spoke to him very recently and he seemed as sane as could be—"

"That doesn't mean he was sane all the time."

"True, but your parents were basing their analysis of

him on random observations as well. There has never been a documented case of life on the moon driving anyone crazy. There were hundreds of people up here during the construction of this base and there are dozens living here now. Some of them might have gotten depressed or desperately homesick, but nothing worse than that."

"Well, what if Dr. Holtz was losing his mind *before* he came here?" I asked. "What if this was Alzheimer's or something?"

Zan shook her head. "Dr. Holtz was thoroughly vetted by NASA's medical staff before being approved for this mission. Because of his age, they were certainly checking for Alzheimer's or any other type of disease like that. If he'd shown even a trace, they would have flagged him. But he was given a clean bill of health, mentally and physically."

"It's been six months since then," I said. "And he wasn't visiting Dr. Marquez like he was supposed to. Although Chang says that probably didn't matter."

"Six months isn't long enough to go from completely sane to imagining great scientific discoveries and thinking that someone is forcing you out the air lock. Trust me on this, Dashiell. I've studied human psychology."

I raised my hands in surrender. "All right. I'm just telling you what my folks said. Dr. Holtz didn't seem crazy to me either . . . up until he signed that the earth had killed him."

"That's not crazy. It's code for something."

I nodded agreement, although I wasn't quite as convinced as Zan about this. "Is there anyone else besides Nina who might have had access to the security footage?"

Zan focused her bright blue eyes on me. "Why do you ask?"

"Well, I know Nina's been acting suspicious through all this, but she doesn't seem to have a motive. Whereas some other people do."

"Like who?"

"Lars Sjoberg. He didn't like Dr. Holtz at all. That's what the whole thing in the gym was about last night. He was saying all sorts of bad stuff about Dr. Holtz, and Chang got upset."

"What kind of bad stuff?"

"That Dr. Holtz did a lousy job making this base fit for humans. Even though that wasn't really his job."

"Hmm." Zan began pacing again. "Lars blew half a billion dollars to come up here. He's probably looking for someone to blame besides himself. And he certainly has a violent side."

"And now, suddenly, he's demanding that Nina put him and his family on the rocket back to earth. Like he's trying to get away from the crime scene as fast as possible."

"That's true."

"Is Nina going to let him?"

"I don't know. Letting the Sjobergs go will cause a huge mess as far as scheduling is concerned. A lot of the other temps would end up stuck here until the next rocket comes. But NASA doesn't want one of the world's most wealthy and powerful men telling people he's being held prisoner up here. They need the money from future tourists to keep this place going. So it's possible that if the Sjobergs sign a contract swearing they won't bad-mouth Moon Base Alpha, NASA will find a way to let them go home tomorrow."

"So he'll get away?"

"He's very wealthy and powerful. I suppose that back on earth he might be able to keep from being arrested. For instance, he could move to a country where the US couldn't extradite him. *If* he's even guilty. We don't really have any proof of that." Zan stared thoughtfully at the big SlimScreen, watching the digital unicorns as they frolicked beneath the rainbows. "Who else do you suspect?"

I paused, not thrilled about what I had to say next. "Chang Hi-Tech."

Zan looked back at me, surprised. "Really?"

"He accused Dr. Holtz of stealing an idea from him a long time ago. He says he's over it, but maybe that's a lie. Last night, in the gym, he was pretty scary when he was angry."

"I suppose. But if he really has been holding a grudge all

this time, why not kill Dr. Holtz on earth? It'd be far easier to cover his tracks there."

"If he did it, he's done a good job covering them here," I said. "There doesn't seem to be any evidence against him at all. Maybe he thought he could make it look like an accident better up here. Or get Lars Sjoberg to take the fall for it."

"Good point," Zan admitted.

"There's also Dr. Marquez," I offered. "According to Chang, he's not a very good psychiatrist. Dr. Holtz tried to block him from coming up here and he knew it."

"Really? That's interesting."

"And Daphne Merritt's up to something too. I saw her fiddling with the station computers last night. I don't know if it has anything to do with Dr. Holtz, but it was suspicious."

"Wow." Zan blew out a big breath. "That's quite a list of suspects."

"There's one more thing," I said. I brought up the threatening text on my smartwatch and showed it to Zan. "This isn't actually from Kira. Someone hacked her account and used it to send me this."

Zan read the text, then looked to me with fear in her eyes. "When did this happen?"

"Last night after dinner. That's why I was trying to find you. I showed it to my parents, but they said it was probably someone like Patton Sjoberg trying to scare me."

"I suppose that's possible, but . . . I think you're right to be concerned." Zan shook her head sadly. "Oh, Dash. I'm sorry. I was hoping something like this wouldn't happen."

"So . . . you think I'm really in danger?"

"I'm not sure. If it was really the killer who sent this, they're not telling you that they're coming for you next. They're just warning you to back off—which probably means they're scared. We've gotten close to them and they're worried they'll get caught. But this certainly isn't something to take lightly, either."

My watch alarm chimed. I glanced at it and groaned.

"What's wrong?" Zan asked.

"I forgot I'm supposed to have a session with Dr. Marquez today."

"About what?"

"Everyone thinks I'm going psycho because I said Dr. Holtz's death was suspicious. And yet here's all this evidence that says it was."

"Even so, it's best to keep this to ourselves." Zan fixed me with a piercing stare. "You *swear* you haven't told anyone else about what we're up to?"

"I swear," I lied.

"Good. Although . . ." Zan trailed off, as though she was embarrassed about finishing the sentence.

"Do you need something else?" I asked.

"I hate to ask, especially given the threat you've received."

"That's even more reason I want to help," I said. "The faster we find whoever sent this, the less chance there is they can hurt me."

That wasn't the only reason. I didn't want to admit it to Zan, but the investigation was exciting. It had shaken up my dull life at MBA and given me something to focus on. Even though I'd been threatened, I didn't want to go back to my boring old routine.

"I just need you to keep your eyes and ears open a bit longer," Zan told me. "I'm going to look into all these leads you've found and try to figure out where Dr. Holtz stashed his phone, but I could still use another brain on this. Sound out Dr. Marquez right now. Watch Daphne to see if she does anything else suspicious. Keep your distance and don't do anything stupid, but pay close attention to our suspects— and anything else you notice that's out of the ordinary."

"That's it?" I asked.

"Trust me, that's plenty. Now hurry. You don't want to be late to your appointment with Dr. Marquez."

"Actually, I do. In fact I'd prefer to miss it completely."

Zan laughed. It sounded so sweet, it was almost like a song. "I understand. And if he wasn't a suspect, I wouldn't push you."

"All right." I headed for the door, opened it a crack, and peeked into the hall.

Mr. Grisan was passing by on the ground floor, but otherwise there was no one around. Once Mr. Grisan was around the corner, I stepped out onto the catwalk and waved Zan through after me.

She hurried for the stairs while I locked the door. She'd only gone a few steps before something occurred to me. "Wait!" I whispered.

Zan turned back, looking nervous to be out in the open with me. "What?"

"I told you about all the suspects I found. Did *you* find any?"

"Yes."

"Who?"

"Trust me, Dashiell, the less you know about what I'm doing, the safer you are." Before I could protest, Zan ducked around the corner, disappearing from sight.

MENTAL HEALTH

At MBA, every effort has been made to create a relaxing,
enjoyable environment for all lunarnauts. However, as you will
be among the first humans to ever live on a non-earth celestial
object, you will be subjected to things that few of your fellow
humans have ever experienced. Therefore, as part of our commitment to provide the finest medical care possible, all lunarnauts are required to visit the base psychiatrist on a regularly
scheduled basis.

Keep in mind, there is no evidence that life on the moon
causes any mental conditions that life on earth does not.*
This psychiatric monitoring and assessment will help us learn
about the effects of lunar life on MBA residents and help us
plan for future voyages—perhaps to places even farther than
the moon! In addition, psychiatric sessions can be relaxing,
enlightening, and even fun. So make the most of them.

---

* Although there *is* some minor evidence that disruption of the standard
earth day can lead to depression.

PSYCHIATRIC EVALUATION

Lunar day 189
Lunchtime

"How are you feeling, Dashiell?" Dr. Marquez asked.

"Hungry," I said. "I missed breakfast today."

"You know that's not what I mean."

"That's how I'm feeling." I held up a plate of recently rehydrated enchiladas. "That's why I've got this. I didn't want to miss lunch, too."

Dr. Marquez picked at something in his teeth. He was seated on an InflatiCube across the table from me in his family's residence. Dr. Marquez usually met patients in the medical bay, but Dr. Holtz's body was still in there, and

everyone figured that having a corpse around wasn't conducive to a good therapy session.

The Marquez family's large SlimScreen was set to an
image of a wheat field: acres of golden grass rippling in a
light breeze. It was probably supposed to be relaxing, but all
it really did was make me hungry for fresh-baked bread.

I'd never enjoyed my meetings with Dr. Marquez, but
I put up with them because I thought they were important. Now that Chang had told me Dr. Marquez wasn't
very good at his job, I was annoyed. His nervous tics and
probing questions were getting under my skin—and it
was hard to hide, since he kept asking me to discuss my
feelings.

Dr. Marquez said, "Your parents have expressed concern
about how you're responding to Dr. Holtz's death. You have
been distressed, distracted, paranoid . . ."

"What did I do that was paranoid?"

"You suggested that the death wasn't a mere accident.
That there might be a conspiracy surrounding it."

"I didn't say anything about a conspiracy." I forked some
of my enchiladas into my mouth, only to discover they
weren't enchiladas. They were liver and onions that had been
mislabeled. I spat it back onto the plate.

Dr. Marquez pointed triumphantly. "Ah! See what you
just did? You told me a lie, and your own body reacted vio-

lently against it. In being dishonest with me, you almost made yourself throw up."

"No, I almost threw up because this food sucks," I countered. "It's liver and onions. I didn't like liver and onions back on earth. No one does. So what NASA moron thought it would be a good idea to dehydrate it?"

"You are displaying a great deal of anger," Dr. Marquez said. "I wonder if this might truly be about something else besides the food."

"It's not," I said. "I'm starving and I just got the worst lunch imaginable. I'd rather eat rat droppings."

Dr. Marquez templed his fingers under his chin. This was a very special weird tic of his, the one he did when he was trying to look smart. He generally followed it with what he imagined was a Very Impressive Observation. "I think you're subverting your anger, Dashiell. Something else is annoying you."

Yeah, you, I wanted to say. But I didn't. Instead I shoved the liver and onions away from me. A little bit sloshed off the plate onto the table.

Dr. Marquez recoiled from it. "Dashiell, I understand the source of this anger. Dr. Holtz's death has been upsetting to all of us—"

"No," I said. "It hasn't."

Dr. Marquez arched an eyebrow. "You mean it's not upsetting to you?"

"No. It's very upsetting to me. But other people here haven't been upset at all. In fact, there were a lot of people here who didn't like Dr. Holtz very much."

"That's not true . . ."

"Like you, for instance."

Dr. Marquez froze. He'd been about to say something, but now a weird, surprised gagging noise came from his mouth. It took him a while to decide what the proper response to my accusation should be. He finally opted for indignation. "Why would you say something like that?"

"Because it's true."

"And what could I possibly have against Dr. Holtz?"

"He thought you were a lousy doctor and tried to keep you from coming up here."

Dr. Marquez made the weird gagging noise again. He was struggling to control his emotions, but he couldn't quite do it. Anger flashed in his eyes. "Where did you hear that?"

I didn't want to rat Chang out, so I said, "Lots of people said so."

"Well it's absolutely false!"

"So you weren't angry at Dr. Holtz?"

"This session isn't about me! It's about you."

On another day I might have backed down, but Zan had asked me to sound out Dr. Marquez. And besides, provoking him was much more fun than answering annoying questions about myself. "All I'm saying is, there are people—like you—who aren't at all upset that Dr. Holtz died. So maybe it's not paranoid of me to think that his death wasn't an accident."

Dr. Marquez gasped. "Are you accusing me of something?"

Rather than answer, I shrugged.

Dr. Marquez shook his head and tutted. "This is very disturbing. Your delusions are worse than I was led to believe. Have you told anyone else this?"

"Some people in security."

"And what was their response?"

"They were already suspicious of you."

It was a lie, but Dr. Marquez bought it. His eyes went wide in surprise. "That's ridiculous! I had nothing to do with Dr. Holtz's death! And besides, there are plenty of people here who were far angrier at Dr. Holtz than me!"

"Like who?"

"Lars Sjoberg and his wife!" Dr. Marquez blurted out, so worked up he forgot all about censoring himself.

I leaned forward, intrigued. "Sonja?"

"Oh, definitely. She *hated* Dr. Holtz. He hadn't wanted the Sjobergs to come here and had been very vocal about it. Sonja was offended—and believe me, that is one woman you don't want on your bad side. Everyone thinks Lars is dangerous, but she's the real hothead in that family."

"Really? She doesn't seem like it."

"Don't believe that icy exterior of hers. Underneath, she's a volcano. Back on earth, at a charity luncheon a few years ago, one of her best friends made a joke about her being shallow. Sonja stabbed her in the leg with an oyster fork. Lars had to spend nearly a million dollars on lawyers to keep her from filing charges."

"I never heard that," I said.

"Lars spent another couple million keeping the story hushed up. I only found out during a hypnosis session."

I was growing more convinced that Dr. Marquez wasn't a very good psychiatrist. I was pretty sure doctors weren't supposed to talk about their patients like this. But as long as Dr. Marquez was doing it, I was going to keep pushing him. "Did she ever hurt anyone else?"

"Oh yes. She once attacked a paparazzo with a high-heeled shoe. And when she caught a butler trying to steal some of her lingerie, she tackled him and bit part of his ear off."

"And NASA let her come up here?"

"They didn't know. Like I said, the Sjobergs spent a lot of money to keep her bad behavior under wraps. But she's not the only enemy Dr. Holtz had up here. There's also Mr. Grisan."

"He didn't like Dr. Holtz either?"

Dr. Marquez started to say something but then changed his mind. "Actually, I can't speak to that."

"Why? Did Mr. Grisan tell you something in confidence?"

"No. In fact, Mr. Grisan doesn't have any sessions with me."

"He doesn't?" I asked. "I thought everyone was required to do that."

Dr. Marquez shrugged. "Not him. I don't know why. I asked my superiors at NASA, but they said to forget about it and just let him be."

"So then why did you suggest him?"

"I don't think he and Dr. Holtz liked each other. I once overheard Dr. Holtz telling Nina he didn't think Mr. Grisan could be trusted."

"Why not?"

"I don't know. That was all I heard. It's no basis to accuse Mr. Grisan of anything. I should never have mentioned it. You got under my skin, and I made a mistake." Dr. Marquez nervously nibbled on his thumbnail.

"So is there anyone else you suspect?" I asked.

"I've said too much as it is."

"I'm not asking for anything you heard in a session—"

"The point is, I shouldn't even be playing this game." Dr. Marquez was calming down now, seeming to realize that he'd blabbed too much. He corkscrewed his index finger in his ear, digging out a glob of wax. "No good can come out of making accusations. No one had anything to do with Dr. Holtz's death except Dr. Holtz. He made an error of judgment and died by accident. End of story."

"But you just accused two people yourself," I said. "You really think this was an accident?"

Instead of answering, Dr. Marquez sniffed the earwax, wrinkled his nose, then flicked the wax across the room, where it stuck to the wall. "Let's talk about *you*, Dashiell. Why do you continue to insist there's a conspiracy at work?"

I sighed. Dr. Marquez had regained his composure. I wasn't going to get any more out of him. Now I'd be stuck talking about my feelings for the next hour.

Although I *had* pried two new leads out of him. Which was very unsettling. A day before, I'd thought that everyone at MBA had loved Dr. Holtz. Now, everywhere I looked, I uncovered more people with a grudge against him—any one of whom might have wanted him dead.

Excerpt from *The Official Residents' Guide to Moon Base Alpha*,
© 2040 by National Aeronautics and Space Administration:

ASSEMBLY

Although MBA is equipped so that all lunarnauts have multiple ways of communicating with one another—e-mail, phone, Com-Link, etc.—sometimes the best way to disseminate information is still the good, old-fashioned group meeting. Therefore, on the first Monday of every month, a mandatory assembly will take place in the rec center for all lunarnauts over age 18. Said meetings will be run by the moon-base commander (unless he or she assigns someone else that duty) and shall cover any topics deemed necessary. If there is something you would like discussed with the group, please submit it to the MBC several days ahead of time.

In addition, the MBC has the right to call additional meetings whenever he or she deems necessary—and for whatever residents he or she deems necessary as well. In these cases, the assembly should be considered mandatory for all whose presence is requested.* Furthermore, if there is a group of lunarnauts whom you would like to call an assembly for, please submit your request to the MBC at least seven days in advance for scheduling purposes. And remember: Everyone enjoys an assembly far more if the person leading it is organized and enthusiastic and doesn't waste their time, so please conduct yours accordingly.

---

* Except in the case of severe illness.

IMPOSSIBLE TRAVEL

Lunar day 189

Afternoon

The memorial service was held for Dr. Holtz that afternoon. Attendance was mandatory.

The Sjobergs didn't show up anyhow.

Everyone else came, though. Even the kids were asked to be there, so the rec room was unusually crowded. There were so many people we'd had to bring extra InflatiCubes from our rooms—and some of us still didn't have a place to sit. I had to stand in the back with Kira. Unlike the other funerals I'd been to before, this one was weirdly casual. No one had anything formal to wear on base. Instead we all looked like we were dressed for a Sunday barbecue.

Although lots of people had been asked to speak about Dr. Holtz, Nina ran the proceedings, which was probably a mistake. Her speech about Dr. Holtz was merely a flat, emotionless laundry list of everything he had done in his life. And I mean *everything*. Short of what he ate for breakfast every day, it didn't sound like any fact had been left out. I could barely keep my eyes open—and I wasn't alone. The little kids passed out within a few minutes. Most of the adults were struggling to stay awake as well. Dr. Howard was slumped against the wall, unconscious, his tongue lolling out of his open mouth.

My parents were up front. They had to be, as Mom was going to speak. Violet was curled up in Dad's lap, snoring softly.

"In 1998," Nina droned, "Dr. Holtz published his first paper in the *International Journal of Astrophysics and Space Science*, concerning the effects of long-term spaceflight on the human intestinal tract . . ."

Kira leaned over to me and whispered, "I have to tell you something about Dr. Holtz."

Before answering, I glanced around to make sure no one was paying attention to us. It seemed disrespectful to talk during the memorial—but listening to Nina one more minute was going to put me to sleep, and that wasn't particularly reverent either. Besides, we were a good distance away from everyone else. "What?" I whispered back.

"I had an idea for a lead this morning. I figured I could

hack the computer and check MBA's phone logs for the night Dr. Holtz died to see who he was talking to when you overheard him in the bathroom."

If I hadn't been in the middle of a funeral, I would have smacked my forehead. NASA certainly would have kept a log of all phone calls made at the base. I couldn't believe I hadn't thought to check it myself. "And? Did you do it?"

"Well, I tried, but . . . there's no record of Dr. Holtz making a call at two thirty that night. In fact, there's no record of *anyone* making a call at any time around then."

I frowned, concerned. "That's not possible. I *heard* him. Someone must have erased the call logs."

"That's what I figured. And who do you think has the authority to do that?"

I looked toward the front of the room. "Nina."

"Exactly."

Nina was still delivering the eulogy without any passion whatsoever. "Dr. Holtz followed his landmark work on the digestive system with a detailed analysis of how zero-gravity travel affects the spleen . . ."

I said, "Although if you and Roddy can hack the computer, there are probably other people who could have done it too—and they could have tampered with the call logs."

"True," Kira admitted. "So have you come up with any leads besides Nina?"

"Plenty."

"Who?"

I glanced around again. Chang Hi-Tech and Dr. Marquez were both close enough to overhear us. Neither appeared to be eavesdropping, but they could have merely been pretending not to. "I can't go into it right now. But what I really need help with is finding Dr. Holtz's phone."

Kira nodded. "Have you figured out how to get into his residence?"

"No, but I'm pretty sure it isn't there anyhow."

Kira's eyes suddenly lit up with excitement. "Maybe the evidence on it is the call from the bathroom the other night! Maybe he recorded it—so we'd know who he was talking to—because he knew someone would erase the call logs."

"Maybe," I agreed. "Of course, that doesn't do us any good if we can't find the phone." I suddenly got the feeling someone was watching us and cased the room. Everyone was still doing their best to listen to Nina and stay awake— except Roddy. Even though he was sitting in the third row, he was facing backward, staring right at us. Or really, he was staring at Kira.

Kira noticed him too, then quickly averted her eyes.

Roddy broke into a big, wolfish smile. He slicked back his hair and, even though Nina was speaking, hopped to his feet and slipped out of his row.

"Uh-oh," I said.

"What's he doing?" Kira asked, keeping her eyes down.

"Coming our way."

"Why?"

"Um . . . I guess because he likes you."

At the front of the room Nina droned on. "Eventually, Dr. Holtz completed the first significant analysis of how spaceflight affected pregnancy and subsequent generations of many species, including rats, mice, and cockroaches . . ."

Roddy sauntered back to where Kira and I were standing. "Hey, there," he whispered, in what he probably thought was a suave tone. "What are you guys doing back here?"

"Nothing," Kira told him.

"Doesn't look like nothing to me," Roddy said. "Were you talking about me?"

"No," I said. "We were talking about Dr. Holtz—"

Roddy turned to Kira, ignoring me completely. "How'd those codes I gave you work out? You find what you needed?"

"Yes, thanks." Kira shrank back from Roddy, looking a bit uncomfortable.

"You ever need anything else like that, let me know." Roddy grinned. "I know the computers here inside and out. It's not like there's anything else to do in this crummy place."

"This place isn't that crummy," Kira replied.

"Give it a few weeks," Roddy told her.

"We're on the *moon*," Kira reminded him. "Have you forgotten how amazing that is? Every kid back on earth is jealous of us. We're going to go down in history. Someday, when humans are traveling to other galaxies, they're going to look back at us and be thankful for the first steps we took for them."

Roddy laughed. "You think we're going to travel to other galaxies? Honestly?"

Behind Roddy's back I shook my head at Kira, warning her not to get Roddy started on one of his rants. I'd heard the one about space travel a dozen times already.

Kira ignored me, though. "Of course," she said. "Someday."

"Fat chance," Roddy told her. "We're not even close to interstellar travel, and we never will be. Right now the fastest spacecraft humans have ever built travels at one hundred sixty thousand miles per hour. At that rate it'll still take a decade just to get past Pluto. The closest star to us, Proxima Centauri, is four and a quarter light years away. It would take us seventeen thousand years to get there. *Seventeen thousand years!* That's equal to all of human civilization, from the cavemen to now. Just to get to some rock that, for all we know, might be even worse than this place." Roddy folded his arms across his chest proudly. He probably figured Kira would be impressed by his knowledge.

Instead she was annoyed at him for picking a fight with her. Now she lashed into him. "Two hundred years ago, people thought that humans living on the moon was impossible. A hundred years ago, no one had even *landed* on the moon. Or even imagined the Internet. Or smartwatches. Or virtual reality. Or evaporators. You have no idea what humans will invent in the next century."

"It won't be warp-speed travel," Roddy told her. "That's a pipe dream."

Meanwhile Nina was still slogging through Dr. Holtz's accomplishments. "As we moved further into the twenty-first century," she was saying, "Dr. Holtz began to focus his research on the lower end of the human digestive tract . . ."

Nearby, Chang lost the battle against sleep and toppled, unconscious, onto the floor.

Everyone looked his way. Nina frowned but soldiered on, unfazed. "His work on the low-gravity toilet was a blessing to us all."

I noticed Zan Perfonic was standing on the far side of the room in a clump of temps. She gave me a barely perceptible nod, then returned her attention to Nina.

Meanwhile Roddy was still pressing his case against space travel. "By the way, that seventeen thousand years? That's only to get to the closest possible planetary system. It'd more likely take twice that—at least—to get to anything resembling earth.

And for all we know, we'll show up on that place and find out it's covered with seas of flesh-eating acid and inhabited by brain-sucking leeches. Whoopee. That'll be fun."

"I don't want to talk about this right now," Kira said.

"Why?" Roddy flashed his wolfish grin again. "Because I'm destroying your argument?"

"No," Kira snapped. "Because we're at a funeral, you nimrod."

"So let's go somewhere else." Roddy waggled his eyebrows suggestively, completely unaware that Kira was annoyed with him. "If you want, I can help you hack the system again."

Kira wormed away from him and sidled up to me. "Not now. We can't skip out on the memorial."

"Why not?" Roddy asked.

"It's mandatory," Kira said. "I don't want to get in trouble for blowing it off."

"Who's gonna notice?" Roddy waved a hand to the crowd. "Everyone's here. In fact, it's the perfect time to hack the system. No one's paying attention to security right now."

I snapped to attention. Roddy had a good point. If someone was going to get up to no good, this was the perfect time to do it. I scanned the room, taking everyone in, suddenly thinking there was something wrong I had missed before.

"I don't want to miss this," Kira told Roddy. "I liked Dr. Holtz."

"So did I," Roddy sighed, "but this is lame. Nina's so boring she could lull a Restless Venusian Flugleworm to sleep."

"Other people are going to speak soon," Kira said.

"Not soon enough," Roddy muttered.

I realized what was wrong in the room. Everyone on base *hadn't* gathered there. One person was missing. "Do you guys see Daphne?" I asked.

Kira and Roddy quickly turned their attention back to the funeral.

"She must be here," Roddy said. "Daphne never misses an assembly."

"Well, I don't see her," Kira said. "Where do you think she is?"

"I don't know," I told them. "But I think we'd better find out."

Excerpt from *The Official Residents' Guide to Moon Base Alpha*,
© 2040 by National Aeronautics and Space Administration:

VIGILANCE

As a lunarnaut, you will be part of the first community of humans to ever live on a celestial body besides earth. While this is certainly exciting, please keep in mind that, as pioneers of lunar living, you may encounter the occasional problem. Therefore, we ask that every lunarnaut—no matter what your age—be extremely alert for any sign of trouble. Keep your eyes peeled and your ears tuned! If you notice *anything* that seems wrong, report it to the base commander at once. Don't be shy. There is no shame in reporting something that turns out to be a false alarm. We have taken every precaution to make sure that MBA is the safest, most durable building ever constructed, but in the very unlikely chance that something *does* go wrong, a vigilant crew is the best defense against disaster!

SKULLDUGGERY

Lunar day 189

Afternoon

Roddy didn't bother making an excuse to leave
the memorial service. He just scurried right out the door.
Kira was close on his heels, excited to investigate.

I held back, though. If Daphne was the killer—which
was hard to believe, but still possible—then she'd be dangerous. I tried to get Zan Perfonic's attention without being too
obvious about it, waving at her.

She looked my way—but so did several other people. So
much for not being obvious.

I pointed out the door, trying to indicate it was urgent.

Wait, Zan mouthed.

"Dash!" Kira hissed from the hallway. "C'mon!"

I reluctantly stepped out of the room, hoping Zan would follow. Kira was waiting in the hall, but Roddy was nowhere to be seen.

"Where is he?" I asked.

"He ran on ahead," Kira told me.

"Why didn't you stop him?"

"What am I supposed to do? Tell him we suspect her in Dr. Holtz's death?" Kira paused. "*Is* she a suspect in Dr. Holtz's death?"

"I don't know," I admitted. "But she's definitely up to something."

"Then maybe we should find her before Roddy does and messes everything up."

I glanced back into the rec room. Zan was still watching me, but she didn't seem comfortable leaving the service yet. She hadn't taken a step toward the door.

"All right," I said.

"He went this way." Kira bounded toward the main air lock. She tried to go quickly, but she was still having trouble in low g, so she flew too high and nearly banged her head on the catwalk.

I caught her leg, yanked her back down, and helped her along. We hooked right through the staging area and quickly came upon Roddy. He was flattened up against the wall of the administrative offices, doing his best to stay out of sight. Kira and I stopped in our tracks. Roddy pointed through the office window and mouthed, *In there.*

I gingerly took a few steps forward until I could see through the office window. Sure enough, Daphne was on the computer. She was typing frantically, bringing up page after page of information, pausing every few moments to touch her watch to the screen and download something. She certainly wasn't supposed to be there. She had the same look that Violet always has when she's sneaking candy without permission.

I was about to step back, out of Daphne's range of sight, when Roddy sneezed.

It wasn't a tiny sneeze either. It was a great big snot-blaster. In the otherwise quiet hallway, Roddy might as well have clashed two cymbals together.

Daphne turned from the computer, saw me through the window, and shrieked.

This startled Roddy, who shrieked as well.

Daphne clutched her heart in shock. "Holy cow! You guys almost scared me to death!"

Kira opened the office door and asked, "What are you doing in here?"

Daphne looked from Roddy to me to Kira, desperation in her eyes. She quickly tried to come up with a lie—and failed. "I'm . . . uh . . . I'm . . . Oh, fiddlesticks. I can't keep this up any longer. I'm a spy."

"*You?*" I couldn't contain my surprise. It was impossible to envision Daphne as a spy. A kindergarten teacher, yes. Or someone who ran a bakery. But a spy?

"Not like for the CIA or anything," Daphne said quickly. "I'm a corporate spy."

"You mean, for a company?" Kira asked.

Daphne nodded, then flushed in embarrassment. "For Maximum Adventure."

"The tourism company?" Roddy screwed up his face in confusion. "Why? They're already running the tourism here."

"They want to open their own hotel on the moon," Daphne admitted, "so instead of bringing up just one family of billionaires at a time, they can bring up lots of them."

"How long have they been planning this?" Kira asked.

"Years." Now that her secret was out, Daphne seemed very relieved, like a weight had been lifted off her. She'd obviously been keeping everything bottled up, and now it spewed out of her. "They've suspected all along that MBA wouldn't really be the perfect vacation place—and now that the Sjobergs are so upset, they're worried all the others they have lined up to come here will start backing out. They've wanted to build a *real* resort here all along. With nice beds and good food and masseuses and low-gravity sports and stuff like that."

"What are you doing for them?" I asked.

"Getting information," Daphne replied. "About how certain systems work. Like the evaporators and the heating and stuff like that."

"You're not *getting* information," Roddy corrected. "You're *stealing* it. NASA spent billions of dollars developing those systems and now you're going to give it all away?"

Daphne hung her head in shame. "You're right. This is bad. Really, really bad. It's just that when Maximum Adventure approached me, they didn't make it *sound* bad. I mean, no one was going to get hurt. And to be honest, I really needed the money. This gig doesn't pay all that well. I could have made ten times what I'm getting here if I'd stayed back on earth and worked for a private robotics company."

Kira asked, "Then why'd you come?"

"Why did any of us?" Daphne replied. "To go to the moon! To make history! And when Maximum Adventure offered me the money, I figured I could have it both ways: live here *and* cash out. But it's been terrible. Maximum Adventure has asked me to do far more than I thought they would. And I've hated living a lie. Just hated it. I like everybody here so much, and I've been going behind all your backs all this time. Look at me! I loved Dr. Holtz, and here I am, skipping out on his memorial to do this dirty work."

"To be honest, you're not missing much," I said.

Daphne heaved a huge sigh. "I can't believe I'm telling you all this. I'm the worst spy in the world."

"Pretty much," Roddy agreed. "We're only kids and you cracked like an egg."

Daphne laughed. "I know. But it just feels so good to tell someone. I've always hated lying. And now I've had to tell the biggest lie of my life for months." She paused as something occurred to her. "Please don't tell anyone."

"We can't lie for you," Kira said.

Daphne looked horrified. "No! That's not what I meant! I meant that *I* should tell everyone what I've done, not you. I've lied long enough. It's time for me to be honest. I'll do it right after the memorial is over."

I looked to Kira and Roddy. It seemed like all of us should be really upset at Daphne, but I certainly didn't feel that way, and the others didn't seem to either. Daphne was simply too nice—and she seemed upset enough at herself for the four of us. "All right," I said.

"We should get back," Kira added. "Nina's probably almost done with her eulogy by now."

"I wouldn't bet on it," Roddy grumbled.

I started back toward the rec room. "Still, I shouldn't miss my mom's eulogy. She worked really hard on it."

Kira began to follow me. However, Roddy stayed rooted to his spot, staring Daphne down.

"You coming?" he asked.

"In a few minutes," Daphne told him. "There's one more thing I need to take care of."

I stopped in my tracks. I liked Daphne, but I didn't completely trust her anymore. "What?"

Daphne put her hand over her heart. "It's nothing for Maximum Adventure, I swear. I'm not even going to send them the files you caught me swiping just now. But while I was doing that, I noticed something strange in the robot log from two nights ago, and I want to follow up on it before I forget."

Kira and I shared a look, the same idea occurring to us at once.

"You mean, the night Dr. Holtz died?" Kira asked.

"Yes." Daphne had turned back to the computer. She wiped away several windows until she came to a log sheet filled with dates and times. "It's probably nothing important. You should get back to the memorial."

I returned to the door of the office. "What was strange?"

Daphne scanned through the log. "Well, as you know, there are hundreds of robots at work here, especially at night. They run all sorts of maintenance tasks while we're asleep: calibrating the evaporators, checking the seals on the exterior of the base for oxygen leaks, cleaning the solar arrays, and so on. They work in carefully timed shifts, so they're not all bumping into one another out there and screwing each other up. The computer logs all their entry and exit times, so I can tell if there's a problem with any of them. Like, if I see that a solar-panel robot is taking longer than usual, I know it might be time to run some maintenance; it probably has moon dust built up in its joints or something. But instead of the usual three hundred sixteen robots two nights ago, the log shows there were three hundred *seventeen*."

Kira and I shared another intrigued look.

Roddy kept his eyes locked on Daphne, suspicious. Now that he'd busted her for spying, it was like he imagined himself to be the base police force. "Why are you only noticing this now? Aren't you supposed to check the logs every morning?"

Daphne sighed. "Yes. But as you might recall, there was a lot going on here yesterday."

"What happened yesterday?" Roddy asked.

I smacked him on the back of the head. "Dr. Holtz died, you moron."

"Oh yeah," Roddy said.

Daphne said, "With all the commotion, I forgot all about checking the robot logs."

Kira asked, "Do you know what the extra robot was?"

"Not yet." Daphne kept scrolling through the log. "But it shouldn't take long to find out. . . . Aha! Here we go!"

Daphne pointed at the screen triumphantly, then looked surprised. "That's weird."

"What?" Kira and I asked at once.

"I was expecting that one of the maintenance robots had glitched," Daphne told us. "That instead of going out once, it went twice. But according to this, a drone went out."

"What's a drone?" Kira inquired.

"A robot we send out for a specific task," Daphne explained. "The maintenance robots do the same thing all the time, day after day. But often we need to handle something more precise. The biologists want a soil sample, so we send out a drone with a drill. Or the geologists want to map a specific crater, so we send out a flying drone to scan it. The thing is, not just anyone can send a drone out. In fact, I'm the only one authorized. Other people are allowed to send them, but it's supposed to be cleared with me." Daphne's fingers were tap-dancing on her keyboard, bringing up more and more information on the suspicious robot.

"What kind of drone was this?" I asked. "Where did it go?"

"And when did it go out?" Kira added.

"It was a rover," Daphne replied. "It went to Solar Array Two, panel thirty-six-B. And it went out at five fifteen in the morning."

"Who sent it?" Roddy asked.

Daphne stopped typing and stared at the computer, shocked. "According to this, *I* did. But I didn't. Which means someone here swiped my command code."

I stepped back from the office, not wanting her to see my face, afraid I couldn't control my excitement—because I had a very good idea who'd sent the probe out.

Dr. Ronald Holtz.

Excerpt from *The Official Residents' Guide to Moon Base Alpha*, © 2040 by National Aeronautics and Space Administration:

THE LUNAR SURFACE

The surface of the moon is deceptive. While it is certainly an amazing, beautiful, and serene place, it is also the harshest environment humankind has ever lived in. In direct sunlight the temperature is 260 degrees Fahrenheit. And yet the moment the sun goes down, the temperature will almost immediately drop to 240 degrees below zero: cold enough to instantly freeze a man to death. In addition, there is no oxygen. Of course, your personal space suit can protect you against all this—temporarily—but keep in mind that, should your suit not be put on properly, the lunar surface can kill within seconds.

For this reason, access to the lunar surface is extremely restricted. Children are prohibited from venturing outside MBA unless an emergency has compromised the safety of the base. As for adults: Unless you have express permission from NASA *and* the base commander, you should never venture onto the lunar surface. And even if you believe you have good reason to go, analyze your options carefully. If your task can be performed by a robot rather than a human, send the robot. And if you absolutely must venture onto the surface, never *ever* go by yourself. Always go with a partner. Check your suits multiple times before passing through the air lock. Don't wander too far from MBA. And exercise extreme caution. Let's not spoil our beautiful moon by having a tragic accident on its surface!

MOONWALK

Lunar day 189

Evening

The way I figured it, Dr. Holtz had sent the robot out to hide his phone somewhere around panel 36B in Solar Array 2. After all, the robot was dispatched shortly before Dr. Holtz stepped through the air lock. Who else besides him (except whoever had forced him to go outside) would have been awake at that time? And it was the perfect place to hide something. If Dr. Holtz's killer suspected he'd hidden evidence somewhere, they'd most likely search the base—but not outside it. When I explained my theory to Kira later, she admitted that not only did it make sense, but she'd been thinking the same thing.

There was only one problem: Getting the phone wouldn't be easy.

The surface of the moon is deadly. Therefore Kira and I—as well as every other kid on base—were banned from going out onto it.

Despite this, Kira was still eager to go. "It was amazing out there yesterday," she told me. This was an hour after we'd confronted Daphne. The memorial was over; everyone else's speech about Dr. Holtz had been much shorter than Nina's. (Mom's had been the most touching by far.) Now Kira and I were huddled in a corner of the staging area while most everyone else mingled in the rec room. Kira asked, "Didn't you think it was incredible when you were on the surface?"

"Of course," I replied, although the truth was, since it had been six months since I'd trudged from the rocket to the air lock, my memory of it had faded greatly. After all, the walk had only taken a few minutes and there had been lots of distractions.

"So let's go," Kira said. "It won't take more than ten minutes to get to the solar array."

"This isn't like sneaking behind the scenes at the art museum or the zoo," I warned. "This is dangerous."

"Not if we're careful. It's perfectly safe out there with our suits on."

"Dr. Holtz just *died* out there with his suit on."

"Because someone forced him to go out with it on wrong. Someone who's still on the loose here in the base, because the evidence against them is out there." Kira pointed out the air lock in the direction of Solar Array 2.

"That's only a guess," I said.

"Well, it's a *good* guess." Kira gave me a frustrated stare. "I can't believe you're trying to weasel out of this. I thought you were going stir-crazy in this place."

"I am."

"So? Think how awesome it would be to get outside again, even for just a few minutes. There's no good reason we're not allowed out there. It's just a stupid rule that ought to be broken."

"It's not stupid," I protested. "And if we break it, we're going to get caught. We'll end up in big trouble."

"Not if we find Dr. Holtz's phone," Kira argued. "We'll be heroes."

I sighed and looked out through the air lock window. Kira was right. I *did* want to go out there again. And I didn't want to wait another two years and six months until my return rocket home to do it. But it was far more dangerous than Kira seemed to understand. Or she was far more reckless than I'd realized.

"There might be another way to get the phone," I said.

"You mean like sending a robot?" Kira asked.

"No. I don't know how to do that, and we can't ask Daphne to help." I looked down the hall, to where Daphne was standing with my parents and Chang.

Daphne had already revealed her secret to everyone. As she'd promised, she'd told Nina right after the memorial, and word had spread quickly. Nina wasn't happy, of course, and told Daphne there'd be some punishment, but everyone else seemed okay about it. After all, Daphne was probably the most-liked adult on the base. The fact that she'd owned up to her mistake and seemed genuinely ashamed only seemed to make everyone like her even more. My father and Chang were teasing her about it at the moment, humming the James Bond theme and calling her Special Agent Merritt.

Kira asked, "So what's the other option, then?"

"We get an adult to do it."

Kira looked annoyed. "Who? Your parents?"

"No," I said. "They wouldn't break the rules like that. And besides, they still think Dr. Holtz was crazy."

"Then who? We can't ask *my* dad. He'd get lost out there and we'd never see him again."

"I can't tell you." I knew Zan was the right person to approach about this. She was an adult and she was determined to find out who'd killed Dr. Holtz. She'd be thrilled to hear I'd learned where the phone was hidden—and she probably had all the security clearance she needed to go out onto the lunar surface. But she'd also made it extremely clear I couldn't tell anyone about our collaboration, no matter how much I wanted to.

"What are you talking about?" Kira demanded. "Don't you trust me?"

"Of course."

"Then why can't you tell me who you're going to?"

"I just can't," I said.

Kira gave me a long, hot stare. "Fine. Whatever. But if this secret friend of yours says no, then we go, okay?"

"They won't say no."

"But if they do . . . we go. Tonight, after everyone's gone to sleep. There's no time to waste. Whoever killed Dr. Holtz is going to find out about the robot soon enough."

"Sure," I said. "We'll go tonight."

"You promise?" Kira stuck out her hand.

I shook it. "I promise." I fully meant it. I just didn't think I'd have to.

I never got to talk to Zan Perfonic. I *saw* her. The first time, she was standing with a bunch of scientists after the memorial service. The second time, she was at dinner in the mess with the other temps. And both times she saw me, too. After the memorial, I signaled that I desperately needed to talk to her. She mouthed, *Not now*, so I backed off, expecting her to come around sooner or later, but she didn't.

So when we were in the mess, I decided to be a little more direct. I started across the room toward her, intending to approach her directly. When Zan saw me coming, though, she reacted with such alarm that I stopped dead. Behind the backs of everyone at her table, she shook her head wildly, panic in her eyes.

I signaled again that we needed to talk.

I know, Zan mouthed. *I'm sorry.*

I started to signal that this was really, really urgent, but all the temps at her table were staring at me now like I was nuts. So I backed down and headed off to get dinner, hoping now that Zan knew I was desperate to talk to her, she'd come find me.

But that didn't happen.

This was incredibly frustrating. I'd found our biggest lead so far—and Zan couldn't make the time to hear it? I understood that we needed to keep our alliance a secret, but it seemed that secrecy was now jeopardizing the entire purpose of our investigation.

I spent an hour trying to chill inside my residence after dinner, figuring Zan would swing by, and after that I went out and combed the base in search of her. I found everyone I *didn't* want to see—Nina, Dr. Marquez, the entire Sjoberg clan—but not Zan. After a dozen loops of the base, I had no choice but to conclude that she didn't want to be found.

I couldn't wait for her anymore. Kira was right about there being no time to waste. If we had figured out that Dr. Holtz had sent the robot to the solar array, his killer would probably figure it out soon as well. And when they did, they'd go right for the evidence.

I sent Kira a text: *We're on for tonight.*

She responded within seconds. *1 am.*

I reluctantly returned to my room and spent the rest of the evening trying to act normal around my family, hoping Zan would decide to throw caution to the wind and show up at our door. I talked to Riley in Hawaii for a bit, pretending everything was fine, then finally got around to making my video log about Dr. Holtz. I wasn't that pleased with it—it was kind of dull, just saying that Dr. Holtz was a nice man and that I'd miss him—but Mom and Dad both said it was perfect. I turned in when everyone else did, acting like I was tired when I was actually buzzing on adrenaline. I tried to read in bed but couldn't concentrate.

Zan never showed.

I slipped out of my residence at one a.m. on the nose. Kira was already in the staging area, pacing like a lion in the zoo.

She brightened when she saw me. "I was worried you were gonna chicken out," she whispered.

"I'm right on time," I told her.

She started to say something else, but I put a finger to my lips. The moon base was deathly silent at night. Even our softest whispers carried.

Kira nodded understanding and opened the storage unit where the kids' space suits were kept.

The suits had been custom-made for us solely so we could get from the rocket to the moon base and back. Each had cost millions of dollars for about twenty minutes of use. Or at least NASA *hoped* we'd only use them for twenty minutes—because the only other reason for them would be an emergency that required us to evacuate MBA. Which is why the suit storage unit isn't locked. (No one has ever told me what we're expected to do on the surface of the moon after all our air runs out. It seems to me that if something really went wrong at MBA, suiting up and evacuating to the lunar surface would only postpone our deaths. But maybe NASA figures that, at the very least, we'd be happy to go outside.)

MBA has mandatory practice emergency drills once a month to keep our evacuation routine well rehearsed. Due to this, I knew how to get my suit on quickly. Even faster than Kira, who'd worn hers just the day before. In the early days of space travel, astronauts had to wear multiple layers of insulation, so suiting up could take several minutes. Now-adays the suit itself is perfectly insulated, which means the person inside is much less constricted. I pulled on the outer shell, stepped into my boots, clamped my helmet, and pulled on my gloves in less than two minutes. Since we wouldn't be gone that long, I opted not to wear the astronaut diaper, which was designed so that anyone who has to be on the lunar surface for a good stretch of time won't have to return to the base to use the bathroom. Then I sealed all the connections and checked them again. And again. And again. Then I had Kira do it for me.

I had no intention of being the second person in history to die on the moon.

I inspected Kira and found she was suited properly as well.

Since my suit had barely been worn, it still smelled like a new car on the inside. I flipped on the fan vent so the glass of my helmet wouldn't fog up. Given our position at the pole, the sun was still out even now, so we both lowered the reflective visors; without them, in the sun's direct heat, undimmed by any sort of atmosphere, our heads would cook like potatoes in an oven. There were radios inside the helmets, so we could now talk to each other without the whole base hearing us.

"Testing, testing," Kira said. It sounded like she was

right next to me, speaking directly into my ear. "Can you hear me?"

"Yes," I replied. "Can you hear me?"

"Perfectly. Let's go!" Kira clapped her hands in anticipation.

We headed for the air lock. Normally, a security door is controlled by a thumb or retina sensor so only certain people can open it. However, neither of those work very well when you're wearing space gloves and helmets, so this one has a large keypad instead. As kids, we weren't supposed to know the six-digit code that would open the air lock, but my parents had taught it to me months before, figuring I might need it in case of an emergency—and that they could trust me not to do anything stupid like head outside without their permission.

In truth, I figured that while heading onto the lunar surface was reckless, it wasn't *insanely* risky. Solar Array 2 wasn't far from the air lock, and I wasn't going solo. If all went well, Kira and I would only be outside ten minutes, if that.

I tapped in the code. The inner door of the air lock slid open.

Kira and I stepped inside and entered the same code on another keypad. The inner door slid closed.

There was a whoosh as the air lock repressurized to match the atmosphere of the lunar surface.

I looked to Kira. Even though she'd been outside only the day before, she was bouncing up and down on her toes in anticipation. While I couldn't see her face behind the reflective visor, she didn't seem to have the slightest bit of concern about what we were doing. I couldn't help thinking of Riley's dog back on earth, pacing at her kitchen door, barely able to wait to get out in the yard.

Kira turned to me impatiently. "C'mon. What are we waiting for?"

I entered the code again on the keypad for the outer door. It slid open.

Kira immediately bounded onto the lunar surface.

I followed her.

For some reason, I'd been thinking that after being cooped up inside for six months, it would physically feel strange to be outside. But it didn't. The suit increased my weight, so I didn't bound as far with each step, but other than that I felt exactly the same as I had inside the moon base.

But mentally it felt *very* different. Like I was an inmate paroled from jail. Or a zoo animal released into the wild. A sense of euphoria quickly came over me.

Kira was certainly experiencing it too, behaving even more enthusiastically. With the added weight of her suit, she seemed more comfortable in low gravity and quickly bounded ahead of me, springing as high as she could with each step, whooping with joy. "This is so awesome!" she cried. "Can you believe it? We're on the moon!"

I took a few more steps. With each one, a puff of white moon dust exploded below my boot. It was like walking across a massive plain of pancake mix.

Since there was no atmosphere outside, there was no sound from the surface, no crunch of my boots in the dust, though I probably wouldn't have heard it anyhow, given Kira's thrilled exclamations ringing in my helmet.

Several well-trod paths snaked through the moon dust from the air lock. The one we wanted veered right, then branched into two others. One of these went directly to the large white dome of the moon-rover garage, while ours continued straight, threading the gap between MBA and the garage, then banked left to circumvent the science pod.

As I took the turn, the robot arm came into view. I'd never seen it up close before. It was an impressive piece of machinery: an intricate combination of gleaming metal, pistons, and wires. Each of the three sections of the arm was more than three stories tall. They were connected with enormous ball-and-socket joints and folded up vertically, like the pincer of a massive praying mantis. The arm was attached to the lunar surface with a swivel, which allowed it to rotate 360 degrees and reach anything between the launchpad and the air lock. The hand was high above me, all four fingers and both thumbs clenched together in a gigantic fist.

"Dash? What are you doing?"

Kira's words caught me by surprise. I spun to find her well ahead of me, looking back my way.

"Sorry," I said. "I got distracted."

"I'll say," Kira teased. "Hey, check this out!" With that she leaped ahead, covering twenty feet with one bound. Then she crash-landed, tumbling onto her back. But she didn't seem to care. Instead she lay there, giggling, and made the lunar version of a snow angel.

Her enthusiasm was infectious. Even though our mission was serious, there was no reason I couldn't enjoy myself a bit. I cocked my legs and launched myself forward. The ground dropped away below me and I sailed well past the robot arm, almost to the end of the science pod, and landed in a great cloud of moon dust.

"There you go!" Kira cheered. "Wow. You practically went into orbit!" With that she got back to her feet and bounded off again.

I followed her. Springing across the lunar surface was more fun than I'd had in months. Exploring a real place was far better than any simulation the computers could cook up. Above us the stars gleamed, and the Milky Way was a gorgeous slash across the ink-dark sky. The earth shone brightly in the middle of it, a beautiful blue jewel. I found a patch of moon dust that had somehow remained pristine and, unable to resist, planted my feet right in it, making myself the first human to ever set foot on that spot.

The fun was short-lived, however. We were covering so much ground with each leap that we quickly reached Solar Array 2. Since it's on the western side of MBA, where there are no windows, I had never seen it before. It was startlingly large, a field of solar panels taking up significantly more space than the base itself. Each panel was five feet square, perched atop a tall metal post from which it could be angled directly at the sun. Currently, the panels were all were tilted southwest, sucking up so much solar energy that I could feel the heat from them as we came close.

"Daphne said the robot traveled to panel thirty-six-B," Kira said. "Any idea where that is?"

I looked over the array. There were more than a thousand panels. Thankfully, they were arranged in an orderly fashion, in perfectly spaced rows, like plants on a farm. I bounded to the closest support post. There was a number etched into the side: 29A. 28A was to my right; 30A was to my left.

"This way," I said, heading left, where the row of panels continued toward the edge of the blast wall that surrounded the launch pad. I returned to walking normally now, not wanting to accidentally bounce up into the solar panels and fricassee myself.

As expected, 36A was six panels down from 30A. And one row in sat 36B.

I glanced at the moon dust at the base of its post. It had been trampled by hundreds of footsteps over the months of installation and maintenance, but a more recent nonhuman track—two sets of treads—sliced across all the boot prints. "Look," I told Kira.

"Dr. Holtz's robot," she said. Even with her reflective visor down I could tell she was smiling.

"Looks like we're in the right place." I circled the post, looking for where the robot had set the phone.

Only the phone wasn't there.

"I don't see anything." Kira now sounded concerned.

"Maybe it blew away," I said.

"A whole phone? How? There's no wind here, brainiac."

"I know. But maybe when the rocket landed, the blast blew it somewhere."

Kira's helmet shifted back and forth as she shook her head. "No way. The blast wall is built to prevent that. Otherwise the rockets would blow moon dust all over the solar panels and mess them up."

I frowned, not feeling quite so super any more. We'd been so sure Dr. Holtz had sent the robot out, but now I wondered if we'd made a mistake. I scanned the area around post 36B, hoping to find some sign that we hadn't.

"Dash," Kira said. "There's something I have to tell you. Before we came out here tonight, I had a lot of time to kill. So I figured I'd search the computer files a little bit more."

My gaze fell on the tracks of the robot in the dust. Something struck me as significant about them. Although I knew Kira was trying to tell me something important, I couldn't help but focus on the tracks too.

"I decided to look for the footage from the bathroom the night you overheard Dr. Holtz in there," Kira went on. "Not to see you on the toilet or anything, I promise. Since the phone log had been erased, I was thinking that maybe if I could watch Dr. Holtz on the call, I could get some idea who he was talking to."

The tracks were from a small robot, I realized. That ruled out the maintenance ones, which tended to be quite large, as they often had to move heavy machinery. It was probably a small probe, which the scientists used more often. Mostly to take geologic samples.

Which meant it was built to dig.

I dropped to my knees and began brushing moon dust away from the base of the post for panel 36B.

Kira stopped talking. She dropped to her knees and started digging as well.

"Go on," I told her.

"Never mind," she said. "It might not be important."

I brushed aside another scoop of dust, and something gleamed in the hole. I plunged my hand inside. It was hard to grasp anything with the gloves, but I finally managed to do it.

A small, clear plastic bag had been buried in the hole. The kind of bag the scientists use to keep sterile samples in.

Dr. Holtz's phone was inside it.

"You found it!" Kira cheered. "All right!" She raised her hand for a celebratory high five.

I gave it to her, but even though I'd found the phone, I didn't feel nearly as thrilled as I should have.

Kira's voice had sounded far more relieved than excited. Like there was something she knew that I didn't.

"What did you find on the computer?" I asked.

"Nothing." Kira stood up and started walking. "Forget I mentioned it. We need to get back to the base."

I stood too, but I didn't follow her. "Tell me."

Kira turned back. "No. I shouldn't have even brought it up. I was rushing to look through stuff, so maybe I misunderstood what I saw."

"Which was . . . ?"

Kira motioned for me to follow her. "Come on. We've been out too long as it is."

I stayed put. "What did you see, Kira?"

She sighed heavily. In the speaker of my helmet it sounded like a hurricane in my ears. "Okay, I'll tell you, but you have to realize I might not be right about this. I wasn't even sure if I should mention it or not until I had time to go over everything again, but then we got here and it looked like Dr. Holtz hadn't hidden his phone here after all, so I started to think that, maybe, he *was* cracking up a bit."

"Why would you think that?"

"Because I found the footage from the bathroom." Kira came back toward me. "The footage of Dr. Holtz's conversation. The reason we couldn't find any record of his phone call in the logs was that he didn't make a phone call."

"That's not possible," I said. "I heard him."

"You heard him *talking* to someone," Kira corrected. "But he wasn't using his phone. I saw him."

"You mean someone else was in the bathroom with us?"

"No. I could see the entire room in the footage. There wasn't anyone else there."

I stared at Kira, wishing I could see her face rather than just a reflection of myself in her visor. "So he was just talking to himself? Like a crazy person?"

Kira's helmet nodded up and down.

I wanted to defend Dr. Holtz, to tell Kira that she certainly had to be wrong—but before I could, I spotted something in her visor's reflection.

Something else was moving on the lunar surface behind me. And it was moving fast.

"Look out!" I screamed, then dove. I slammed into Kira, knocking her flat.

A second later the massive hand of the robot arm crashed to the ground where we had just been. It came in with such speed that it sliced clean through the support post of solar panel 36A and landed hard enough to make the ground shake. The panel toppled and shattered, strewing glass all over the lunar surface.

"What was that?" Kira gasped. "A malfunction?"

"No," I told her. "Someone's trying to kill us!"

As if to prove me right, the robot arm reared up again, preparing for another attack.

Excerpt from *The Official Residents' Guide to Moon Base Alpha*, © 2040 by National Aeronautics and Space Administration:

EMERGENCY PREPAREDNESS

Although every precaution has been taken to make sure that MBA is as safe as any place on earth—if not safer—given the nature of the base's location on the moon, there is always the chance that an emergency might occur. Rest assured that MBA is equipped to withstand anything the solar system can dish out, be it a fire, solar flare, or meteor strike. However, in the unlikely event of an emergency, your safety will depend on your being prepared. So remember the three F.A.R. steps:

1) Familiarize yourself with all emergency systems and know how to use them.

2) Attend all monthly emergency preparedness sessions and evacuation drills.

3) Rehearse emergency procedures on a weekly basis—if not more often!

Familiarize. Attend. Rehearse. F.A.R. It's easy!*

---

* Actual emergency procedures and evacuation plans may not be easy for young children. All parents need to be prepared to handle their children's safety during emergencies.

BAD ROBOT

Lunar day 190

Possibly the last minutes of my life

"Run!" I ordered Kira.

At the exact same moment, she yelled at me to do the same thing. Her scream echoed so loudly in my helmet that my ears rang.

Meanwhile the robot arm was bizarrely silent as it rose above us. It was kind of like watching an action movie with the sound off—only I was in it. The arm stretched to its full hundred feet and the hand made a fist. A fist the size of a small car. Which then swung down toward us.

Kira and I were already moving.

In our fear we hadn't thought to coordinate. Each of us

went a different way. I bolted back the way we'd come, while Kira plunged deeper into the forest of solar panels.

The robot fist thudded down right where we'd been, shattering several more solar panels. Glass exploded into the air and sailed far and wide in the low gravity, the shards sparkling in the sunlight as they rained down around me.

"Where are you going?" Kira screamed at me.

"Back to the air lock!" I yelled. "Where are *you* going?"

"Where there's cover! You're right out in the open!"

She was right. There was nowhere for me to hide on the route to the air lock—and the robot could reach me anywhere on the way. I'd planned on outrunning it, but I'd forgotten something very important:

It's very hard to run on the surface of the moon.

I could only bound along, like I was in slow motion. It was like one of those nightmares where someone's coming after you, and no matter how hard you try to run, you can't. Only it was real.

And now that I'd made the decision, there was no way to double back. The robot arm reared up again between me and the solar panels, its giant fist blotting out the sun.

It was only about fifty yards from the solar array to the air lock. But despite my best attempts to run, I'd only covered a third of the distance.

On earth the sound of the robot arm would have told

me where it was—and whether it was going for me or Kira. On the stupid, soundless moon I had to watch it, and with a space suit on I couldn't just glance back over my shoulder. I had to turn my whole body, which wasn't exactly conducive to speed either.

Behind me the arm pivoted downward.

It was coming for me, not Kira.

I suddenly wished I'd worn that space diaper. Though somehow, despite the fear of being pounded into paste, I managed not to evacuate my bladder.

"Look out!" Kira cried.

I couldn't outrun the giant fist. I had to try to dodge it.

I watched as it arced downward, then sprang as it came in, using the low gravity to my advantage.

This time, however, whoever was controlling the robot had changed their attack. Instead of simply trying to squash me flat, the hand suddenly extended its fingers and swooped in sideways. It was like being slapped by King Kong. One of the huge metal digits caught me flush in the chest and I went flying.

I tumbled through the air, soaring so high that I cleared the rover garage. For a moment I feared I might actually break free of the moon's weak gravity and go into orbit. I found myself high enough to see the roof of MBA and the blinding panels of Solar Array 1 on the far side of the base.

But then, thankfully, I began to arc downward again. Gravity yanked me back and I face-planted on the lunar surface. In low gravity you don't come down that fast, but I still landed hard. Every part of my body felt like it had been punched at once, and the wind was knocked out of me. I skidded across the surface, leaving a deep trough through the moon dust, until I slammed helmet-first into a large rock, which stopped me dead.

There was a soft, terrifying clink inside my helmet.

I'd closed my eyes as I'd braced for impact. Now I opened them to have my worst fears confirmed.

The glass of my helmet had cracked.

A tiny web of fractures had appeared where I'd impacted the rock, looking like the divot a stone leaves in a windshield. But the cracks were spreading. My helmet wouldn't be able to take another hit. The glass would go—and I'd suffocate in seconds.

"Dash!" Kira's terrified voice rang inside my helmet. "Are you all right?"

I rolled over and took stock of where I was. The robot arm had knocked me thirty yards, so I was now on the opposite side of the air lock from where I'd started. The rover garage was between me and the field of solar panels; I could no longer see Kira over there.

By the garage, the robot arm reared up on its pivot

again. The hand swiveled back and forth, the palm angled at the ground.

I realized it was looking for me.

Whoever was controlling the robot had to watch me on the cameras, but the arm had swatted me so far I'd flown out of sight. There were several cameras mounted on the arm itself, though, and now my attacker was using them to scan the area to see where I'd landed.

The air lock wasn't too far away now, only a bit more than ten yards. Temptingly close. But I didn't run for it.

Instead I stayed where I was, not moving an inch.

The lunar surface was gray and white. My suit was gray and white—and it now had a layer of moon dust coating it. Hopefully, I'd blend right into the surface. I wasn't going to disappear completely, like a chameleon changing color, but on the monitors I'd be much harder to spot lying still than I would moving.

"Dash!" Kira screamed again. It sounded like she was crying. "Are you okay? Answer me!"

"I'm okay," I told her.

"Thank goodness! Where are you?"

"By the launchpad," I lied.

The robot hand immediately swiveled that way.

Which meant the killer was eavesdropping on our transmissions. But I'd figured as much. And now I'd diverted them and bought a few seconds.

There was another clink from my helmet. A small crack extended from the impact point, spreading across the glass like the fissure of a miniature earthquake.

I didn't have much time.

I sprang to my feet and tried to run for the air lock.

"Hold on!" Kira told me. "I'm coming to help you!"

"No!" I cried. "Stay where you are! Stay under cover! I'm fine! I'll send help for you!"

Of course I couldn't run at all. I only bounded slowly. But the air lock came closer.

And then I spotted something shimmering in the sun to my right.

I turned that way and saw the bag with Dr. Holtz's phone, lying in a patch of moon dust.

I'd tried my best to hold on to it as I'd flown through the air, but it had obviously slipped from my gloved fingers, probably when I crash-landed. It now lay only a few feet out of my path.

I tried to bank toward it and pick it up.

Only it wasn't so easy in low gravity. On earth the detour would have taken only a few seconds, if that. But it was much harder to change direction on the moon. I skidded in the dust once as I tried to stop my forward momentum, and again as I tried to grab the phone, squandering precious seconds each time.

I plunged my hand into the moon dust, fumbling for the phone.

"Dash!" Kira screamed.

I risked a look back at the robot arm.

It had spotted me—and was on the attack again.

It was hurtling my way, the palm open, only this time it was swooping around to nail me from the side. I figured that at the speed it was coming, one swat would send me sailing over the entire moon base like a home-run ball. I'd land in Solar Array 1 and fry to death on the panels.

I moved toward the air lock, but there was no way to outrun the arm.

However, I only wanted whoever was controlling it to *think* I was trying to outrun it.

I took one bound, then dug my heels into the lunar surface as hard as I could, bringing myself to a stop.

The arm had extended, trying to catch me right by the air lock.

Now I sprang in the other direction, diving for the lunar surface again.

The palm rocketed past my feet while the arm soared over me, close enough to clip the back of my helmet. The fingertips scraped the base hard enough to furrow the wall as they swept past. Whoever was controlling the arm tried to stop it, but now they had to fight the low-gravity inertia of the moon. They failed. The arm crashed into the rover garage.

The cracks spread farther across my helmet.

I scrambled back to my feet, spun around, and lunged for the air lock.

The arm had slammed into the garage so hard the wall had collapsed, and the arm was now tangled in the wreckage. It was jerking about, trying to wrest itself free. Pieces of the garage—and possibly the rovers—were tearing loose and flying away.

I reached the air lock. There was no keypad on this side, only a big red button clearly marked OPEN. There was no point making entry difficult from the outside, as there was no one else on the moon. I slammed my fist into the button.

The air lock slid open.

There was another red button beneath the first, in the event that the air lock was jammed. This one was marked ALARM.

I punched it as well.

The robot arm tore free from the garage, leaving a gaping hole. It then pivoted upward . . .

And suddenly froze. Whoever had been controlling it had abandoned the controls, probably frightened off by the alarm inside the base.

I leaped into the air lock and punched the red button on the inside.

The outer door slid shut.

A moment later the glass of my helmet shattered.

I felt the staggering heat of the lunar surface and held my breath, hoping it wouldn't be my last.

There was a blast of air as the air lock repressurized to match the atmosphere of the base. As it did, I could hear the alarm wailing through the inner door. The air was blessedly cool as well.

"Are you all right?" Kira asked again.

I tentatively inhaled. Oxygen filled my lungs. Even though this had happened a half a billion times before, it was still the greatest feeling of my life. I sighed with relief.

"I'm in the air lock," I told Kira. "And whoever was controlling the arm took off, so it's safe to come back now. Are you okay?"

"Yes. Just frightened. I've been hiding in the solar array the whole time. I'm sorry I didn't come help you—"

"Don't be. There was nothing you could do."

"I guess not." Kira still sounded guilty. "Okay. I'm on my way back."

I pressed another red button, which opened the inner air lock door.

Inside, the alarm was much louder, designed to ruin everyone's sleep and rouse them from bed. I glanced toward the robot control room. The door hung open; my attacker was long gone.

Nina was already up and out her door, perched at the edge of the catwalk. "You!" she yelled, glaring down at me. "What were you doing out there?"

"Just getting a little exercise."

Nina stormed down the stairs toward me. "You think that's funny? Well it's not! This is a serious violation of protocol!"

"Are we in trouble?" Kira asked through the radio.

"Big trouble," I told her.

"Maybe I'll stay out here a bit longer," she replied.

Behind Nina on the catwalk, our door flew open. My parents emerged, panic in their eyes. I figured they'd woken to the alarm and discovered I was missing. Dad had Violet in his arms. She actually seemed pretty excited by all the noise.

Mom and Dad spotted me and at once looked relieved and worried. They came down the stairs behind Nina, who was still chewing me out.

"Not leaving this base is the number one safety directive for every child here!" she shouted. "What were you thinking? Or were you even thinking at all? And what happened to your helmet? Are you aware how lucky you were not to have died out there?"

"Yes," I told her. "I'm very aware of that."

Nina reached the ground floor and stormed toward me,

flushed red in anger. "Then what possible reason did you have to go out there?"

"To get this." I held up Dr. Holtz's phone triumphantly. Only now that I had a moment to look at it, my sense of accomplishment quickly faded.

Somewhere, during the robot's attacks, the phone had been hit too. The glass was shattered and the casing was cracked almost in half.

The object I had just risked my life to get was destroyed.

Excerpt from *The Official Residents' Guide to Moon Base Alpha*, © 2040 by National Aeronautics and Space Administration:

EMERGENCY PREPAREDNESS (CONTINUED)

In the unlikely event of an emergency, it is imperative to respect the chain of command. The base commander has had far more training in emergency procedures than anyone else, has studied all possible crisis scenarios, and will be the primary liaison with Mission Control in the event of trouble. Therefore, in a state of emergency, any orders issued by the base commander must be followed immediately. Failure to do so will be considered mutinous behavior and will be punishable upon return to earth.

Should the base commander have been rendered unconscious, dead, or in any other way unable to carry out his or her duties, then the second in command will take over. Rest assured, though, that the chances of such an event occurring are exceedingly small. In all likelihood, your stay at MBA will be calm, relaxing and trouble free!

CORRUPTED EVIDENCE

Lunar day 190
Really early in the morning

There may be no better way to cause chaos at a
moon base than to set off the emergency alarm, rouse everyone from sleep, and then reveal that someone has just tried
to kill you with a giant robotic arm.

Nina was so apoplectic she didn't know what to get
angry about first. Instead she kept starting to yell about one
thing, then changing her mind and yelling about something
else. Within only thirty seconds she freaked out about my
irresponsibility, the wrecked rover garage, the shattered
solar panels, how expensive the robot was, and how I had
deliberately violated a direct order from her by pursuing my

investigation. At no point did it ever occur to her to ask how I was doing after my near-death experience.

However, my family was plenty concerned about me. My parents hugged me tightly and fawned over me, at once relieved to see that I was alive, annoyed that I'd done something so risky, and angry at Nina for how she was treating me. Violet's usual gleefulness had soured upon learning that I'd been in danger. She clung to me and cried while I tried to reassure her that the threat was over and everything was all right.

Meanwhile, around us in the staging area, the Moonies were all going nuts. Lars Sjoberg was his standard jerkwad self, yelling at everyone within earshot about the alarm, as though this were merely another instance of bad service at MBA, like a hotel wake-up call that had come too early. Daphne was devastated by how her precious robot had been used for evil—and severely damaged in the process. Some people, like Chang and Dr. Kim, were trying to make sense of what had happened, while others, like Roddy, were panicking and wanting to know if the alarm meant we had to evacuate the base. Even Dr. Howard was displaying emotion for the first time since he'd arrived. Once Kira returned through the air lock safely, he threw his arms around her and began sobbing. The only people who remained silent were Mr. Grisan, who was figuring out how to shut the alarm off, and Zan Perfonic, who hung back by the wall, studying everyone carefully and taking everything in.

Eventually, I got the chance to tell my story: how I'd gone out to retrieve Dr. Holtz's phone and been attacked, but the attacker had fled before I could see who it was, and the phone was now a total loss.

Chang took the phone from me and examined it closely. "Maybe not," he said. "Mind if I try to salvage something?"

I wasn't sure I could trust Chang, but no one else volunteered to help. I glanced at Zan and she nodded that she thought it was okay, so I handed over the evidence. Chang promised to stay within sight and went to work on it at the computer station in the control room.

Meanwhile Nina finally settled on one thing to be angry at: me. "Do you have any idea how much damage your reckless behavior has caused?" she demanded. "Millions of dollars for sure. Maybe billions!"

Mom placed herself between Nina and me, anger flaring in her eyes. "Dashiell's behavior didn't cause any of this! Whoever was controlling that robot did. So why don't you stop chewing him out and try to find whoever just tried to kill him?"

"Because for all I know, your son made the whole thing up!" Nina shot back.

"Oh, right," I said. "Kira and I decided to play with the

robot arm, destroyed it by accident, and then went outside to fake our own deaths to cover it up."

"I wouldn't put it past you," Nina snarled at me.

"Oh, for heaven's sake!" Dr. Howard yelled. "Give it a rest, Nina!"

His words caught everyone by surprise, because few of us had even heard Dr. Howard speak, let alone raise his voice. Every last Moonie stopped what they were doing and turned his way.

He was standing beside Kira now, still clutching her tightly, glaring at Nina. "We all know you're afraid of a scandal here, but there is now irrefutable evidence that there is a killer on the loose at this base! So stop pretending that Dr. Holtz's death might have been an accident and face the facts!"

It turns out, the second best way to cause chaos on a moon base is to reveal that one of the residents is a killer.

Everyone who had finally calmed down now went nuts again. Moonies ran off to lock themselves in their rooms, or demanded Nina explain why she'd covered up the crime, or pointed accusing fingers at who they thought had done it.

"I'll bet it was Lars!" Roddy announced, and half the other Moonies quickly agreed with him.

"This is an outrage!" Lars shouted. "I am sick and tired of being treated like a common criminal!"

"This sounds like a job for *Squirrel Force!*" Violet announced.

"Silence!" Nina roared. And when everyone kept talking, she added, "The next person I hear a peep out of gets thrown out the air lock!"

Everyone shut up.

"I have never covered anything up about Dr. Holtz's death," Nina informed us. "Until now, all evidence has indicated that he died due to reckless behavior and personal error. And as of this moment there is still no evidence that indicates otherwise. However, the Gibsons and Dr. Howard are correct. Someone on this base has caused some serious damage to our robotic arm and some of our facilities, most likely while Dashiell and Kira were on the lunar surface. Now, I intend to find whoever did this—and if their motives were, in fact, to bring harm to Dashiell and Kira, then I will see to it that they are prosecuted for what they have done. However, until that point, we are going to have order on this base! There will not be a witch hunt! So, for everyone's safety, I'm sending you all back to your rooms right now until further notice."

"You mean you're grounding us all?" Lars asked indignantly.

"I'm *ordering* you," Nina growled. "As is my right as base commander, per the bylaws of Moon Base Alpha, section seventy-eight, subheading A. Anyone who sees fit to violate that order will be locked in the medical bay with Dr. Holtz's corpse and held there until I see fit. Is that understood?"

Everyone nodded obediently and started back to their rooms.

As my parents reluctantly turned away, Chang whispered from the control room, "Not so fast."

He'd only wanted my family, the Howards, and Nina to hear. We all looked that way.

"I found something," he said. "It's not much, and it's in bad shape, but I'm guessing it's what Dr. Holtz wanted us to see."

Mom called to Dr. Brahmaputra-Marquez, "Ilina, can you take Violet back to your room for a bit?"

"Sure," she replied.

"Are we having a slumber party?" Violet asked, thrilled.

"Just for a little bit." Mom kissed Violet on the head and handed her off. Then she and Dad led me toward the control room. The Howards fell in beside us.

"Hold on now," Nina said. "I'm okay with the parents, but I don't think Dashiell and Kira need to be a part of this."

"I think they became a part of this when they nearly died getting the phone," Dad told her. "And frankly, I'm not about to let them out of my sight again with a killer on the loose. So why don't you just remove that stick from your rear end and let them see what they found?"

Nina steamed, but she didn't say another word.

As we filed into the control room, I caught sight of Zan, hanging back behind the other Moonies as they headed to their residences. She gave me a reassuring wink and, behind everyone's back, followed us to the control room. No one noticed her as she stopped outside the door, watching the proceedings inside.

Instead everyone was focused on Chang and the computer. He'd jury-rigged some wires to connect the phone to it.

"This phone is trashed," he told us. "We're talking terminally ill. The ports are wrecked, the wireless is blown, and most of the files bit it out there on the moon. However, between the computer and me we've managed to salvage something. Given our time constraints, with there possibly being a killer on the loose and all, I only focused on the most recent items stored, figuring those would be the most relevant. Turns out, Holtz recorded a video only thirty minutes before he went out the air lock."

A murmur of excitement rippled through the room.

"Well?" Nina demanded. "Show it to us."

"I'm about to," Chang told her. "But it's pretty corrupted. I tried to clean it up as much as possible, but it's still in lousy shape. Or at least the bit I've seen was. I didn't want to watch it all without you."

"Duly noted," Nina said. "Now run it."

"All right," Chang sighed. "You've been warned. Computer, play the footage."

"It would be my pleasure," the base computer replied.

A video sprang to life on the monitor before us. Only it didn't look much like a video at all. It looked like a great sea of static with an occasional image flashing for a split second. Not that any of the images seemed to matter. The few we could see were blurry or partially blocked, as though Dr. Holtz might have had the phone hidden somewhere—or perhaps cupped in the palm of his hand.

"I can't make out any of this," Nina griped.

"Doesn't matter," Chang told her. "What's important is the audio. I think Dr. Holtz only wanted us to hear this, not see it."

"Well, the audio's garbage too," Nina muttered.

She was right. What we could hear pitched back and forth between garbled speech and a loud static buzz that sounded like a nest of giant hornets.

"Give it a moment," Chang told her. "It gets clearer."

No sooner had he said this than the audio improved. Slightly. The voices were still terribly distorted, so it was impossible to recognize the speakers, but at least we could finally understand them.

It began in midsentence. We'd missed the beginning of the conversation.

". . . thought I might be seeing you this morning," some-one said.

"That's Dr. Holtz," Chang told us.

"Oh?" the other person asked. "And why's that?" Their distorted voice was several octaves too low. It made me think of what a rock might sound like if it were trying to speak.

"Who is that?" Mom asked.

Chang could only shrug in response.

"You might have fooled everyone else," Dr. Holtz said on the video, "but not me. I figured out what you were really here for shortly after we all got to the moon."

"And what might that be?" the other person asked coyly. With the distortion I couldn't even tell if it was a man or a woman.

"To keep an eye on us all," Dr. Holtz said. "Not for NASA, though I suspect they were forced to give their approval. My money's on the military."

The other person laughed mockingly. "Dr. Holtz, I think you're being a bit paranoid."

"Really? You've obviously been watching *me*. Why else would you be talking to me at five o'clock this morning?"

There was a brief pause. Then the other person said, "Touché."

"So what's the purpose of this visit?" Dr. Holtz asked.

"It seems you've discovered something important."

"Yes. Did you eavesdrop on my conversation in the bathroom this morning?"

The other person ignored the question. "What is it that's so amazing?"

Dr. Holtz hesitated for a moment, unsure whether to answer, but then his enthusiasm got the better of him. Even with his voice distorted, I could tell how excited he was. The news he'd been keeping inside just burst out.

"I've identified an alien life form," he said.

I gasped in astonishment. Practically everyone else in the control room did too. My parents' faces lit up with excitement.

Even the other person on the tape seemed caught by surprise. It was quite a while before they spoke again. "Confirmed?"

"Of course," Dr. Holtz replied. "Many times over. The evidence is concrete."

"Are we talking about microscopic life here? Unicellular? Some kind of bacteria or something?"

"No." Dr. Holtz's voice brimmed with excitement. "A complex life form. An *intelligent* life form. In fact, a life form far more intelligent than we are!"

Another wave of elation rippled through the control room. I was almost as amped on adrenaline from Dr. Holtz's news as I had been while fighting for my life.

The only person who didn't seem excited was the other person on the video. Their voice barely modulated, as though Dr. Holtz had just told them something routine, such as "I like bagels."

"How many of these extremely intelligent life forms have you encountered?" they asked.

"Only one."

"And have they made contact with any humans besides you?"

"Not that I'm aware of."

"Why you?"

"I don't know," Dr. Holtz said.

There was another pause. "I think you do," said the other person. "Don't lie to me, Ronald. This is extremely important."

"I know it's extremely important!" Dr. Holtz exclaimed. "It might be the most important event in all human history! Actual contact with intelligent life from another planet!"

"What other planet?"

Dr. Holtz didn't answer right away. Something about his visitor seemed to have put him on guard. "You'll find out soon enough, when everyone else does. I'm going to announce my findings to the base—and to NASA—this morning."

"No," the other person said menacingly. "You won't."

Beside me Kira shivered. Her eyes were wide with fear.

Dr. Holtz was taken aback too. "What are you talking about?"

"Your announcement isn't going to happen. The people of the world aren't prepared for something like this."

"Of course they are!" Dr. Holtz's voice sounded different now. I couldn't tell if he was angry or worried, though I would have bet on worried. "People have been hoping for a moment like this as long as there have been people!"

"No. They've been dreading it. Humans have never been prepared to meet the unfamiliar. Throughout our history, every time two cultures have encountered each other, it has resulted in war rather than peace. That's the root of all human conflict, thousands of years of bloodshed: us versus them. And that's just when people meet other people: people who are exactly like they are, save for the color of their skin or the language they speak or the god they worship. Can you imagine what would happen if humans learned that there really are other intelligent life forms out there? Ones who are smarter than us? Who know how to come to earth? There'd be a worldwide panic."

"I don't think that's true at all," Dr. Holtz replied. "I think the people of earth will be thrilled to hear the news."

"That's not a risk I'm willing to take," the other voice told him. With the distortion it sounded extremely ominous.

"Well, it's not your decision," Dr. Holtz said defiantly.

"It's mine. I'm revealing that I've made contact today—and there's nothing you can do to stop me."

"Oh, there is, Dr. Holtz," the other person said. "Believe me, there is. I have a lot of people at my disposal down on earth. And at this very moment a team of them is positioned outside your daughter's home."

Dr. Holtz gasped. Even with the distortion we could hear the fear in his voice. "You wouldn't dare!"

The video suddenly ended. There was a burst of static, and that was it.

Everyone turned to Chang. I could see shock and dismay on all their faces.

"Where's the rest of it?" Nina demanded.

"I don't know," Chang said. "Destroyed, I guess. We were lucky to get as much as we did."

"Lucky?" Nina snapped. "We've got garbage. We can't even tell who confronted Dr. Holtz!"

"But we know *someone* confronted him," Mom said. "And that to keep his discovery a secret, they forced him to go out the air lock."

"We can't even tell if the killer's a man or a woman," Nina groused. "And we don't know *how* they forced Dr. Holtz out—"

"They blackmailed him!" Dad cried. "You heard them! They threatened his family!"

"We don't know if that worked," Nina shot back.

"It would work for *me*," Mom snapped. "And Dr. Holtz is dead. What else do you need?"

"Uh, guys," Chang said, "I know we're all freaked out by the murder and everything, but . . . Dr. Holtz said he made alien contact! This is huge!"

"We don't have any proof of that," Nina said curtly. "Only Dr. Holtz's say-so. And as we're all aware, he might have been going insane."

Dad glared at her. "I think the fact that we have a murderer on tape proves that Dr. Holtz didn't wander out the air lock by accident."

"But it doesn't prove he wasn't crazy," Nina countered. "He could have merely imagined this alien contact and the killer mistakenly believed him. But then we can't question the killer, because we have no idea who they are!"

"Check the security feeds," Kira suggested. "Whoever was controlling the robot arm would be on them."

Nina shook her head. "Whoever it was shut down the security system before coming after you. All the recordings from tonight were stopped hours ago." She pointed toward the computer. "That recording was the best lead we had."

My mind was racing. Despite Nina's argument, I still believed Dr. Holtz's story of alien contact—but the thrill of that had already been dulled by frustration and anger. I couldn't believe that the recording I had worked so hard to get had failed to identify the killer. And yet it seemed to me that I was missing something. There was a clue I had overlooked somewhere during the last few days.

"It's not like the killer can get away," Dad pointed out. "It's someone on this base. We'll simply have to question everyone about the events. I'm sure the killer will slip up somehow."

"Not necessarily," Nina sighed. "We could go through the whole dog and pony show and end up right back where we are now."

"Well, we have to do something!" Dr. Howard exclaimed. "This person didn't only kill Dr. Holtz. They nearly killed two children! And if we don't find them soon, what's to say they won't try to kill again?"

Mom turned to Chang. "Isn't there some way you can get some other data from that recording?"

"I've done my best," Chang said. "I'm only a genius, not a miracle worker."

I wondered if Chang was telling the truth. Maybe *he* was the killer and he hadn't tried to clean up the recording at all. Or maybe the recording had been fine and he'd done the damage himself, covering up his own presence on it.

"Please," Mom said. "Can't you try?"

Chang sighed and turned back to the monitor. "Computer, is there any way to clean up this recording?"

"Perhaps," the computer replied. "What would you like me to lean it up against?"

"Not *lean* it up, you stupid machine!" Chang snapped. "*Clean* it up! Can you *clean* it up more?"

"I'm sorry," the computer said. "The recording is in very bad shape. I'm afraid this is the best that can be done."

Everyone sagged, looking defeated.

Except me. I'd just realized something important.

Computers could make mistakes. Despite all the amazing things they were capable of, they were still fallible. The base computer misunderstood and misinterpreted things all the time.

The problem was, we tended to forget this. We tended to think the computers were perfect and trust them completely.

I had done exactly that the day before. I'd trusted the computer when I shouldn't have.

"I think I know who killed Dr. Holtz," I said.

Excerpt from *The Official Residents' Guide to Moon Base Alpha*, © 2040 by National Aeronautics and Space Administration:

COMPUTERS

For your convenience, MBA has been designed with the latest state-of-the-art computer technology.* The base computer can handle many of your day-to-day needs, ranging from establishing ComLinks with earth to analyzing lunar-soil samples. And since it is equipped with the latest voice-recognition software, all you have to do is ask it! The computer is always listening, everywhere, all the time, so whenever—or wherever—you need help, it will be there for you!

---

* As of the time of construction. Computer technology will most likely have advanced by the time you read this manual.

IRRATIONAL FEAR

Lunar day 190

Really early in the morning

Everyone turned to me at once.

"Who?" they demanded.

"Well," I hedged, "I'm not one hundred percent sure—"

"Great," Nina muttered.

"—but there's a way to check it out," I finished quickly. "You see, Dr. Holtz *tried* to name his killer the other night—only we didn't understand what he was saying."

Everyone asked questions at the same time. "When?" "Why?" "How do you know?"

"Hold on!" Dad told them all. "Give Dashiell time to

explain himself." He then looked to me expectantly, as eager to hear my thoughts as everyone else.

I suddenly found myself very nervous, wondering if I was right. But I pressed on anyhow. "Kira found footage of Dr. Holtz inside the air lock, right before he went out onto the moon. He was using sign language in it, but neither of us speaks sign language, so we asked the computer to translate it for us. Unfortunately, I think the computer got something wrong, though at the time we didn't realize it. We assumed the computer was right—and that we just didn't understand what Dr. Holtz meant. Or that he had space madness or something."

"What did he say?" Nina asked.

"That he was being murdered. And that earth had killed him."

When everyone looked at me quizzically, I said, "That's the part the computer screwed up. I have the footage right here."

Despite the fact that I'd been smacked around by a giant robot arm, my space suit had protected my watch well (not to mention myself), so it was in much better shape than Dr. Holtz's phone had been. I touched it to the computer in front of Chang, transmitting the video file, which popped up on the screen. "You can still speak sign language, can't you, Mom?"

"Oh," Mom said. "I could never speak it fluently, Dash.

I only tried to learn it to communicate with my grandfather when he was sick."

"But you know *some*, right?" I pressed.

"I suppose," Mom said. "It's been a long time, though."

"Well, try," Nina ordered.

I scanned through the footage until I got to Dr. Holtz signing inside the air lock. "Here," I said. "This is where he says he was being murdered."

We all watched as he pointed beneath his open hand.

"That's the sign for murder, all right," Mom said.

Dr. Holtz began to make the quick series of movements with his hands.

"This is where I think the computer got it wrong," I told her. "Where it translated 'earth killed me.'"

Mom watched and nodded. Then she paused the footage. "You're right," she said. "That's not the sign for 'earth.' He's making letter signs."

"You mean he's spelling?" Dad asked.

"Yes," Mom said. "In American Sign Language there isn't a sign for every name. Instead you spell them out, letter by letter."

"Then why did the computer say 'earth'?" Kira asked.

"It must have thought Dr. Holtz was spelling 'earth,'" Mom suggested. "And it simply interpreted that as a name. So it said 'earth killed me' in the same way it would have said 'Jim killed me.' Only Dr. Holtz was probably spelling something else and the computer misread it."

"So what was he spelling instead?" Chang asked.

"Let's see." Mom scrolled the footage backward to the point where Dr. Holtz began spelling.

The first thing he did was raise his hand with a finger pointing to the side.

"Oh my," Mom said. The color drained from her face.

"That wasn't an *E*, was it?" I asked.

"No." Mom still seemed to be in shock.

"Was it a *G*?"

Everyone looked to me, surprised, then to Mom for confirmation.

She nodded. "Dr. Holtz wasn't spelling 'earth.' He was spelling 'Garth.'"

Everyone in the room reacted at once. I saw astonishment, disbelief, and betrayal.

"Mr. Grisan?" Kira asked, shocked. "He's a spy for the military?"

"I guess, if that's what Dr. Holtz thought," I said. "Whoever he works for definitely has some power over NASA. Dr. Marquez told me Mr. Grisan was the only person here who didn't have to sit with him every week."

"Computer," Nina demanded, "where is Garth Grisan right now?"

"Dismantling the main air lock," the computer replied calmly.

Everyone gasped in alarm.

Nina was the first to race out the door. The rest of us were right behind her.

"Stop right there," Mr. Grisan ordered.

As the computer had said, he was standing by the main air lock. The control panel had been ripped off, and wires dangled out of it.

Mr. Grisan was wearing a full space suit, helmet and all. He no longer looked like the reserved, meek man we knew. That had all been an act. The real Garth Grisan was a daunting presence with a cold look in his eye and a commanding voice. He warned, "If anyone comes a step closer, I'll open both doors at once and depressurize the whole moon base."

"That's not possible," Nina said.

"It is now," Mr. Grisan told her. "I overrode the safety protocols. Although I won't do anything unless you force me to." He placed a thumb on the keypad and shook his head sadly. "I was really hoping things wouldn't come to this."

It was twenty feet to the air lock from where we all stood. There was nothing but open space in between us. There was no way to get ahead of Mr. Grisan.

Nina raised her hands, signaling him to calm down as she edged closer to him. "Take it easy . . ."

"Stop!" Mr. Grisan ordered. "I'm not bluffing!"

Nina froze where she was.

I noticed Zan Perfonic wasn't with us anymore. I had no idea how long she'd been gone—or how much she'd witnessed in the control room. I could only hope that she was circling around to get the jump on Mr. Grisan somehow.

"What do you want from us?" Dad asked.

"Your cooperation," Mr. Grisan replied. "Unfortunately, you have all become privy to information that should have remained secret. And I am prepared to take drastic measures to make sure it goes no farther than this spot."

"Are you crazy?" Chang asked. "If you open that air lock, you won't just kill us. You'll kill everyone else here."

"Desperate times call for desperate measures," Mr. Grisan said calmly. "There are forces at work here you don't understand."

"Then explain them to us," Mom pleaded. "Why is it so important that no one learn that there has been alien contact?"

"That's not the case," Mr. Grisan informed us. "The *right* people can know about it. In fact, they *should* know about it. Dr. Holtz wouldn't listen to reason, though. He wanted to tell everyone. He wanted the whole world to know. And I knew I couldn't trust him to keep his mouth shut."

"Why *can't* the whole world know?" I asked.

"Grover's Mill," Mr. Grisan said.

"Oh, come on," Chang groaned. "You can't be serious."

"What's Grover's Mill?" Kira asked.

Chang started to explain, but Mr. Grisan beat him to it. "On October thirtieth, 1938, an actor named Orson Welles did a radio broadcast in which he reported that martians had landed in Grover's Mill, New Jersey. Although Welles warned people before the broadcast that it was merely for entertainment, people who tuned in during the middle believed it—and they were terrified. There was a massive panic."

"Because in the story the martians were attacking earth!" Nina argued.

"And they were imaginary!" Mr. Grisan shot back. "Now think what would happen if the citizens of the world learned that *real* aliens were coming. The public is primed to think that any aliens are dangerous. Even if you tell them this new race you've found comes in peace, they won't believe it. Frankly, *I* don't believe it."

"So that's what this is about!" Chang exclaimed. "This isn't about real people at all. It's about *you*—and all your fellow psychopaths at the Pentagon. *You're* the ones who are afraid!"

Mr. Grisan's brow furrowed in anger. "You think that's foolish? You think an alien race is really going to come halfway across the galaxy just to make friends? That's not how the universe works, pal. The Europeans didn't sail across the ocean six centuries ago to make nice with the Native Americans; they wiped them out and stole everything they had. And there's no reason to believe that another race would do any different."

"Of course there is," Chang protested. "Just because humans are evil doesn't mean the rest of the galaxy is too."

"Fine," Mr. Grisan said dismissively. "You can go right on believing life's just like *E. T.* When the aliens come, we'll all link arms and sing 'Kumbayah' together. But my job is to be prepared for the alternative. Any life from another planet is most likely hostile—and any contact they make with us, no matter how friendly it seems, is most likely a ruse to learn our weaknesses."

"Wow," Chang gasped. "Is everyone at the Pentagon such a paranoid whack job—or are you just special?"

Mom squeezed Chang's arm and said under her breath, "Don't taunt him."

Mr. Grisan was shaking his head, sneering at Chang with disgust. "Dr. Holtz was just like you: a naive optimist, thinking his alien contact couldn't possibly be dangerous. So much that he was willing to give up his life for it. I gave that fool options. He could have turned over the alien to me, let me talk to them, and get a sense of their intentions. But rather than do that, he chose to force my hand."

"So you threatened his family back on earth?" Dad asked. "Told him you'd have them killed if he didn't go out the air lock?"

"I wouldn't necessarily have had them killed," Mr. Grisan said.

"But you still threatened them, right?" Mom demanded. "Because that's what you do, isn't it? Threaten those who are weaker than you. You sent that text to Dashiell, didn't you?"

"It was for his own good," Mr. Grisan argued. "It was for *all* of your own good! If your son had backed off and kept his nose out of this, none of us would be in this position right now!"

"This isn't Dashiell's fault!" Mom cried. "You're the one who's threatening our lives! You're the one responsible for Dr. Holtz's death! And you have the gall to accuse the *aliens* of being monsters? They couldn't possibly be any worse than you!"

"I did what I had to!" Mr. Grisan shouted. "While you're all up here playing with moon rocks, I'm trying to prevent riots on earth and make sure we're prepared for alien invasions! Yes, I took out Dr. Holtz to ensure the safety of billions of other people—and if you're not prepared to cooperate, I'll happily do the same to you!"

"Hey!" Lars Sjoberg suddenly appeared on the catwalk, wearing his robe, slippers, and a furious expression. "What's with all the shouting? I'm trying to get back to sleep!"

Startled, Mr. Grisan turned to him, taking his eyes off the rest of us for a moment.

Chang leaped into action. He launched himself at Mr. Grisan, soaring across the twenty feet between them quickly in the low gravity.

Mr. Grisan spun for the controls to the air lock, but Chang slammed into him, knocking him off his feet. Mr. Grisan fought back, head-butting Chang with his helmet so hard that Chang tumbled off him, but by that point Dad and Nina had rushed to help as well. Together with Chang, they overpowered Mr. Grisan, flipping him onto his stomach and wrenching his arms behind him.

"Garth Grisan," Nina said. "You are hereby under arrest for the murder of Dr. Ronald Holtz—as well as the attempted murders of Dashiell Gibson and Kira Howard, sabotage, blackmail, and destruction of federal property."

"You don't know what you're doing!" Mr. Grisan snarled.

Nina continued, "You will be handcuffed and placed under lock and key in the medical bay until tomorrow, after which you will be returned to earth under guard on the Raptor and turned over to the proper authorities there."

Mr. Grisan shouted something about the Pentagon having his back, and that he wouldn't stay under lock and key for long, but I didn't hear all of it, because Mom pulled me aside.

"You were right about Dr. Holtz," she told me. "He was sane, after all—while Mr. Grisan was apparently the one we should have been worried about. I'm sorry we doubted you. I'm sure that, wherever he is, Ronald is thankful for what you've done for him."

"What about the aliens?" I asked. "What happens to Dr. Holtz's discovery?"

Mom lowered her eyes sadly. "I don't know. Dr. Holtz was the only one who'd had contact. Now that he's gone . . . there's no proof they exist at all."

"Rose!" Nina called. "There are handcuffs in the top left desk drawer in my room. Could you get them?"

"All right." Mom broke away from me and raced up to Nina's quarters.

Everyone else was gathered around the air lock. Dad and Nina were pinning Mr. Grisan down while he writhed angrily and told us what fools we all were. Chang was inspecting the air lock to see if he could figure out what Mr. Grisan had done to it. Lars Sjoberg was shouting at Nina, upset that Mr. Grisan would take the precious return seat on the rocket that one of his family members wanted. Kira and her father were off to the side, quietly watching it all.

The other Moonies were pouring back out of their quarters, defying Nina's orders, to see what all the commotion was about.

I thought about what my mother had just said to me about Dr. Holtz's proof being gone. It seemed so wrong. Perhaps he'd left some more evidence on his phone, but if he had, it was probably destroyed. Which meant it would all remain a mystery until the aliens ever chose to make contact again.

And then, suddenly, understanding dawned on me. A realization so powerful I had to lean against the wall to steady myself.

Then I walked around the corner, leaving the chaos behind, looking for some privacy.

The mess hall was on my left, the greenhouse on my right.

As a kid, I wasn't supposed to enter the greenhouse, but I went in anyhow.

The greenhouse wasn't working out nearly as well as we'd hoped. Growing food on the moon was a big priority, but it had proved much harder than expected and the plants were barely surviving. The brochures for MBA had displayed artists' renderings of a greenhouse so thick with plant growth it was practically a rain forest. In real life, the greenhouse looked more like the Great Plains after a drought. All around me straggly bits of greenery struggled to survive.

I sat down, looking away from the door. I focused on a few pathetic tomato plants that had yet to produce a single fruit.

"Hello, Dashiell."

I turned around. Zan Perfonic was standing behind me. I hadn't heard her come in. But then I hadn't expected to.

She seemed to read my thoughts. "You were hoping to talk to me?"

"Yes," I said. "Tell me: What planet are you from?"

Excerpt from *The Official Residents' Guide to Moon Base Alpha*,
© 2040 by National Aeronautics and Space Administration:

ONE LAST NOTE

Thanks for taking the time to read this guide to your new home in its entirety. Hopefully, you found it useful and informative. Now it's time to start your great adventure as one of the first humans to ever live on a celestial body other than earth!

Although there will be a great deal of work ahead (or school, if you're a child at MBA), we at NASA would like to take this opportunity to remind you to enjoy yourself. We have taken great pains to make the base just as comfortable as your home on earth—if not *more* comfortable—so have fun up there! Make friends with your fellow lunarnauts (if you haven't already). Be part of the community. Organize events. Start a book club, or an amateur theater group, or a low-gravity square-dancing society.

Remember: Moon Base Alpha is going to be your home for a long time. The more you get involved, the better it will be.

Have a great trip! And remember, the world is watching you!

MIND-BLOWING DISCOVERY

Lunar day 190

Morning

"How long have you known I'm an alien?" Zan asked.

"Not very long," I admitted. "In fact, I wasn't completely sure until right now."

Zan smiled, and her big, blue eyes sparkled. It now occurred to me why I'd never seen any eyes like hers before.

They weren't human.

"My planet isn't that far in galactic terms," she told me. "It's only about ten light years away. You humans call it SG 61109b. We call it something that can't be pronounced in your language. So Dr. Holtz and I just called it Bosco."

"Bosco?" I repeated.

Zan shrugged. "Dr. Holtz said it was better than SG 61109b."

"Good point."

Above us the greenhouse roof had a large skylight in it. It had been one of the most expensive parts of MBA to transport and install, but it was necessary for the plants to have sunlight. I looked up and saw the earth above us, along with several thousand stars. "Where's Bosco?" I asked.

Zan pointed northward. "That way. In the constellation Draco."

I looked back at her. There were a thousand questions in my head, all vying to be asked at once. Finally I went with, "I'm the only one who can see you, right?"

Zan's eyes sparkled again. "You figured that out?"

"The only time you've ever spoken to me is when we were alone," I explained. "I've seen you near other people, but I just realized I've never seen you speak to any of them. Or interact with them. The only person you've done any of that with is me. And the other day, when Kira overheard us talking in my room, she could only hear me . . . not you."

"Dr. Holtz was right about you," Zan said. "You're a smart kid."

"He was talking to you that night in the bathroom, wasn't he? But the cameras couldn't see you, so it looked like he was talking to himself."

"Yes. I probably shouldn't have approached him there, but it seemed private at the time. I didn't realize you were there."

"I asked you before if you were talking to him then. And you lied to me."

"Technically, I didn't," Zan told me. "You asked if I was on the *phone* with him that night, and I said that I wasn't."

I frowned, realizing she was right. "Well, you misled me. About that and a whole lot of other things."

"I didn't think you were ready for the truth."

"I wasn't the only one who overheard Dr. Holtz speaking to you. My mom did too. And some other people here. But they all thought Dr. Holtz was talking to himself, going crazy."

Zan nodded. "Dr. Holtz knew that had happened. It was one of the reasons he wanted to reveal my existence. He didn't think we could keep this all a secret much longer."

Outside the greenhouse, across the hall, I could hear Garth Grisan being locked inside the medical bay. He was yelling the whole time, telling Dr. Janke and Chang they were fools for not seeing things his way. "When the aliens attack and we're not prepared for it, you won't be so pleased with yourselves!" he warned.

Then the door slammed, silencing him.

"What a nut job," Chang sighed.

I stared at Zan. She didn't seem remotely evil. In fact I got a feeling from her that I couldn't explain, a sense that she was nothing but goodness, warmth, and light. And yet, somewhere in the back of my mind, I found myself wondering if this could all be a trick, as Mr. Grisan had warned.

"So how do you do it?" I asked. "How do you make yourself invisible to everyone but one person?"

"Because I'm not really here," Zan said, like it was the most obvious thing in the world.

Only it wasn't obvious to me at all. "What do you mean?"

"Your friend Roddy was right the other day about how difficult space travel is. Our civilization is far more advanced than yours, and even *we* haven't figured out how to go from planet to planet in less than a generation. However, contrary to what your scientists tell you, there is one thing that can go faster than the speed of light. Much faster, in fact: thoughts."

I'd been kind of proud of myself for figuring out who'd killed Dr. Holtz, and what Zan's secret was. But this revelation caught me completely by surprise. "So . . . you just *think* yourself here?"

"In a sense. It's not quite as simple as that. In fact the process is quite complicated. But yes, that's the general idea."

"If you're only a thought, how can I see you? Or hear you?"

"Because thoughts are extremely powerful—if you know how to use them right. Has there ever been a time when you knew what someone was thinking without saying anything?"

"I guess."

"It's kind of like that. I'm communicating directly with your brain. And since your brain controls what you see and hear, I can let you see and hear me. Or at least I can let you see and hear a representation of myself that isn't alarming to you."

"You mean you don't look like a human?"

Zan smiled again. "Not at all. I've merely tried to model the image I project to be as human as possible. Do you like it?"

I stared at her amazing blue eyes. "Yes. Though I don't think you got the eyes quite right. You made them *too* good, somehow."

"I couldn't help it. Dr. Holtz told me something once: that you humans consider the eyes a window to the soul."

The greenhouse was right across from the mess hall. I could hear Kira and her father in there.

Dr. Howard was saying, "Promise me you'll never go out

on the surface without permission—or do *anything* risky like that—ever again. I don't know what I'd do if I lost you."

"Trust me, Dad," Kira said, "I've had enough excitement to last me a long time."

I returned my attention to Zan. As amazing as her revelations were, I found them surprisingly calming as well. Many strange things from the last few days suddenly made sense. Like why Zan had never opened a door, or touched me—or touched *anything*, for that matter. Or why she had looked so alarmed when I approached her in the mess hall when other people were around. It was because she wasn't really there. Every time I'd seen her, whether she was with other people or hanging out by herself, she had merely been pretending to exist physically.

"How long were you in contact with Dr. Holtz?" I asked.

"Only a few weeks. But my kind have been watching you humans on earth for quite some time now. I suppose you could say we've been thinking ourselves there without choosing to interact with any of you."

"For how long?"

"We first became aware of humanity about a hundred of your years ago, when you started detonating nuclear bombs. Such violent activity has effects your kind hasn't figured out yet. In a sense, it sends ripples through the fabric of space-time. When we realized that you existed and what you had done, we deduced where you were and sent out our first explorers."

"You've been coming for a hundred years?" I asked, startled. "And you've never been in touch with *any* humans that whole time?"

"No," Zan said. "We have decided to be very cautious about this. Besides, much can be learned about a species through observation."

I heard Lars Sjoberg storm past the greenhouse. He was chastising Nina. "You promised us *all* space on that rocket home."

"That was before I had a murderer to get rid of," Nina replied. "Trust me Lars, I'd love to send you back on the same rocket with him. Even better, I'd like to put the two of you on a rocket together and send it off into deep space for the rest of eternity. But NASA's saying no, so for the time being I'm stuck here with you and your horrible family."

I waited until they were out of earshot before speaking again. "So why did you decide to make yourself known after all this time?"

"Because of this base. You humans are making a sincere attempt to colonize planets beyond your own. You're a long way from getting out of your own solar system, but it's a step. Which means that someday down the line, you might be coming our way. So we decided that a connection should be made. After a great amount of deliberation, Dr. Holtz was selected. I have to admit, given how many of your movies are about evil aliens attacking your planet, I thought Dr. Holtz might be frightened at first. I was pleasantly surprised by how thrilled he was to make contact. And then when he kept pressing me to let him reveal our existence . . . well, his enthusiasm was contagious. He was very convincing." Zan lowered her eyes sadly. "I had no idea it would end so tragically. Sadly, I wasn't aware it was even happening. . . ."

"Why not?"

"I can't be here constantly. That requires tremendous thought and focus. On my own planet I need to sleep—and do other things. So I was busy when Mr. Grisan got to Dr. Holtz. When I returned . . . his death was as big a shock to me as it was to you."

"So that's why you came to me?" I said. "To try to find out what happened to Dr. Holtz?"

"Yes. It was a serious breach of protocol, but I feared there was no other way to find out. I wanted to know the truth, but no one else here seemed willing to investigate the death—except you. Though I figured you might need a little push."

I now heard Roddy entering the mess with his brother. "I suspected it was Mr. Grisan all along," Roddy boasted. "I never trusted that guy. He always seemed shiftier than a Neptunian Blorkbeast."

"Roddy," Cesar said. "Unless you want that new girl to think you're the biggest dork in the universe, you *have* to stop saying things like that."

I returned my attention to Zan, putting all the pieces from the last few days together. "You also picked me because I was a kid, didn't you? An adult would have known there was no Zan Perfonic scheduled to come here. They wouldn't have followed your orders so blindly."

"Maybe not," Zan said, "But I saw other reasons to choose you as well. Your intelligence, for one. In fact you proved to be much smarter than I expected. I didn't think you'd figure out what I really was. I originally planned to learn what happened to Dr. Holtz, then pretend to return on the rocket today and disappear from your life forever."

"So you lied to me. About pretty much everything. Your job. Why you wanted my help. What you really are . . ."

"I apologize for that. I didn't know what else to do. Just because I'm highly evolved doesn't mean I'm perfect." Zan fixed her brilliant blue eyes on me. "Although, now that you *have* figured out what I am, you seem as qualified a human contact as Dr. Holtz was. Perhaps even better."

I was so startled by this, I actually forgot to breathe for a moment. Finally I gasped, "Really?"

"Yes. Approaching a human subject is no easy task. Not everyone would handle it as well as you have. I suspect most would, as you humans often say, 'freak out.' Therefore, I would very much like to continue our discussions. Although, sadly, I think that given the events of the past few days, we must keep our contact a secret. Humanity doesn't seem to be ready for this yet."

"I'm sure Mr. Grisan's reaction wasn't a normal one . . . ," I began.

"Even so," Zan told me, "I wouldn't want anything to happen to you. So, what do you say? Are you willing to continue human-extraterrestrial contact?"

Of course, I wanted to shout. I couldn't believe Zan was asking me. I was so thrilled by the idea, I could barely contain myself. And yet I did. I stayed so calm I surprised myself. "I'm not sure."

For the first time, Zan looked surprised. "Why not?"

Outside, I could now hear my own family in the halls, calling to me. Violet was back with my parents. I'd been in such a hurry to talk to Zan, I'd forgotten to tell them where I was going. Since I'd almost been killed less than an hour before, my parents sounded a bit worried. Violet didn't. She was acting like it was a big game of hide-and-seek, singing "Dashiell! Come out, come out, wherever you are!"

I was going to have to show myself to them soon.

"I can't do it because of *them*," I said quietly. "Dr. Holtz lived on his own up here. I don't. It's going to be very hard to keep you a secret from my family. Sooner or later they're going to catch me talking to myself and think I've cracked up."

"We'll take precautions," Zan told me. "This would mean a great deal to my planet as well as yours. In fact, it is more important than you could possibly understand."

I looked up through the skylight at earth once again. It suddenly occurred to me that, for the first time in months, I wasn't longing to be back on my home planet. My anger at being stuck on the moon had vanished. But it wasn't only because of Zan's offer. I also had a new friend in Kira. And I'd finally stopped grousing about having nothing to do at Moon Base Alpha and started actually doing things there.

Although making alien contact *was* kind of a big deal.

"All right," I said. "I'll do it . . . with one condition."

Zan beamed, her eyes brighter blue than ever. "Of course. What is it?"

"The way you travel between planets. Is that something only your species can do?"

"I'm not sure," Zan admitted. "I suppose others could do it, although it isn't easy."

"I'd like to try. Will you teach me?"

Zan stared up through the skylight thoughtfully. For a moment it seemed that she was no longer with me. I could still see her body, but her mind appeared to be light years away. I got the sense she was communicating with someone back on her home planet. Her eyes were eerily vacant, the sun and earth and a million stars reflected in them.

Then suddenly she was back. The life returned to her eyes. She looked at me.

And smiled.

Don't miss *Spaced Out*, the next Moon Base Alpha mystery from Stuart Gibbs!

Earth year 2041
Lunar day 216
Bedtime

If I hadn't made the mistake of showing *Star Wars* to an alien life form, I never would have ended up fighting Patton Sjoberg with the space toilet.

But then, being friends with an alien had been one problem after another. It was far more difficult than I had ever imagined. For starters, there was no end of things I had to explain.

Every single aspect of my life was strange and unusual to Zan Perfonic. She wanted to know the reasons for everything I did. But it turns out, there's not much reason behind half the things we humans do.

For example, blessing someone after they sneeze.

One day, Zan overheard me do this and later, she asked why I'd said it.

I had to think for a moment before admitting, "I have no idea. It's just something we humans do. It's supposed to be good manners."

"Like when you use napkins to blot partially eaten food off your faces?"

"Kind of."

"What does 'bless you' mean?"

"Um . . . that you want good things to happen for someone. I think."

"So every time someone involuntarily blasts snot out of their nose, you humans tell them you want good things to happen to them?"

"Er . . . yes."

"Do you say 'bless you' for other involuntary actions? Like when someone burps?"

"No."

"Or farts?"

"Definitely not."

"Why not?"

"I guess because farting is considered rude."

"And yet, is also considered funny?"

"Not by everyone."

"Your sister seems to think it's funny."

"Well, she's six."

"Your father does too. He's not six."

"Good point."

"So why do some people find involuntary emissions of noxious gases from their rectums funny while other people find it rude?"

"I don't know."

"Do you think it has something to do with the sound?"

It went on like that for twenty minutes, with Zan asking me to try to explain everything from whoopie cushions to "pull my finger" until I was mentally exhausted. For this reason, I'd taken to showing Zan movies whenever I could. They made life easier. I'd used them to help explain everything from dinosaurs to World War II to professional sports.

I know I sound like a crazy person with all this talking-to-an-alien stuff. Like the kind of lunatic who stumbles through the streets babbling gibberish and wearing a tinfoil hat.

But I'm not crazy. My name's Dashiell Gibson and I'm a totally sane twelve-year-old boy who happens to live on the moon. You've probably heard of me. All of us up here are pretty famous, seeing as we're the first families to colonize someplace that isn't earth. There's so much coverage of us down there, you might think you know everything about us.

But you don't. You only know what the government wants

you to know. And a lot of that is lies. Like when you hear that Moon Base Alpha is a really amazing, incredible place? Or that we're all getting along great up here and having the time of our lives? That's all a big, steaming pile of garbage.

Plus, there are things we all keep to ourselves. Like being in contact with aliens from the planet Bosco.

Zan's planet wasn't really called Bosco. But I couldn't pronounce its real name. When Zan said it in her native language, it sounded like a bunch of dolphins who'd sucked the helium out of a Macy's balloon. It was so high-pitched it made my ears hurt. So we went with "Bosco" instead.

No one else at MBA knew I was in contact with Zan. I was the only one who could see her. Or hear her. Or speak to her.

There was a perfectly good reason for this: Zan wasn't really there. You see, her species hadn't mastered interstellar travel yet. (Not that we humans have come anywhere close to figuring it out ourselves.) Zan's species had found a short-cut, though. They could *think* themselves to other places.

I had no idea how it worked. Zan had been doing her best to explain it to me, and it always left me feeling like I was an idiot. But then, even Albert Einstein would have looked like an idiot to Zan.

The point being, I wasn't really seeing Zan with my eyes. Instead she was connecting directly with my mind, inserting herself into my thoughts. I didn't even see the *real* Zan. Instead I saw an image of her that she wanted me to see: a beautiful, dark-haired thirty-year-old female human with startlingly blue eyes. In truth, I didn't know what Zan really looked like, because she hadn't shown me yet.

Communicating with Zan wasn't actually that difficult. She had learned English and could speak it better than half the humans I'd met. The hard part was that she insisted our friendship remain a secret. However, she had a very good reason for this:

Zan had befriended only one human before me, Dr. Ronald Holtz, who had been the doctor at Moon Base Alpha. Dr. Holtz had wanted to reveal Zan's existence to all humanity, but he never got the chance. Because the second person who learned about Zan was another Moonie named Garth Grisan, a whacked-out, ultra-paranoid spy for the military who believed humanity wasn't ready to learn we're not alone in the universe. Garth killed Dr. Holtz to keep the secret safe, though he made it look like an accident. I'd figured it out with Zan's help, though, and Garth had been shipped back to earth to stand trial for murder.

So Zan wasn't in any rush to reveal her existence this time. I understood. Frankly, I was surprised she was willing to give humanity another try. And it was absolutely thrilling to get to talk to an alien.

It just wasn't easy.

Maybe things wouldn't have been so much trouble if I still lived on earth. Back there, if I wanted to spend some private time with Zan, I could simply go to my room and lock the door. But on the moon, I don't have my own room. I share a cramped one-room residence with my parents and my little sister, Violet, and my "bedroom" is a niche built into the wall. On earth, I could go for a walk around the neighborhood. On the moon, I can't. I'm not allowed outside, because I could die out there. On earth, there were a million places I could go to be by myself. On the moon, there are none. I have no privacy whatsoever. There are security cameras everywhere, half the base is off-limits to me, and even the bathrooms are communal.

So, basically, the only way I could spend any serious time with Zan was late at night, after everyone else had gone to bed.

The night I showed her *Star Wars*, it was well after dinnertime. Mom and Dad had already tucked Violet into bed for the night and were playing chess in our room, while all the other Moonies seemed to be settling down in their residences as well. I wasn't trying to explain anything to Zan by showing her the movie. I had simply referenced it so much, she demanded to see it.

It was hard to talk about life in space without talking

about *Star Wars*. Or *Star Trek*. Or any other space movies. Because space travel always looked so cool in those films, when it wasn't in real life. In the movies, you never saw anyone having trouble walking in low gravity or eating disgusting rehydrated space food or vacuuming their poop out with a space toilet. Instead, gravity was always exactly the same on every planet, the food was delicious, and no one ever even went to the bathroom. Without thinking about it, I'd referenced *Star Wars* over and over again, and finally Zan had said, "Are you ever going to show me this movie?" So I did. I brought her to the rec room and uploaded *Star Wars: A New Hope* onto the SlimScreen.

Zan thought it was hilarious.

She laughed hysterically the whole way through it. And laughter was something that didn't really translate between us. Zan's species actually *had* humor, which was nice, but they didn't express it by laughing; that was a human thing. Instead they made a high-pitched whine that was shrill enough to rattle my eardrums. Plus, there was a strange side effect where Zan would lose control of her projected self and her eyeballs would swell up like beach balls. It was all very disconcerting. Finally, about halfway through, I had to pause the movie and tell her, "It's not a comedy."

She stopped whining, her eyeballs shrinking back down to normal size, and said, "It's not?"

"No," I told her. "It's a science-fiction adventure movie."

"But all the spaceships and the weapons and everything are so ridiculous. Like the laser guns. When they shoot lasers at each other, you can see them moving through space, whereas in real life, light moves so quickly that the shot would be instantaneous. . . ."

"Er . . . yes," I admitted, although this had never occurred to me before. "But . . ."

"And the ships keep jumping to warp speed, which is faster than light speed, which is simply impossible."

"Well, just because you haven't figured out how to do it doesn't mean it *can't* be done."

"Yes, but if it *is* done, it certainly won't be in spacecraft as ludicrous as the ones in this movie. Half of them seem to be using the same type of rudimentary combustion engines that you use on your rockets. They'd be lucky to break the gravity of their planets, let alone travel dozens of light-years in a second."

"I suppose. . . ."

"Plus, all the space creatures are absurd. They're all modeled on humans with two arms and two legs, when there are thousands of other ways a body could be constructed."

"There are?"

"Certainly. Look at your own planet. There are billions of species of insect and only one species of human. And yet there isn't a single creature in the movie with an insect body structure."

"You mean, you'd think *Star Wars* would be *less* funny if Chewbacca looked like a giant cockroach?"

"Well, it would certainly be more realistic. The chances of Wookiees being so structurally similar to your species is staggeringly improbable. And don't even get me started on the fact that Luke Skystalker and Princess Leo and Ham Bolo look exactly like humans, even though they live in some galaxy far, far away."

"Those aren't their names. . . ."

"Well, you know who I mean. Honestly, the entire film is laughably earth-centric and the physics are preposterous."

I turned the TV off. "Obviously, showing you this was a mistake."

"No!" Zan cried. "It wasn't. I'm really enjoying it. I haven't laughed so hard in a long time." She giggled at the thought, her eyes swelling up again.

"Do *you* look like a giant cockroach?" I asked pointedly.

Zan stopped laughing. Her eyes returned to their normal size. "Why do you ask?"

"Because I don't know anything about you," I told her. "We always talk about me and earth and humanity, but never about *you*. I don't even know what you really look like."

"I don't think you're ready to see me as I really exist. For the time being, it's much better if I appear to you in human form."

"Why?"

"Because it's far easier for you to relate to something that appears similar to you than something that appears alien."

"You don't know that for sure."

"It seems logical to assume as much."

"Now you sound like Mr. Spock."

"Who?"

"Never mind." If Zan had an issue with Wookiees looking too human, she'd probably flip out when she learned about Vulcans.

"I sense frustration in you," Zan said.

"Yes." There was no point in denying it. One of the side effects of Zan communicating directly with my mind was that she could read my emotions as well as I could. Better, sometimes.

"Why?"

"When you first approached me about being your human contact, you said it was extremely important," I reminded Zan. "More important than I could possibly understand. But you haven't told me *why* yet. You haven't told me *anything*. Not one thing about you or your family or your planet. While I've told you plenty. I've answered all your questions, and you've had a million of them."

"Dashiell, when we began this relationship, I warned you it wouldn't be easy. . . ."

"You can't tell me what we're doing here? Or why our contact is so important?"

"Certainly you must realize how significant contact is between humans and an alien species for the first time."

"Yes, but there's more to it than that, isn't there? What's so important about it that I couldn't possibly understand?"

"If I told you, you wouldn't understand it."

"See?" I snapped. "Answers like that are why I'm frustrated! Can't you at least *try* to tell me?"

"I don't have authorization for that yet."

"Is the earth in some kind of danger?" I asked.

Zan didn't answer. But something changed in her. I couldn't tell what, exactly; it was almost as though her image had distorted for a fraction of a second. I got the idea that I'd caught her by surprise.

"I'm right, aren't I?" I demanded. "The earth *is* in danger."

"No," Zan told me. "It's not that dire."

"You're lying."

"I'm not," Zan said, but I had the distinct feeling that she was. Or at least hiding something from me.

"What is going on here?" I asked.

Before Zan could respond, voices echoed in the hall outside the rec room. Someone was coming our way.

I suddenly realized that, in my frustration, I'd forgotten to not speak out loud to Zan.

I always tried to keep all our conversations inside my head, but that took a great deal of focus and concentration. When Zan appeared to me, it didn't *feel* like she was only an image being projected into my mind. She seemed as real as any person on the base, and over my twelve years of life, I'd learned that when you speak to someone, you use your mouth, not just your brain. It was a tough habit to break. Often, I thought I *was* keeping quiet, only to realize in midsentence that I wasn't.

Zan's eyes flicked toward the door. "We can't discuss this now. I have to go."

"No," I said. "Wait. . . ."

"I'm sorry," Zan told me, then vanished.

A second later, Patton and Lily Sjoberg stormed into the room. Patton and Lily were the biggest bullies at Moon Base Alpha. They were twins, aged sixteen, and at that moment, they were very angry and obviously looking for trouble.

Unfortunately, they'd found me instead.